Sycamore Promises

OTHER FIVE STAR TITLES BY PAUL COLT

Historical Fiction

Boots and Saddles: A Call to Glory (2013)

A Question of Bounty: The Shadow of Doubt (2014)

Bounty of Vengeance: Ty's Story (2016)

Bounty of Greed: The Lincoln County War (2017)

Great Western Detective League

Wanted: Sam Bass (2015)

The Bogus Bondsman (2017)

Sycamore Promises

Paul Colt

FIVE STAR
A part of Gale, a Cengage Company

GALE
A Cengage Company

Farmington Hills, Mich • San Francisco • New York • Waterville, Maine
Meriden, Conn • Mason, Ohio • Chicago

GALE
A Cengage Company

Five Star™ Publishing, a part of Gale, a Cengage Company

LIBRARY OF CONGRESS CATALOGING-IN-PUBLICATION DATA

Names: Colt, Paul, author.
Title: Sycamore promises / Paul Colt.
Description: First edition. | Waterville, Maine : Five Star publishing, a part of Gale, a Cengage Company, [2018]
Identifiers: LCCN 2017029702 (print) | LCCN 2017031525 (ebook) | ISBN 9781432838140 (ebook) | ISBN 1432838148 (ebook) | ISBN 9781432838133 (ebook) | ISBN 143283813X (ebook) | ISBN 9781432838218 (hardcover) | ISBN 1432838210 (hardcover)
Subjects: LCSH: Frontier and pioneer life—Fiction. | Landowners—Fiction. | GSAFD: Western stories.
Classification: LCC PS3603.O4673 (ebook) | LCC PS3603.O4673 S97 2018 (print) | DDC 813/.6—dc23
LC record available at https://lccn.loc.gov/2017029702

First Edition. First Printing: January 2018
Find us on Facebook–https://www.facebook.com/FiveStarCengage
Visit our website–http://www.gale.cengage.com/fivestar/
Contact Five Star™ Publishing at FiveStar@cengage.com

Printed in the United States of America
1 2 3 4 5 6 7 22 21 20 19 18

The Five Star Team

Producing a book takes teamwork. The author's name goes on the cover; but the book wouldn't happen without the rest of the team. So, this book is for the team at Five Star, especially:

Tiffany Schofield. If western literature has an "energizer" advocate, beating the drum these days, it's Tiffany. She's the driving force behind Five Star and a person willing to take a chance on a newbie. My thanks.

And Hazel Rumney. Hazel is more than an editor, she's my partner. She brings professional expertise and experience to the process of making a book. When we finish a book, I know it's right, when Hazel says it is. Thanks for another one.

AUTHOR'S GUIDE

This is a work of historical fiction. More particularly, it is historical dramatization where the author animates characters and events while remaining faithful to the historical record. There are challenges in undertaking a work of sweeping scope, spanning more than a decade. Most obvious is remaining true to characters, period, and events.

These historical events are played out by a large cast of characters that goes beyond simple protagonist, victim, and villain. This challenges author and reader alike. Change the facts and dilute the history; or crowd the reader's attention with a complex cast of characters. There is no easy answer to the trade-off, hence this guide.

In this work, the author opted to preserve the historical record with one creative license. The important characters are there. As in life, they take the stage, play their part, and depart. You will recognize them by their spare descriptions. Take them for their part in the story as you might in a newspaper account and let them go. Some are more consequential than others. They play larger roles you will recognize by a more vivid description and recurring appearances. You will get to know them as the story unfolds. I have taken the liberty of animating these characters with dialog that advances the story while endeavoring to keep their roles in character.

The fictional characters, settlers Micah and Clare Mason, former slaves Caleb and Miriam, along with landholder Titus

Thorne and a few others, give the story continuity and humanity. They are the characters the reader will want to know in the conventional sense.

In the end, I hope the reader finds a deeper understanding of a complex historical period fraught with challenges that yet echo in our own time.

Paul Colt

Sycamore Promises

Lo the mighty sycamore, her branches brush the sky
She buds forth summer promise, shelter is her shade
She scatters golden coverlet, o'er season's earthen end
Bare she stands the winter long, sentinel in the snow
So the mighty sycamore, her promise bears you home

Prologue

Washington City
1852

There has to be a way. Senator Stephen Douglas stood at his office window, hands clasped behind his back, gazing across the Potomac into a crisp, November sky. His thoughts rode a wispy mare's tail cloud west toward his home in Chicago. A diminutive firebrand, Douglas made up for his lack of stature by intellectual brilliance, adroit political skill, spellbinding oratory, and a ruthless intensity of purpose that rendered him a giant among lesser men over whom he found power and influence.

He saw the way forward as clearly as the destiny that drove the nation's westward settlement. They'd accomplished much in that regard. By purchase and the spoils of war, American territorial possessions now spanned the continent from Atlantic to Pacific. A vast, rich land stretched forth before the nation, waiting to yield promises of unimagined wealth and greatness. As chairman of the Senate Committee on Territories, Douglas knew this. Expansion would realize the promise of commerce. Commerce followed the National Road across the Appalachians. Commerce would similarly follow the nation's young rail system. The rail gateway west would become the heart of prosperity's promise. That gateway must be Chicago.

Chicago had a natural claim on the prize with its Great Lakes port, agricultural center, and proximity to commercial shipping interests along the Mississippi. It should be a simple matter of economics, but it wasn't. The question that vexed him was how a divided nation might muster the will to realize the dream of her full potential.

Slavery divided the nation north and south as it had since the very foundation of the republic. Douglas personally opposed slavery, believing it to be economically impractical and doomed to eventual extinction. Nonetheless he believed states had the right to govern the practice. The issue dominated every question of territorial expansion, owing to a delicate balance of power maintained in the Senate by a like number of slave and free states. This balance became law thirty years before by enactment of the Missouri Compromise. By provisions of the law, territories south and west of Missouri's southern border would be admitted to the Union as slave states. Territories north and west of this boundary would be admitted as free states. Therein lay the problem. Sighting any rail route to the Pacific would necessarily favor the formation of states slave or free and thereby incur the fevered opposition of the other side. The vexing question then: how to unravel such a Gordian knot?

Douglas concluded the problem too strident and controversial to be solved by a single stroke. Reasonable steps would be required to advance the cause, beginning with justifying the need for a Pacific rail route to the American people. He could put forward that argument in favor of commerce and, more importantly, national defense. A railway to the Pacific was needed to defend the rich gold and silver deposits in California and newly acquired western territories. Without rapid, reliable transport west, these territories were indefensible should any hostile foreign power decide to seize them. That message could be clearly presented in the national interest. Route selection would be the controversial question. It must necessarily be settled by geographical considerations of difficulty and cost. Surveys would be needed to determine both. That would take time—time that could be used to defuse the tinderbox issue imposed by the Missouri Compromise. But how? Legislation would be required. The Missouri Compromise must be repealed while preserving balance in the Senate. *There had to be a way that favored Chicago. Perhaps . . .* He nodded.

Chapter One

Hudson, Ohio
January, 1853

A cheery fire popped and crackled, spreading a halo of warmth beyond the hearth. Outside winter wind howled at the eaves of the three-room cabin that once served as the Mason family homestead. Micah Mason, eldest son of Hiram and Eugenie Mason, had moved into the old homestead with his new bride the previous spring. Micah worked the family farm along with his father and three brothers that summer and through the fall. Sandy haired and boyishly handsome, he exuded a thoughtful confidence. Hard work rendered him well made without the advantage of imposing stature. Little else set his homespun appearance apart save thoughtful blue eyes that spoke a wisdom beyond his years. He thumbed a week-old edition of the *Cleveland Plain Dealer,* absorbed in an editorial advocating the national imperative of a rail route to the Pacific.

Across the parlor, his newlywed wife, Clare, sat mending the knee of a worn pair of britches. She squinted at fine stitches in firelight, giving a sober expression that denied her ready smile. Large, brown eyes dominated delicate features, dark, curly hair, and a tawny, satin complexion. She wore her womanhood with a gentle grace that captured Micah's heart the day they first met in that one-room schoolhouse.

Micah folded the paper. "I believe they will build it."

"Build what, dear?"

"A railway to the Pacific."

"Oh, my, that seems a near impossible task."

"I expect it will be terribly difficult. The land is vast. Mountains and rivers must be negotiated. Hostile Indians will surely resist."

"Those are all formidable obstacles. Still, you believe they will succeed?"

"I do. We must. The Louisiana lands we've purchased and those obtained from Mexico after the war must be brought into the Union. Manifest Destiny they call it. Senator Douglas of Illinois speaks of it as a national imperative. We have gold and silver deposits in the West we cannot defend should the need arise."

"I never thought of it that way."

"A Pacific railroad will open new territory to settlement. It will make produce accessible to new markets, east and west, all along the route."

"I should think that land will become valuable one day."

"It will, Clare. It will."

"Does the article say where the railroad is to be built?"

"No. The senator is recommending legislation that would survey northern, southern, and central routes to determine the most practical and efficient. That makes good sense, though choosing any one of them is certain to provoke dispute over the slavery issue."

"That barbaric practice again. When will it end?"

"Who is to say? Feelings are strident on both sides."

"As a Christian, I can't abide the notion of enslaving another human being."

"We see it that way. Southerners have grown up with a different view."

"Then how can you believe they will ever choose a route for a Pacific railroad?"

"There's too much at stake not to. It won't be easy. No one knows how, but a route will be chosen. A Pacific railroad will be built. Fortunes will be made when it is. Our own Baltimore and Ohio is building west to reach the commercial centers in Chicago and St. Louis. That routing seems as likely a course as any."

Micah got up from his rocker and crossed the dirt floor to sit beside his wife on the thread-worn settee.

"There's a future to be made in the west, Clare."

"You mean leave Ohio?"

"People do it every day."

"Our families are here."

"Our family has just begun. Don't you want our children to have better opportunities than the ones we've had here?"

"I do, but the idea of leaving is frightening."

"There is a practical problem with staying. The farm is too small. Father and the boys can more than manage without me. We need to provide for our own children. Land here costs money, money we haven't got. Land in the West is plentiful and there for the taking if a man is only to improve it by the sweat of his brow. Don't you see that for opportunity?"

"I suppose I do, it's only . . ."

"It would be an adventure."

"Where would we go?"

"West; I don't know more than that now. We must study it. Think about it."

"You're serious, aren't you?"

"I am."

"Then I shall think on it."

"Good. Now, come to bed before the warmth of this fire dies out."

The White House
March 20, 1853

Early spring warmth lay glorious upon Virginia. A lightly scented, gentle breeze ruffled the curtains in the president's office. Franklin Pierce sat at his desk, his attention drawn to the south lawn emblazoned with blossoms basking in a sun-splashed mantle of fresh greenery. Scarcely more than two weeks in office and events that would define his presidency were already beginning to unfold. Slightly taller than average, the forty-nine-year-old president presented a sober countenance. Dark-blue frock coat, dove-gray vest and cravat suited the austerity of his office.

A knock at the door drew him back to the moment.

"Secretary Davis is here, sir."

"Send him in."

Secretary of War Jefferson Davis appeared at the office door. "You sent for me, Mr. President?"

"I did, Jefferson, come in. Have a seat."

Davis crossed the polished wooden floor on purposeful strides. Lean and angular with ruffled, dark hair, he bore a softer, more comely likeness to his soon-to-be adversary Abraham Lincoln. He folded himself into a guest chair drawn up before the president's desk.

"How are you adjusting to the war department, Jefferson?"

"I've barely gotten my chair warm, sir. I might ask the same of all this." He gestured to the trappings of presidential office.

"Two weeks and counting for me. I can scarcely find the privy."

"We're even then. What can I do for you, Mr. President?"

Pierce reached for his desk copy of The Military Appropriations Act of 1853. "It's about your budget appropriation, more specifically the Pacific railroad provisions. Have you had a chance to study them?"

"As a matter of fact, I have. The survey appropriations seem rather straightforward. It's the motivation behind them that gives me pause."

"Yes, I expect we share similar concerns in that regard."

"I'm pleased to hear that, sir. I wasn't sure."

"I'm not a southerner, Jefferson, but I am a Democrat. I am sympathetic to southern interests, particularly where state's rights are concerned."

"Then you understand the problem of choosing a rail route to the Pacific."

"I do."

"As long as the Missouri Compromise stands, a Pacific railroad cannot be built without jeopardizing the balance of power in the Senate."

"I understand. So does Senator Douglas. This railroad is largely his vision."

"So I'm told, and there of course is the rub. This issue is too vital to southern interests to entrust it to a northerner."

"Senator Douglas may be a northerner, but he, too, is a Democrat and no wild-eyed abolitionist. I think you'll find the senator and me like minded on the issue. As chairman of the Senate Committee on Territories, Senator Douglas is in a position to influence the way forward to an acceptable resolution."

Davis studied the president. "I see his position in the Senate. We know he has a reputation for getting things done. The proof of all you say will be in the pudding. I suspect my fellow southerners will wait to have a taste before passing judgment on the acceptability of his resolution."

"I'm sure you're right about your colleagues in the southern caucus, Jefferson. We've been friends long enough; I hope you will trust my judgment where Senator Douglas is concerned. But, as you say, the southern delegation will have to be convinced as events unfold. All that aside, you still have a survey to conduct. Have you given that as much thought as the longer-term ramifications of a Pacific railroad?"

"I've discussed it with my engineers and surveyors. They recommend five survey parties."

"Five? Doesn't that seem rather excessive?"

"Not five routes, sir. Three parties will survey routes west across the northern plains, across the central plains to the Rockies, and a southern route through our newly acquired possessions. The other two will survey passages east from California that might link to the three primary choices."

"I see. That seems a reasonable plan. When might you begin?"

"Preparations are already under way. I should think we might begin in May, June at the latest."

"Excellent, Jefferson. Find us a good route, and leave the politics to the politicians. Those matters are in capable hands."

"I hope so, Mr. President."

"Come now, Jefferson, I have a taste for pudding myself."

Hudson, Ohio
July, 1853

"West?" The question rolled off Hiram Mason's tongue, leaving behind a sour taste.

"You can't be serious, Micah." Eugenie dabbed at her eye with a handkerchief.

"I'm sorry, Ma, but we are." Micah wrapped a protective arm around Clare's shoulder, standing together on the news that struck Sunday's family dinner silent. "We've given it a great deal of thought. There is a future to be had out there."

"But you have a future here," Pa said. "We have the farm."

"We do have the farm, Pa, with more than enough mouths to feed without Clare and me adding to the number. We need to make our own future."

Pa considered the practicality of his son's point.

"Hiram, you must make him see reason."

"He does see reason, dear. We may not feel it in our hearts, but Micah sees it clearly in his thinking. Where might you go, son? 'West' takes in a great deal of territory."

"We're not certain yet, Pa. Somewhere we might take advantage of prosperity brought by the railroad."

"Railroads? What do you know of railroads?"

"I know they make opportunity wherever they go. You've only to look around us to see the effects on commerce."

"Commerce? You're a farmer."

"I am a farmer, a small farmer. With a railroad to transport crops to markets too far to serve by wagon, cash crops become practical. Cash crops can be grown on a large scale."

"Farming is a family business."

"It doesn't have to be. Our farm is small because we have a limited amount of land. Land here is expensive. That keeps us small. Land in the west is plentiful and there for working it."

"The size of a farm is limited by the labor needed to work it."

"Farming on a large scale can be done. Consider the cotton plantations in the South."

"They do so with slave labor! You can't possibly be thinking of that."

"Not slave labor, Pa. Cash crops can pay hired help."

"Hmm."

All eyes were riveted on Micah, brothers and sisters open mouthed at the power of his argument.

"Hiram, please talk sense to the boy."

"Eugenie, he's not a boy. He's a man with a wife and the prospect of a family to provide for." Hiram paused to fold his napkin. "What sort of cash crop are you thinking?"

"I don't know. It will depend on the suitability of the land. I'm studying corn and wheat."

His father nodded. "I can see those possibilities."

"Oh, Hiram." Ma rose, signaling the girls to begin clearing the dishes.

Chapter Two

Washington City
November, 1853

Cold, gray afternoon lit the office window. Senator Douglas sat at his desk reading draft legislation. He set it aside and removed his spectacles. He'd found the way, of course. He always did. The irony of it appealed to him. The way forward from the current impasse was simply a return to the condition that created it in the first place. Fashioning the legislation had been trivial. Navigating it through the crosscurrents of a bitterly divided Congress would require every ounce of his considerable political acumen. That started with securing the confidence of the greatest skeptics, his own Democrat colleagues in the southern caucus. He might be a Democrat, but as a northerner he could not be completely trusted. He'd chosen his co-sponsor candidate carefully with that difficulty in mind.

"Senator Atchison to see you, sir."

He glanced at the door. His secretary waited expectantly. He rose to greet his guest. "Send him in, Robert."

Senator David Rice Atchison of Missouri strode into the office.

"David, good afternoon. Good of you to come." Douglas crossed the floor, his hand extended.

"When the chair of a committee as important as Territories calls, what choice has a good soldier but to obey?"

"I should hope you think of it more as the invitation of a colleague. Please have a seat." He gestured to the settee drawn up before the fireplace.

"I shall judge the occasion by the subject matter for discussion."

The guarded reservation suited Atchison, who personified the stiff demeanor of a fire and brimstone preacher. Long of feature, his dour expression became exaggerated by a mop of wavy, brown hair swept back from a broad forehead. He wore a severe frock coat, cravat, and vest. He folded his frame into the offered cushions.

"Ever the vigilant pragmatic." Douglas retrieved the draft legislation from his desk and took a wing chair beside the settee.

"So, what's on your mind, Stephen?"

"I need your help, David."

"Of course you do. That's why I'm here. The question is help with what?"

"Right to the point. Help in building a rail route to the Pacific."

"I've listened to the arguments. I've read your opinions as reported in the press. One can hardly argue the notion on merit. It's the sensitivity of where it will be built that gives us pause."

"Which is precisely why I need your help."

"Help to deliver the southern caucus to be sure, but deliver it to what purpose? The surveys have yet to be completed."

"True, they haven't been completed, but it doesn't matter. No matter the route recommended, any proposal will run afoul of the Missouri Compromise."

"You propose to repeal it?"

"It no longer serves the purpose for which it was intended."

"At the risk of speaking for my colleagues, I must tell you anything that upsets the balance of power in the Senate will never be enacted."

"Which is why I need your help. I've had a bill drawn. I'd like you to sign on as a co-sponsor."

"And champion it in our caucus."

"If you believe it to be the way forward." He handed Mason the bill.

"The Kansas-Nebraska Act. Two territories—one slave, the other presumably free."

"That's how the old formula worked."

"And this bill of yours would repeal the Missouri Compromise?"

"Not yet."

"What do you mean 'not yet'?"

"It will after you discuss it with your caucus. They'll demand it, and we'll give it to them."

"Clever. That should appeal to my side, but your northern friends will never stand for it."

"True. They'll scream bloody murder. They will support the Pacific railroad on merit just as you do. They will see the need to replace the compromise in order to achieve that noble purpose. In return for repealing the compromise, we will delegate determination of the slavery issue to the territories."

Mason handed the bill back to Douglas. "I shall never ask my colleagues to support anything so uncertain."

"David, do you honestly expect you can get certainty? Do you seriously believe you can long oppose the national destiny this railroad represents? Consider the practicalities. Slavery is an agrarian institution in the south. Abolition is high-minded morality in the industrial north. How do you think the territories will decide for themselves?"

"If that is your plan, why doesn't your bill provide territorial sovereignty on the issue?"

"My good friend, we need something to give our northern friends when they do raise hell."

"I see. You are a clever bastard, Stephen. One last question. Why now?"

"We have a sympathetic White House. Will you join me then?"

"Let me think on it. May I discuss it with some of my colleagues?"

"Please do."

Two Weeks Later

"Senator Atchison to see you, sir."

Douglas waved him in.

Atchison strode across the office without formality. "Stephen." He took a wing chair across from the senator's desk.

"I take it you've had a chance to think over my invitation."

He nodded. "That and discuss it with a few of my colleagues."

"And?"

"Senator Dixon of Kentucky has the ear of the caucus. He was both strident and eloquent in stating a case my colleagues wholeheartedly embraced. We can't support your Kansas-Nebraska Act, I'm afraid, without repeal of the Missouri Compromise."

"What did you tell them?"

"I told them I would make their position clear to you."

"You have. I accept."

"I thought you might. Now we shall see if your brokered horse trading can bring the other side along."

"No brokered trading this time. We'll introduce the bill to the new Congress next year. Let the fireworks start on the floor so our friends have the luxury of vigorous political opposition, before we surrender to our victory."

"You are a devious bastard, Stephen."

Douglas smiled. "Merry Christmas, David."

Chapter Three

Washington City
February, 1854

"The chair recognizes the honorable senator from the great state of Massachusetts for the purpose of debate."

Senator Charles Sumner strode across the chamber floor to the podium. His angular frame hunched forward, his lion-like dark mane bent in concentration. His demeanor rendered grim by the gravity of the matter at hand. A formidable orator, Sumner's abolitionist views were well known and widely anticipated. He was rumored to be aligning himself with those who sought to form a new Republican party. He mounted the podium and let his gaze wander over the assembled chamber. A cough here, a shuffle of paper there was all that could be heard from a chamber in anticipation.

"Gentle friends," he paused, allowing the timbre of his voice to draw his audience to attention. "I stand before you today in opposition to the legislative proposal known as the Kansas-Nebraska Act. By its repeal of the Missouri Compromise, this bill seeks to further the sinful stain of slavery on the moral fabric of this great nation."

The Democrat delegation shifted in uneasy courtesy while members of the southern caucus could be heard to grumble under their breath.

"If that causes some in this assembly discomfort, so be it. The keeping of slaves, even those certain societies may deem of inferior station, is morally repugnant. It cannot be justified in a free society founded under the guidance of almighty God. For thirty-four years, the Missouri Compromise has provided a bulwark against the spread of the moral contagion that is slavery. Now, the measure before this body, this Kansas-Nebraska Act, seeks to restore the immoral quid pro quo progression of this sin against God and nature.

"How can we, as men of conscience, contemplate such an action?" He paused. "Ask yourself that question. Bow your head in prayer over the answer. Do we justify such an action in the name of some destiny to westward expansion? Some say such a destiny is manifest. Manifest by whom? Manifest by our Divine Creator? Are we to believe that the highest power foreordains the spread of this evil? Nay, I say! Never! We are called to put aside this evil practice, not perpetuate it.

"I call on all members of this body and all men of clean heart and clear conscience to join me in opposition to this travesty. Surely our ambition to westward expansion can be accommodated without subjecting the weaker among us to a life of involuntary servitude. This nation was founded in freedom. It can no longer abide denying the disadvantaged the nectar of freedom so as to profit the advantaged few. How can we, as men of conscience, contemplate such an action? Ask yourself that question to the depths of your soul.

"Mr. President, I yield the floor."

Abolitionists, Whigs, and Republicans rose in an explosion of support. The southern delegation scowled disapproval restrained by decorum. Their northern Democrat sympathizers sat in uncomfortable solidarity. The gavel rang calling the chamber to order.

"This body stands adjourned until two o'clock for midday recess."

Senator Sumner crossed the floor and marched up the aisle,

accepting the congratulations of fellow abolitionists and the chill disregard of those who opposed him. As he neared the chamber entrance, he noticed a diminutive figure awaiting him. Senator Douglas would no doubt have sharp words of disagreement. Sumner meant to pass him by. They had little to discuss.

"Eloquent as usual, Charles. May I have a word?"

Sumner paused. "Was it something I failed to make clear?"

Douglas smiled. "Of course not. You made yourself perfectly clear. In fact, you said something I rather agree with."

"Good heavens, you don't mean I've changed your mind on some point."

"On this point, I've no need to change. You said there must be a way to accommodate our ambition to westward expansion. We both agree on that. There's too much at stake here not to. We've only to find the accommodation. May we talk?"

"Where? I've not much time, but I'm listening."

Douglas glanced around the chamber slowly emptying for lunch. "This way." He led them to the cloak room off the foyer.

A cloak room, Sumner thought. One of the most divisive issues to come before the Senate in decades, and they turn to a cloak room to discuss it.

"Is there some accommodation you have in mind, Stephen?"

"Not that I can specifically propose. As I understand your position, it's repeal of the Missouri Compromise that causes your opposition, not the prospect of a Pacific railroad."

"True."

"Our southern friends of course have a deeply vested interest in maintaining a balanced representation between slave and free states in this body."

"A balance that can't last. You're a pragmatic man, Stephen. Surely you know that."

"I do know that. I don't hold with slavery myself. My position may not be as fervent as yours, but I don't believe the practice can withstand the test of time. It's more a matter of when and how it comes to an end. You make the point morality will guide people of good conscience to that conclusion. The practice of slavery is a southern tradition. We don't see it much in the north where, for the most part, people of good character have rejected the practice. Frankly, I think if the question were left to people of good character, the practice would come to a natural end."

Sumner knit his brows. "You might be on to something there, Stephen."

"On to what?"

"Popular sovereignty. Let the people decide the disposition of the issue in the expansion territories. After all, morality is on the right side of the issue."

"That does make some sense. Would your members go along with such a thing?"

"They might. I can ask."

"Do that. We'll still have to repeal the Missouri Compromise to retain southern support. With luck, they won't see the moral imperative the way we do. It just might work."

"It might at that." Sumner drew a watch from his vest pocket and popped the lid. "You'll have to excuse me. All this accommodation has me late for my next appointment."

"Talk to your colleagues, Charles. I'll wait to hear from you." *Popular sovereignty*—perfectly reasonable.

Chapter Four

Hudson, Ohio
March, 1854

Lean and gnarled as an old hickory, John Brown sat hunched over the kitchen table reading by lamp light. The House of Representatives passed the Senate's Kansas-Nebraska Act. The *Cleveland Plain Dealer* editorial expected President Pierce would sign it into law by the end of the week. The editor sounded a cautionary note. Repealing the Missouri Compromise ceded the slavery issue to the sovereignty of the subject territories. The sovereignty issue would first be tested in Kansas. The editorial pointed to pro-slavery sentiments in neighboring Missouri and the potential for both sides of the issue to be represented in territorial elections. Brown smelled a fight, a fight that must be won.

He held deeply religious convictions against the practice of slavery. He'd taken a vow to see it abolished, by violent means if necessary. Increasingly, it appeared violence would be needed. He couldn't foresee the time or the place that might be decisive, but he had a strong feeling the next skirmish must take place in the west. He felt honor bound to rise up in opposition to any attempt to advance the sinful practice beyond its current borders. Contain it first—his dark eyes flashed in the lamplight—then crush it. That would be his message to the congregation come Sunday. He would testify to his conviction. He and his sons would rise up to lead a righteous opposition. They would embark on a sacred mission—a crusade west to weed out Satan's work before it could take root in new soil.

Harness chain jangle and wagon wheel creak broke his reverie. Brown set the paper aside, picked up the table lamp, and stepped into the cool spring evening. The horse-drawn wagon disappeared into the barn. He crossed the yard to the barn as his eldest son, Salmon, stepped down from the wagon box. A strapping lad, taller and heavier than his patriarch, he wore a slouch hat over shoulder-length hair, a homespun shirt, and overalls.

"Any trouble?" the elder Brown said.

Salmon shook his head. He pulled back the canvas covering the bed of the wagon. Three pair of wide eyes stared up from the shadows, their anxious faces reflecting the lamplight.

"Welcome. My name is John Brown. You're safe here." He turned to his son. "Have they had anything to eat?"

"Not since morning."

"Make them comfortable in the shed. I'll send Mary Ann with victuals. Come, please."

A powerfully built black man climbed down from the wagon box. He held out his hand to a handsome young woman and a young girl of perhaps four or five. All three were shabbily dressed in ill-fitting clothes likely given them as they made their way north on the so called underground railroad. These would be numbered among the fortunate who managed to escape the trackers empowered to apprehend them by the punitive Fugitive Slave Law.

Brown handed the lamp to his son and set off for the house.

Sunday

Buggies and wagons scattered about the sun-soaked yard of the little white church. Hobbled teams cropped grass or slept hip shot in their traces. Bees danced across patches of spring flowers in a pleasant counterpoint to the fat, black flies buzzing fresh horse and mule droppings. A lark took up a melody to the fading organ chords of the final hymn.

Inside, the small congregation sat in muted golden glow, spilling through windows lining both sides of the church. The wooden pews smelled a mixture of wood polish and beeswax. The parson raised his arms as the strains of the final hymn died away.

"Please be seated. Elder Brown has requested a moment to address you before we adjourn our service this day."

Micah and Clare settled into the pews with the rest of the congregation.

Elder Brown rose from the front pew. His family filled the first row and much of the second. He ascended to the pulpit resplendent in black frock coat and starched Sunday shirt. Flashing dark eyes gathered the congregation up to him.

"Brothers and sisters, I come before you today with a heavy heart. I am grieved by the scourge of slavery that oppresses our land. You know I have committed myself and my family to the extermination of this plague Satan works in our midst. He and those possessed by him enslave our Negro brothers and sisters. He condemns them to servile existence, as beasts of burden. Satan and those who practice his abomination buy and sell our fellow men and women like chattel. They beat them and subject them to all manner of degradation. They tear families asunder. Fathers separated from the mothers of their children. Children torn from their mother's breast.

"For too long now these sinful depredations have continued a dark stain on the soul of this nation. This moral abomination must be brought to an end by whatever means may be required. If it be by blood, let it be blood. If it be by fire, then let it be fire. If it be by God's righteous wrath, let it be God's everlasting condemnation. For our part, my sons and I can no longer stand idly by. It is time to heed God's call. It is time to mount righteous action.

"In the coming days, I fear we face yet another outbreak of this blight on our society. Westward expansion will follow the route yet to be chosen for a Pacific railway. Even now the dark fingers of Satan's minions plot the spread of this vile leprosy in the name of the nation's westward destiny. If we are indeed a God-fearing people, we cannot allow this. We cannot permit this to happen. My sons and I will not permit it to happen. We will stop it by whatever means may be required. If it be by fire, let us kindle the blaze. If it be by blood, let it be by our blood. If it be by God's righteous wrath, let us be the instrument of His fury. We will be victorious or die in the trying. So be it! So help me God."

His fire slacked to an ember, he returned to his seat. No one moved for a time. Then slowly, quietly, the church emptied from the rear pews. The light, sociable mood that accompanied departure from service most Sundays was eerily absent this day. Families departed in silence to their carriages and wagons for a thoughtful ride home.

Micah helped Clare up to the buggy seat. He unfastened the tie-down and hefted the weight into the back bed. He climbed up beside her and clucked to the bay. He wheeled out the churchyard and up the dirt road toward home.

"Do you think it will come to that?" Clare said.

"Come to what?"

"Blood and fire."

"I suspect so. Brother Brown has strong sentiments for abolition. I expect we could have attended services in a similar church in the south and heard an equally strident defense of their way of life."

"But it is morally wrong. You believe that, Micah, I know you do."

"I do. I'm only saying there are blood and fire on both sides. The cause Brother Brown advances will not be easily settled."

They drove in silence for a time.

"Brother Brown's views on slavery are well known," Micah said. "I was little surprised by what he said today. But he did say one thing that spoke to me."

She lifted her chin, her bonnet shading her eyes.

"They will build the Pacific railroad to lead the way west. When they do, that is where a man might make a future for his family."

"The route is yet to be chosen. Who would know where to go?"

"All the signs favor a central route. If Brother Brown is right and the fight will be about slavery, then the route will go west from Missouri. The wagon routes west did. Missouri is the northernmost slave state. The western plains are well suited for farming. A man might stake out his claim and let the expansion come to him."

"It's such a long way. What if the expansion doesn't come?"

He wrapped an arm around her shoulder and hugged her to him. "It will, my dear. It is . . . destiny."

Chapter Five

Jackson County, Missouri
April, 1854

The overseer mounted on a smart bay horse led them down a dusty country road. Barefoot slaves padded along behind in file followed by the underboss mounted on a gray gelding. Songbirds lifted melody to the hum of insects already busy at first light. Cool early morning slowly warmed, absorbing the coming heat of the day.

At planting and harvest times the massas pooled their slaves to make shorter work of the chores. Today Massa Ruben sent his crew to Massa Morgan Walker's farm to finish the spring planting. Caleb walked along with the rest, distinguished only by being among the taller more solidly made men in the party. He wore an ill-fitting, plaid shirt and tattered overalls suspended by a single shoulder strap. A male of twenty-two, according to plantation records, he'd been born to be a field hand. He had broad shoulders and long strapping muscles forged of hard labor. A mat of close cropped, black curls framed finely carved features with wide-set, dark eyes lidded in long lashes that spoke to a gentle heart. Early spring morning, heavy with the promise of a warm day, gave his brow a sheen of polished ebony. Redding, the overseer, considered him a docile, willing worker. The practiced demeanor pleased Caleb, though he ruled the simmer within by firm resolve.

A short while later they turned up a new road, passing under an arch that marked the Morgan Walker property. The road climbed a low rise past planted fields and gardens toward an imposing white house, standing watch over Massa Walker's holdings. They passed by the house, barns, and slave quarters beyond on the way to the north section they would plant this day.

The Morgan Walker slaves were already at work, plowing, planting, raking, and sprinkling new sowings with their first taste of water. A pair of sturdy mules stood harnessed to a plow, awaiting the new arrivals. Redding wasted no time. He nodded to his counterpart.

"Caleb, take the plow and keep them furrows straight." He called others to shoulder heavy burlap sacks filled with seed. Younger boys and those less hardy were given rakes and watering cans. The filled watering cans made heavy lifting for those unused to it but were sure to build the strength for heavier labor in seasons yet to come.

Caleb gathered the mule team lines, set the plow blade, and clucked the team off up the fence row. He'd schooled himself on managing mules. It was a worthwhile skill. Master the cut of a straight furrow and you had a skill for a job where mules worked for a man. He fancied that poetry over the work crew strung out behind him, men working like mules for the man on a horse with a whip.

To be fair, Redding seldom resorted to the whip. Massa Ruben frowned on the abuse of valuable property, though beatings were not unheard of. Like that time Muddy Rivers run off. They sent the slave catcher Jacob Herd after him. That man was one mean son of a rabid bitch dog. They brought Ole Muddy back. Massa Ruben said make an example of him. Redding stretched him out on a hitch rack. He made them all watch while he laid on with that black snake 'til Muddy Rivers run red in his own blood. Redding cleaned the wounds with a bucket of brine. That's when Ole Muddy passed out. No one watching that day had run off since.

He'd finished his fourth row when she came with the water bucket. Planting, harvesting, Sunday church socials, weddings and such . . . you got to know folks. He remembered this one growing up. She handed him a dipper of water with eyes so soft and brown he wondered if they even had a bottom. He stopped to take notice. She'd surely grown up all of a sudden since last harvest. She stood a head shorter than he, though she filled out a faded, gingham dress in fine form. An earthy beauty poured out of creamed coffee skin, black, curly hair tied up in a red bandanna, and high cheekbones to go with them eyes.

"Thank you."

"Miriam."

"Miriam?"

"My name. You was fixin' to ask me my name."

"Was I now?"

She nodded.

"I'm Caleb."

"I know. I asked when you was about my age."

"What age is that?"

"Eighteen, this summer."

"Caleb!" Redding said. "Quit your lollygaggin'. That field ain't gonna plow itself. You got a whole crew waitin' on you."

He smiled. Her eyes smiled back.

The sun rode high onto lunch time. Caleb unhitched the mules and drove them down to the creek to water. By the time he came back, most of the crews had scattered to shady spots to take their lunch. He was the last in the food line. The girl, Miriam, fixed his plate.

"Has you had your lunch?"

She shook her head.

"Why don't you fix yourself a plate and join me by that tree over yonder?"

She looked around. The overseers were all gone up to the big house to take their meal. She smiled.

"That'd be real polite." She filled a plate and followed him along the fence line to the shade of a stately oak. They settled side by side.

"So, Miriam, eighteen this summer, they treats you all right here?"

She shrugged. "So far mostly."

"You don't sound so sure. I hear Massa Morgan's a good man." He took a bite of ham sandwich.

"He is. It's the son worries me."

"The son—why?"

"He looks at me."

He chuckled. "Why that's no surprise. I s'pect a lot a' boys look at you."

"Some may look, but they ain't doin' nothin' less I says so. That one wants his daddy to make me a house slave."

"House slaves get a pretty good life."

"Not like that. Not with him. Not for me."

"You do have your opinions, girl. So what's to be done about it?"

She munched a pickle. "I thought maybe if I was to jump the broom, he'd lose interest in a married woman."

"Well you's old enough for that. You must have some prospects on a place this size."

"None that comes up to my standards."

"There go them opinions again."

She cast a sidelong glance with a merry glint peeking from inside. "Now, if a fella like you was to suggest such a thing, any girl with a lick a' sense wouldn't think twice."

"What? Did I just hear you propose to a man you don't even know?"

"Oh, I know you. I been watchin' you since I was old enough to know why."

"If that's not the craziest thing I ever heard, I don't know what is."

"You don't like me?"

"I didn't say that."

"Then you do like me."

"I didn't say that, either. I got blood in my veins is all I said."

"Well, you should like me."

"Oh, should I. Now why would that be?"

"On account a' it wouldn't be right."

"What wouldn't be right?"

"You jumpin' the broom with a woman you didn't like."

"There you go again, girl, jumpin' to that broom with your opinions."

"Ain't no opinion. It's settled."

"How's what settled? Other than maybe you been out in the sun too long. Even if I was to like you some, we don't even belong to the same massa."

She grinned. "See, you do like me."

"Likin's got nothing to do with it. Who's gonna sell who? Your Massa Morgan's son got a fancy for you? My massa thinks I plow a straight furrow?"

"We'll figure it out. I sees it written in the stars. You just have to think about it."

She stood, collected his plate, and set off for the serving tables.

Just think about it. Miriam, eighteen this summer, jumpin' the broom. Written in stars, no less. My, my, she do cut a fine figure walkin' that way.

Chapter Six

Hudson, Ohio
April, 1854

Hudson awakened slowly on a sunny spring Saturday morning. Micah made it into town early walking the dirt road from the family farm. Now that they'd made the decision to make a life in the west, they had much to do in the coming days. They put their small savings into outfitting the trip. He had a long list. He could only hope the money would cover it.

Jethro Hardy's blacksmith shop and livery stood at the west end of town. Hudson may be lingering over morning coffee, but Jethro was hard at work at his forge.

"Mornin', Jethro."

The barrel-chested smithy in a scorched, stained leather apron smiled through a bush of black whiskers. He extended a meaty, calloused hand. "Micah, what can I do for you?"

"I'm interested in that old Conestoga freighter you've got out back. Is she serviceable, and if she is, is she for sale?"

The smithy chuckled. "In my business, everything's for sale. Is she serviceable? That depends on what you have in mind for her."

"Clare and I are moving west."

Jethro scratched his beard. "Just the two of you, usual provisions, and some household items . . . I expect she'd handle that as long as you're not plannin' to haul any pianos, anvils, or organs."

Micah chuckled. "Nope, none of that."

"Come on, we'll have a look at her."

He led the way around to the back of the shop. The derelict old wagon stood parked in the shade of a gnarled oak. The bows arched over the wagon bed without a canvas cover like skeleton ribs. Micah walked around her. The box springs and wheel rims were rusted, though they appeared to be sound. He hefted the tongue and examined it for rot. It, too, appeared sound.

"The wheels will need greasing, and I expect she'll need fresh tar to water tighten her," Jethro said.

"What do you want for her?"

He scratched his chin again. "She'd run three hundred new."

Micah winced. That would take most of a third of the money they had for the whole outfit.

Jethro read his expression. "You're gonna need stock to pull her and harness for the stock. I got a matched pair of mules that'd do a good job for you. Handle your plowin' once you get where you're goin', too. Tell you what I'll do: you take care of the grease and the tar, and I'll let you have her as she sits with the mules and harness for two hundred fifty dollars. I'll even throw in her old canvas cover. Needs some patchin', but she'll do."

Micah brightened. "Let's have a look at them mules."

The matched pair were five-year-old buckskins, a jack and a jenny. Micah spent the morning greasing the wheels. By early afternoon he had the team hitched for the drive up the street to the Hudson Mercantile Emporium. He climbed into the box, waved to Jethro, and clucked to the team. The old schooner rocked up the street without much complaint. He hauled lines at the mercantile, set the brake, and climbed down with his list. He checked the items he needed to buy against those the family might stake them to.

No one was happy about their decision to leave home, especially Ma. Pa saw the practicality of it. The family farm had all it could do to provide for the mouths it already fed. His brothers had yet to grow into their own families, and the girls would soon enough marry off to their own. He climbed the boardwalk and stepped into the welcoming smells of coffee, smoked meat, burlap, and coal oil.

"Afternoon, Micah." Marlin Fitzweiler, the proprietor, smiled from behind the counter. "What can I do for you today?"

"I've got an order to fill."

Marlin glanced out the front window at the wagon. "That mean what I think it means?"

Micah nodded. "Clare and me are movin' west."

"I'm sorry to hear that, though these days a body can surely understand why. I suspect it's a rather large order."

"It is." He slid the list across the counter.

"Might take a day or two to fill all of this."

"I thought as much. I've got some work to do on the wagon. How about if I come back for it next Tuesday."

"Tuesday should be fine."

The arrival of the wagon brought reality to their leaving. Conversation around the family supper table that evening was noticeably subdued. They'd quietly assembled the hard goods needed for the journey. That had gone more or less unnoticed. Now they had a place to load it. That would begin as soon as the wagon bed was sealed.

"Pass the potatoes," Pa said. "That's a fine pair of mules Jethro sold you, son. They'll get you wherever you want to go. Let's hope that wagon is as serviceable."

"It's sound, Pa. Maybe not pretty, but she's sound. She'll get us as far as we need to go."

"How far is that?"

"Northwest of Missouri, eight or nine hundred miles I reckon."

"They say the land out there makes for good farming," Pa said.

"It does, best I can figure."

"Still planning to farm a cash crop?"

"I am."

"Cash crop needs to get to market."

"It does. We might not be able to start with a cash crop right off, but once the railroad comes, we'll be able to get a cash crop to market."

"Waitin' on the railroad could take some time."

"It likely will, Pa, but it will come; and when it does, it will change everything."

"I hope you're right, son. For both your sakes, I hope you're right."

Ma reached for her handkerchief as she did each time the subject came up.

Chapter Seven

The sun was full up by the time the cow was milked and the stock fed. The boys went off to the house for breakfast. Micah crossed the yard through a flock of pecking chickens to the cabin in the sycamores. He clumped up the step and swung through the door to the smells of bacon and coffee.

"Sure smells good in here to a hungry man."

Clare glanced over her shoulder at the stove, turning sizzling bacon strips. "Food always smells good to you."

"Wagon seal looks set up good enough to start packin'. Have you finished patching the canvas cover?"

"I have; it's ready to put up. I've also made a list. It's on the table."

"I've got the list. I've been checkin' things off right along as we collected them."

She smiled. "Not that list. This list puts things in order for packing. Hard goods we'll need when we homestead go first near the front. Stores go next in the middle. Daily things we'll need while we travel toward the back where they're easy to unload for the night."

He picked up the list and read. He shook his head, set the list down, and crossed the dirt floor. He wrapped his arms around her waist and kissed her neck below the ear. "You do think of everything."

"Just bein' practical is all. Now you be practical, too, Micah

Mason, or you'll have me burn this bacon."

There. Micah wiped sweat from his hands on his britches. He surveyed the first part of his wagon load, estimating the room remaining for the balance of the load. He started with the awkwardly shaped plow. He took it apart and lashed the frame and blades snug against the back of the wagon box. He packed smaller farm implements and basic building tools next, along with seasonal items like snowshoes. He lashed that part of the load to the sides of the wagon in a fashion to hold it from shifting. He brought the team up from the barn and hitched the mules to the wagon. Clare stepped out of the cabin, adjusted her sunbonnet, and stepped off the porch. Micah smiled.

"Just in time."

She peered over the wagon gate to inspect the long-term load, mentally checking that the butter churn was properly packed. Food stores would come next, followed by the items they would need daily along the trail.

"May I?"

He helped her up to the wagon box. He walked around the team checking the harnesses as he made his way to the driver's side. He climbed into the box, released the brake, and clucked to the team. The traces engaged with a lurch down the road into town.

Marlin Fitzweiler wiped his hands on his apron, greeting them with a wave from the boardwalk outside the Hudson Mercantile.

"Pull around back to the loading platform, Micah. It'll make handling an order this size easier."

Moments later Micah and Clare stepped off the wagon box onto the loading platform at the back of the store. Marlin met them there with a hundred-pound sack of flour. The rest of the order was assembled, waiting for them inside. Micah let down the wagon gate and stepped inside. He hefted the flour and carried it to the front of the wagon. Clare stood on the platform with the list checking off the items as Marlin brought them out to the wagon.

Thirty pounds of hardtack, seventy-five pounds of bacon, ten pounds of rice, five pounds of coffee, twenty-five pounds of sugar, ten pounds of salt, and one keg of vinegar. Marlin rolled an empty thirty-five-gallon barrel out to the platform.

"You'll need this for water, Micah. You can mount it on the wagon when you get back to the farm. No charge for the barrel."

"Much obliged for that, Marlin. What do we owe you for the rest of it?"

The shopkeeper wiped his brow on the hem of his apron. He drew a slip of paper from his shirt pocket and handed it to Micah. "A hundred forty-three dollars should do it."

Clare opened her purse and counted out the bills.

"Where you folks headed?"

"Kansas."

"What takes you there?"

"Land. Land and the promise of a rail route to the Pacific. When that happens the market for a cash crop like wheat or corn will stretch as far as the rails will take it."

"Sounds like a lot depends on a rail route that hasn't been chosen yet."

"No, it hasn't, but look at the Baltimore & Ohio. They're betting a whole lot more than we are on a central route that picks up commercial interests in Chicago and along the Mississippi."

"Well I sure hope that part works out for you. Paper says according to that Kansas-Nebraska Act, the vote will decide slavery for the territory. The *Plain Dealer* says it's likely to be controversial with Missouri for a neighbor. Controversial sounds violent to hear Brother Brown tell it."

"We've heard Brother Brown testify in church. I'm hopeful the right of it can be resolved peaceably."

"I hope you're right about that, too, but I'd be careful if I were you. You didn't order caps, powder, or lead. Are you properly armed?"

"I am, though you make a good point. Best add some of all that to the order."

Clare furrowed her brow and followed the men into the store.

They finished packing that afternoon. They added ground corn, canned tomatoes, and half bushels of apples and beans to the food stores. Clare oversaw the last of the load, arranging the things they would need on the way west. They made a bed for sleeping and covered it with a small table, two chairs, a bench, and spare clothing. Last came the coffee grinder, pot, cookware, dishes, water bucket, oil lamp, and candles. Clare nodded, brushing an errant strand of hair off her smudged cheek.

Micah closed the wagon gate as the sun drifted behind the cabin roof. He'd carry the smooth bore cap and ball musket in the wagon box along with a .44 Colt Dragoon and first-aid kit. There'd be time for that in the morning. He put his arm around Clare.

"Ma'll have supper on pretty soon."

"Do we say our good-byes tonight or in the morning?"

"Let's let Ma and Pa decide that. Any other good-byes you feel needful?"

She glanced far away. "Maybe we could stop by the cemetery on the way out of town. I'll take a bouquet for my parents' last respects."

They walked up to the family farmhouse as the supper bell rang.

★ ★ ★ ★ ★

Next morning, they were all there at sunup to see them off. The girls cried. The boys put on their best manly demeanor. Jimmy, the next oldest, shook Micah's hand and accepted responsibility for helping Pa. Pa choked a little on "Good luck, son." Ma gave both of them a tearful hug.

"You be sure to write and let us know when you settle."

Micah nodded around a lump in his throat and helped Clare up to the wagon box. He climbed into the driver's seat and gathered the lines. He took one last look at the family and farm he'd known as home the whole of his life. He released the brake with a wave and clucked to the team. They rocked down the dirt drive to the town road and turned southwest to pick up the National Road west at Columbus.

Jackson County, Missouri
June, 1854

Hot. High summer afforded folks precious little relief from heat's vise-like grip. Even the wind blew hot when it blew. When it didn't, the air shimmered in steamy layers, soaking a person to the pores. Today Caleb didn't mind the heat. He added rock salt to the churn and cranked. He wiped sweat from his eyes with a faded bandanna long gone damp with the chore. A hot summer Sunday was good for fishing or splashing in the creek. On a day like today, it was also good for an ice cream social.

Massa Ruben invited his neighbors to come by after church. Caleb was put to making ice cream. He kept making it, too, even after they had enough for the white folks. Massa Ruben gave him a wink and nod to be sure to make enough for his folk and them as came attending the massa's guests. They'd have a cool, sweet treat from the heat this afternoon.

Massa Morgan Walker was among the first to arrive with his wife and son. Miriam, eighteen this summer, come along, too.

Eighteen this summer, she might be by now. She spotted him while she helped Mrs. Morgan Walker down from the carriage. The family went off to the plantation house. Miriam come down to the ice house, where ice cream making was in progress. She sashayed down the path through the trees with a saucy swivel to her step, wearing that half smile that always made him wonder what might be coming next.

"Afternoon, Caleb."

"I believe it is. Yes, sir, it surely is."

"Don't 'sir' me. I'm a woman."

"Promoted yourself from girl already? Why you must be eighteen now, huh."

"Close enough. Records ain't none too certain on such matters. I reckon you're glad enough to see me," she said, taking a seat on a hay bale.

He added more salt to the ice. "Oh, I don't know, you seem glad enough for both of us."

She pulled a pout and crossed her arms across her chest. "That's a poor way for a man to greet his intentioned."

"That again."

"Yes, that again. You ain't forgot, has you?"

"I ain't forgot you got the notion. How's the house work progressin'?"

"So far he mostly leaves me be 'cept for the watchin'. I 'spect it'll come to no good afore too long. You want me, Caleb, it be time we get to jumpin' that broom."

He paused the crank. "I believe this batch be stiff enough."

"All you got to talk about is ice cream?"

He chuckled. "That be firmin' up, too. What if it don't work?"

"What do you mean?"

"What if he don't lose interest over you bein' taken to wife?"

"We won't know lessen we try."

"We still ain't got the answer to which one of us gets sold.

Won't do no good to wed if we ain't together."

"I told you to think on that. You mean you ain't come up with a plan yet?"

"Not one with a ghost of a chance it might work." He waved over a boy to run the finished batch of ice cream up to the house. He poured cream batter and maple syrup into the churn. "Make yourself useful and fetch me some ice."

She knit her brow in a scowl and did as she was told.

Caleb repacked the churn in ice, added salt, and returned to turning the crank.

Miriam sat on the hay bale, hunched elbows to knees, and rested her chin on her fists. She fixed him with those deep, brown eyes no man could deny.

"There's one way we can jump the broom and be together."

"Well that's good to know. How could I have missed it? And what would that be?"

"Run away."

He stopped mid crank. "And I thought jumpin' broom was a crazy notion. You ever seen what they do to runaway folks?"

"I heard stories."

"I seen it. Miriam, eighteen this summer, you don't want no part of that."

"That's only if they catch you."

"But that's what they do. They send Jacob Herd and them dogs of his after you. They catch you and bring you back to teach the folks watchin' a nasty lesson. You might not think them carnal house chores is so bad compared to that."

"You don't care enough for me you'd let that snot nose white boy have his way with me?"

"I care enough not to want to see you bad hurt for a runaway slave."

"Good. That'd be it then."

"That'd be what?"

"We jump the broom tonight after supper."

"You're crazy, girl!"

"Crazy in love with you. And you're in love with me. You just ain't admitted it in so many words just yet."

"Jump the broom and live apart." He shook his head.

"Like I said, we run away."

"That's silly talk."

"All we got to do is get us to Kansas. It ain't far, and it's fillin' up with Abolitionist Yankees who run them railroads under the ground. We'll be safe there before that slave catcher can round up his dogs."

"You mean underground railroad. The heat must a' got to your mind, girl. You wouldn't have the least notion how to find one."

"Get on with makin' ice cream. We got us a celebration tonight."

"You're serious."

"I am."

"And here I thought this all might just be a bad dream."

"What do you need bad dreams for? Look at me. You got a better offer?"

Chapter Eight

Indiana
June 1854

The National Road stretched a broad thoroughfare from its trans-Appalachian origins all the way to Illinois, paving the way to westward expansion. This leg of the journey rolled across a flat, grassy landscape punctuated by small farms, cultivated fields, scattered hamlets, and inviting inns. The towns offered brief respites from the rigors of the road, but most nights they camped beside the road and slept in the wagon bed. The folks they encountered on the road were freighters shipping produce east or manufactured and imported goods west. Others were neighborly to some nearby town or the occasional drummer peddling his wares. They didn't see much by way of other travelers headed west. That'd likely come further on toward St. Louis.

After a few weeks on the road they had their daily routine down. They'd drive until late afternoon, then find a shady spot or an inviting stream to camp alongside. They'd first see to the mules. Much to Micah's surprise, Clare took a hand in that. She seemed to enjoy tending them with a brush or the water bucket. With the mules picketed to graze, they'd unpack the table and chairs along with the cookware to get on with the business of fixing supper. Most nights they relaxed at table after the meal, enjoying a little restful conversation. One pleasant evening with crickets chirping and frogs croaking Clare said, "They're such sweet willing workers."

"Who?"

"The mules. They're not at all what folks lead you to expect."

Micah glanced toward the shapes picketed in shadow beyond the circle of lamplight near the creak. "They are a good pair." He smiled.

"What's funny?"

"I just never figured you for a mule-skinner."

She wrinkled her nose. "Please, that sounds so nasty."

"That's why it's funny."

"Well, I've been thinking. They're both so sweet they deserve names."

"I call 'em Jack and Jenny. That seems good enough."

"You gonna call your children 'boy' and 'girl'?"

"They're mules. They're not children."

"All the same, they deserve proper names."

"Well since you been thinkin', I expect you've got that figured out, too."

"I may. I favor Samson and Delilah."

"Seems kind a' high and mighty for a pair of mules, but if it makes you happy, Sampson and Delilah it is."

"Good. Now let's clean this up and get some rest. We've still got a long way to go."

Towers of dark cloud billowed out of the west to greet the gray light of predawn. Clare fixed coffee and a breakfast of biscuits and bacon while Micah harnessed the newly dubbed royal couple. The mules took their new-found status in stride, more intent on browse and water before the day's travel.

Clare eyed the threatening sky as she handed Micah his plate. "Looks like we may get wet today."

"Part of traveling. Keep the slickers handy," he said around a bite of bacon.

She blew on a steamy cup of coffee. "How much further do

you figure we have to go?"

"Depends on how far it is to a place that strikes us as home. Best part of six weeks I reckon."

"Seems like we've come a long way already. How far west is west?"

"Once we cross the Mississippi, we can figure we're west. Best get to it before the rains slop up the roads."

They watched the young couple pack up their camp and hitch up the team. Rough-cut men, drifting west, living off opportunities the journey presented.

"Sodbuster with a pretty wife," said the burly man with cold eyes and a bushy, black beard.

"Easy pickin's," the ferret-faced, skinny one said in a reedy voice. "Where do you figure to take 'em?"

The big man glanced at the sky. "Sooner rather than later. Rain comes, that wagon would make for some dry shelter while we pick over the take and take our time with the woman."

Ferret face bobbed his head in anticipation.

The burly man turned to his horse, adjusting the ball and cap Colt at his hip.

Clare sensed them before she heard hoofbeats. She glanced over her shoulder through the canvas tunnel.

"Riders coming fast."

Micah nodded.

Two shabbily clad men of rough description loped past the wagon. A short way up the road they drew rein and wheeled their mounts to meet the wagon head on.

Unease tightened Micah's gut. He slipped the hammer thong off the Colt on his hip. He'd never had to use it in defense of life or property. He hoped he didn't have to now. If he did, he hoped he could. He drew the team to a halt.

"Good morning." He forced a smile.

The bearded man's hand appeared from inside his coat, gun in hand.

"We aren't carryin' money, friend, just household goods. You're welcome to some food if you're hungry."

"Ma'm, ease that gun out of your husband's holster with two fingers and drop it over the side of the wagon."

Clare cut her eyes to Micah.

"Do as he says, Clare."

She lifted the gun and dropped it as instructed.

"She sure is purty," the skinny one said.

"Shut up," the bearded man said. "Now climb down from the wagon. Both of you on the driver's side."

Micah set the brake. He climbed down, willing his knees to support him. He turned his back on the two men and reached up to help Clare, fighting to remain calm. He brought her to the ground shielded from the gunman by his body. Over her shoulder, he could see riders coming down the road toward them. He squeezed her arms in his hands, hoping she got the message to stay there. He turned back to the gunmen.

"Company's coming." He tossed his head up the road. "I should think they'll wonder why you're holding that gun on us."

The bearded man looked up the road. "Tell 'em you had a breakdown. We come by to help like good Samaritans. You've no need to delay them. Remember the gun may be out of sight, but there's nothin' in this coat gonna stop a bullet."

As the riders approached, Micah recognized Salmon Brown, Brother Brown's eldest son. The two men with him were younger brothers Frederick and Owen. Clare recognized them, too. She caught his eye. He directed his gaze under the wagon with unspoken instruction. She nodded.

Salmon drew rein. "Brother Mason, is that you?"

"It is, Salmon." He made a finger pistol hidden from the

bandits' view. "We had a bit of a breakdown. These two gentlemen stopped to help."

Salmon cut his eyes to the two mounted men fronting the team. "Anything my brothers and I can do to help an old neighbor?"

"Things is patched up now," the burly man said. "No need to trouble yourself."

"How about I have a look," Salmon said. "You know how good I am with wagons, Micah." He stepped down and rounded the front of his horse with a shotgun leveled at the burly man. "Now, lemme see your hands."

The man lifted the gun from his coat.

"Drop it. Now!"

The gun hit the ground.

"We can do this one of two ways. You two can get gone and never let me see either of your ugly faces again; or, in about ten seconds, I'm gonna air out this eight-gauge at your considerable expense."

They wheeled their horses and galloped up the road.

Micah let out a breath he'd forgotten. "Brother Brown, the angel Gabriel himself couldn't have looked no better than you boys did just now. We're mighty grateful."

"Honest folk shouldn't have to put up with the likes of them. You do travel armed don't you, Micah?"

"I do. He got the drop on me."

"When it comes to strangers on the road, it pays to get the drop on them first until you figure the difference between friend and foe."

"Sound advice. I shall remember it."

Clare walked around the wagon and retrieved Micah's gun.

"We heard you was moving west before we left Hudson," Salmon said. "Where you headed?"

"Kansas."

"So are we. Pa says it'll be the next front in the struggle against slavery. He sent us to prepare his way to the coming conflict. Tell you what. We'll ride along with you folks today and camp the night just to be sure them two don't come back to give it another try."

"We'd be much obliged for that," Clare said. "I'd be pleased to fix you boys a home cooked meal away from home."

That evening they sat about their campfire with the Brown boys enjoying cooking better than their own. The fire licked at the darkness, holding a shower of stars at bay to the tune of crickets and frogs singing their night songs.

"Where in Kansas you fixin' to settle?" Salmon asked.

Micah shrugged. "We're thinking of farming wheat. That's about all the plan we have. We'll figure it out when we get there. How about you boys?"

"Father has friends in the New England abolition movement. They're assisting right-minded folks to settle the Lawrence area. Father figures them for the bulwark of resistance. We'll prepare a place close enough by to be of some help when the need arises."

"Do you think it will come to violence?" Clare said.

All three boys met her eyes across the firelight. "Father believes it inevitable," Salmon said.

"Oh, dear. That sounds so dire."

"It is, I'm afraid. Nothing more to be done than face it."

"With the good Lord's blessing, cool heads may yet prevail," Micah said.

"One can hope, though I'd do my hopin' with my arms close by."

Chapter Nine

Morgan Walker Farm
Jackson County, Missouri
July, 1854

Bright morning sun filtered through lace curtains softened to a mellow glow. Miriam fitted fresh sheets on the massa's great four-poster bed with its soft feather mattress and gauzy drape to keep the skeeters away. She could scarcely imagine sleeping in such elegant comfort, but the massas did, every night.

She felt his presence at the door. She'd developed a sense for it since moving up to the house. She turned her thoughts to Caleb, wishing he were here. She ignored the presence and continued with her chores. Watching did no harm other than annoy her. The sound of the door closing caught in her throat. She glanced over her shoulder.

He stood there watching. She reckoned him about sixteen. Big for his age, dough-like from soft living with dull, colorless eyes, fleshy cheeks, and slicked-back, brown hair.

"Was you needin' somethin', Massa Andrew?"

"I believe you know what I need, Miriam."

He took a step toward her. She stepped back.

"Don't be shy, girl. If you're nice to me, it'll be real nice for both of us."

"Does your daddy know where you are, Massa Andrew?"

He smiled mirthlessly. "You can start by seeing to those buttons on your dress."

He took another step. She backed into the edge of the bed.

"My buttons is just fine. I'm a married woman, you know."

He laughed and took another step. "That just makes you breeding stock. I ain't interested in breeding. All I want is a little sportin' fun. Now get them clothes off and let the fun begin."

He had her trapped. She couldn't figure but one way out. She smiled.

"Well, if it's just for fun." She undid a few buttons at her throat.

He was close now. So close she could smell him. He stared at her, eyes fixed on her fingers.

"You is fallin' behind. We can't have no fun with you all dressed up like that. Here, let me help." She knelt, looking up. She unfastened his belt and unbuttoned his britches. His eyes glazed.

"Now you're fallin' behind. Let's see some more."

She undid a couple more buttons, watching his excitement grow.

"Hurry up, girl."

"Yes, Massa." She pulled his britches down with her best fetching smile and bolted from the room.

After lunch, Missa Morgan Walker retired to her afternoon nap. Miriam slipped out of the house carrying a berry basket and started for the patch between the fields. No sooner was she out of sight then she hiked up her skirts and ran. The sun was hot, the air thick as wet toweling. Sweat poured down her face, gathering in a rivulet that trickled between her breasts. Her dress darkened with the effort. She didn't care. She had to see him.

The Good Lord His-self must a' run with her. She found Caleb working a field not far from the Morgan Walker property. She hid in the trees until she spotted Redding, the overseer on the opposite side of the field. She straightened herself and walked calmly out of the trees, crossing the field like she belonged there.

Caleb blinked. He couldn't believe his eyes. What was she doing here? She run away in broad daylight? Something must be wrong. He glanced around. Redding had his back to them, busy with some other chore at the far side of the field. Caleb turned back to meet her.

"Get down between the rows, girl."

She did as she was told, frightened, dark eyes looking up to him from between the rows of corn. He continued tasseling.

"What bring you here?"

"I had to see you."

"What's so all fired necessary you run away in broad daylight?"

"He tried more than watchin'."

"The Walker boy?"

She nodded. Caleb took in the news, his slow to boil anger growing hot.

"He hurt you?"

"No. I got him in a bad way and got away."

"You got him in a bad way? You didn't go get you-self in real trouble, did you?"

She giggled.

"What's funny? This ain't no time for jokes."

"You get a man's pants down, he don't run so good."

Caleb got the picture. It must have been kind a' funny.

"Caleb, it's only a matter of time before he come after me again. There ain't but so many ways to stay away from him in that house."

"Maybe you should tell your missa. She likely wouldn't cotton to that boy be-devilin' you."

"That might help some. Then again, it'd surely make Massa Andrew angry. He might decide I'd be fit for worse than fun. We gotta run. No two ways about it, and the sooner the better."

"I been thinkin' on that some."

"Praise the Lord."

"The harvest fandango be the time. Folks stay up late, drink too much. We might be in Kansas before they know we is gone."

"Harvest is two months away."

"Best I can come up with."

"But what if he . . ."

"It ain't just runnin' away, Miriam. It's gettin' away without gettin' caught. Now you have a talk with your missa. Hopefully that'll slow the boy down until harvest. Now you best get yourself back before them Walker folks figure out you is gone."

Chapter Ten

Kansas City
August, 1854

A ragged settlement emerged out of the haze sloping down to a river. Micah drew the team to a halt.

"There she is, Clare." He wrapped an arm around her. "That's Kansas City. Kansas is just across the river."

"You mean Kansas City isn't in Kansas?"

"No, dear, it's still in Missouri, but it's our gateway to Kansas. We'll stop there for a few days to replenish our supplies and gain whatever news we might learn of settlement on the Kansas side."

"Tell me we don't have to float this wagon across that river."

He smiled. "Not this time. There's a ferry that'll take us across when we're ready." He clucked to the team.

Kansas City sprawled along the east bank of the Missouri River, a sizable town of some twenty-five hundred. The commercial center radiated out from the ferry dock, freight docks, and riverfront warehouses. By late afternoon the day's commercial activity tapered off to a sleepy river town thinking about supper and a little relaxation. Micah drew up at a blacksmith shop and livery on the east end of town. He found the smithy at his forge. A bear of a man wearing a sweat-soaked shirt and heavy, leather apron smiled through a thick, rusty beard.

"Afternoon, stranger. What can I do for you?"

"I got a couple of mules I'd like to put up for a day or two, if you don't mind my wife and me parking our wagon in your yard."

He wiped his hands on his apron. "Two bits a head. No charge for the dirt under your wagon. It ain't doin' nothin' I know of just now." He punctuated this last with a toothy grin.

Micah handed the man a dollar.

"You folks headed west?"

"We are. Bound for Kansas."

"You're pretty near there then."

"Kansas covers a lot of territory. We need to better figure where to settle."

"What do you plan on doin'?"

"Cash crop farm soon as we can get a crop to market."

"You're thinkin' railroad then."

Micah nodded.

"That might take a while. 'Course that muddy river yonder takes crops to market every day. Some fella's building a flour mill down near the docks. That'll create markets for wheat and cornmeal."

"Markets far and wide open once the railroad comes."

"That'd be the way I see it. Charles Goodwin's the name." He stuck out a calloused hand.

"Micah Mason."

"Where you hale from, Micah?"

"Hudson, Ohio."

"You come a long way."

"We have."

"If you need any work done on that wagon while you're here, I'd be happy to look at it for you."

"Much obliged. I'll let you know if we need anything. Maybe you'd favor me with some advice on what lies across the river."

"I'm happy to pass along what I know."

"That'd be a good sight more than I know. My wife and I will be fixin' some supper directly if you'd care to join us."

Goodwin brightened. "You're talkin' to a man who can't muster much more'n biscuits and beans on his own account. What time should I come by?"

They had a simple supper of biscuits, fatback, vegetable stew, and coffee. Sitting around the table finishing their coffee, haloed in lamplight, the day's heat lifted as crickets serenaded the stable yard. Up the road in the direction of town a piano tinkled faintly from some distant saloon.

"I'm sorry I don't have a pie to offer you, Mr. Goodwin. I don't have much time for baking when we're on the road."

"Thank you, Mrs. Mason. You've been more than kind sharing this wonderful meal with me."

"It was nothing special."

"It was if you had a steady diet of my cooking. I'll be sorry to see you folks move on."

"Do you have any suggestions on where we might look when we cross into Kansas?" Micah said.

"You'll find good land for farming most places. If you stick close to a river, you'll be able to get a cash crop to market that way until the railroad comes." He paused and stroked his beard. "There's one more thing you might want to consider."

"What's that?"

"You might want to consider your position on slavery. I don't hold with it much myself, but most folks here in Missouri do. Kansas is divided on the subject. They'll likely vote on it next year. No tellin' how it might come out, but there's strong sentiments on both sides."

"We don't hold with it, either, but how would that affect where we settle?"

"If I was you, then, I'd favor the Lawrence area, about forty miles west of here. Folks settlin' there is comin' from the north and east. They're mostly opposed to the idea. I'd feel best bein' among like-minded folks. Everyone hopes the matter can be settled peaceably, but I reckon for most folks, peaceably means settled their way. Like I said, feelin's run strong on both sides."

"That strikes me as sound advice, Charles. We understand the threat of violence. Brother John Brown of Hudson, Ohio, is a strong abolitionist. He believes Kansas and Nebraska will be the next battleground over slavery in the expansion west. He's already sent three of his sons out to Kansas. We met them on the road on our way here. I'm sure they're there by now. They expect Brother Brown himself to join them."

"I'm not familiar with your Brother Brown; but men of his persuasion, you'll likely find in Lawrence."

"His sons said as much. I thank you for the advice, though. We'll start looking for somewhere to settle around there."

Chapter Eleven

Lawrence, Kansas
August, 1854

Micah and Clare drove south along Massachusetts Street to Seventh Street. The town sprawled south and west between the Kansas River to the northeast and Mount Oread on the west. Micah drew the team to a halt in front of the three-story Eldridge House Hotel. The red brick structure looked more like a fortress than a hotel, with its third floor ringed in gun ports. The imposing façade dominated the center of town. After more than two months on the road west, Micah deemed it time for a rest. He set the brake, climbed down, and anchored the team. He held out a hand to Clare.

"Why are we stopping here?"

"We're getting a room for the night."

She took his hand. "Can we afford it?"

"Not really, but it's been two months of rough living. We'll start looking for land tomorrow. Tonight, we are going to have a civilized meal and a proper night's rest." He gave her his arm and led her up the boardwalk steps to the hotel lobby. The registration clerk welcomed them with a smile.

"Afternoon, folks. Welcome to Eldridge House. How may we be of assistance?"

"We need a room for the night," Micah said.

The clerk spun the register.

Micah took the pen from its inkpot and signed. "We'll need a place to park our wagon."

"Stable yard is around back. The stable boy will keep an eye on it for you. That'll be a dollar for the room and fifty cents for the stock."

Micah slid two dollars across the counter.

"How far west you headed?"

"We plan to look at farmland in the area."

"Well then, welcome to Lawrence. Where you folks from?"

"Hudson, Ohio."

"We had some guests from Hudson not so long ago. I believe they're still somewhere here abouts."

"Salmon Brown and his brothers?"

"Why, yes, they're the ones. Abolitionists they said, come here to secure the vote. If you're of the abolitionist mind, you'll find Lawrence a more agreeable place than a more southerly community such as Frederick, if you get my drift."

"I believe I do."

The clerk slid a key across the counter. "Room two-o-six."

Micah handed the key to Clare. "I'll put up the team and bring in some things."

Next day, the stable boy loaned Micah saddles and bridles for Sampson and Delilah. Saddled and mounted, Micah led the way west out of town. They passed below the shadow of Mount Oread standing northwest sentry over the town. They followed the river, taking in rolling hills on a sunny, warm late summer day.

"It's beautiful," Clare said.

Micah nodded.

"How far out do you plan to go?"

He shrugged. "Until we find a good spot."

"Should we look so close to the river? They flood, you know."

"Hmm. I'd thought to be close enough to make shipping

crops easier. You make a good point, though, for finding higher ground." He turned south, climbing a shallow river valley wall a half mile from the river. He swung west again, following a broad plain until they came to a tree-lined creek bed spilling north to the river. Micah drew rein and stepped down. He helped Clare down.

"What do you think?"

She shaded her eyes and turned slowly. "It's lovely and so peaceful."

Micah drew his knife, crouched, and turned over a slice of earth. Rich, black soil crumbled through his fingers. He held his hand up to Clare.

"It smells good."

"It does." He stood. "Can you see a house there by the creek?"

"I can. Oh, and look there. Is that a sycamore?"

The old tree stood near the creek bank, lifting powerful branches to a cornflower-blue sky as though guarding the river valley below. "It is a sycamore," Micah said.

"Ah, that reminds me of home."

"Perhaps it's a sign. Let's ride on a bit further."

They remounted and crossed the creek. Clare looked toward the river.

"We could plant a vegetable garden here."

Micah lifted his chin to the south. "I can see an orchard there."

They continued west across a broad fertile plain, waving in green-gold prairie grass.

"How much land should we claim?" she asked.

"I'm thinking wheat or corn. Two to three hundred tillable acres would give us room to grow." He wheeled Sampson around to look back at the tree line along the creek. "Looks to be about a three-quarter mile or so." He stepped down. "We need some stones to mark this boundary."

They ground tied the mules and spread out, gathering stones they piled to a height visible above waving summer grass. They remounted and rode south yet another three-quarter mile, repeating the process.

Micah collected the mules. "We'll set the east boundary on the far bank of the creek, allowing a plot for a house."

"What about a north boundary?"

"We'll claim the land all the way to the river. That way we'll have access for shipping crops, lumber, and such."

Clare swept her eyes along the creek bank toward the river. They came to rest on the giant sycamore. She listened to the soft rustle of a breeze.

"Oh, Micah, it feels like home already."

"It does."

Sun bent to late afternoon as they stacked the last stones to the east boundary marker. They stepped into the saddle for the return to town, tired and excited by the claim they'd staked. They'd put the mules up in the stable and take a room for a second night.

The old tree spread her shade over the young folks as they rode back toward town. Fresh markers bound her land to some new purpose. Seasons of serenity reached deep to her roots. The creek, the river, wild flowers, and vegetation provided forest critter needs. Peaceful, simple, and all about to change. Slanting sun warmed the possibilities. Unspoken promises awaiting discovery.

Lawrence

The following morning dawned sunny with a crisp break in the summer heat foretelling an urgent need to provide shelter for winter in the coming weeks. Micah found the land office was a short walk down Massachusetts from the hotel. He waited patiently on the boardwalk while the potbellied clerk with a handlebar moustache unlocked the door and flipped the window sign to "Open." He followed the man inside. Dirty window-smeared sunlight lit the dusty office confines. The clerk let himself through a gate behind the counter, hung his coat on a tree, and rustled an officious looking stack of papers while Micah waited at the counter. The man lifted a pair of spectacles from his vest pocket and fitted them over his ears. He turned to the counter as though just noticing Micah was there.

"Now, then, young man, what can we do for you today?"

"I'd like to register a claim."

"I believe we can arrange that. Is the claim properly staked?"

"It is."

The clerk spread a map on the counter. "Can you show me where this claim is located?"

Micah traced the river five miles west of town to the creek. He followed the creek south. "Three-quarter mile south and three-quarter mile west of the east creek bank."

The clerk nodded, marking the boundaries with the stub of a pencil. "That's a handsome piece of property. River side of the Thorne place."

"Thorne place?"

"Titus Thorne . . . owns a large spread south of you. You'll be neighbors. What do you plan to do with it?"

"Farm it."

"Good land out that way. What are you planning to farm?"

"Wheat . . . maybe corn."

"Either one of them ought to do right well out there. The land cost is a dollar an acre due within three years. You pay the taxes and work the land to hold your claim until you complete the purchase. Is that acceptable?"

"It is."

"Fine, then. I'll draw up the paperwork. I should have it ready for you to sign later this morning. That'll be ten dollars."

"Ten dollars?"

"First year taxes. You're a property owner, son."

Chapter Twelve

Micah drew the team to a halt at the creek bank under the spread of the old sycamore. He settled an arm around Clare.

"Home sweet home."

She smiled up at him. "It is. Or soon will be. Where do we begin?"

"The first order of business is shelter for the winter."

"Do we have time to build a cabin?"

He shook his head. "A dugout will have to do."

"Dugout?"

"A sod house. I've given it some thought. Come along—I'll show you." He helped her down from the wagon box and led the way north along the creek bank to the ridge that dropped to the river valley below. He climbed down the slope to a level break in the ridge wall before it continued down to the valley floor.

"How do you like your front yard?"

"Front yard?"

He nodded. "We'll tunnel into the hillside here, hollow out a braced-up living space, sink a pipe for a stove, frame in a front entrance with a door and a window, and be snugged up for the winter."

"What about the mules?"

"We'll make do with a pole corral and a lean-to for shelter. We'll have to gather fodder for them and firewood for us, but we should be able to get that done before the snow flies."

"What about a proper house?"

"That will need to wait a year or so until we've cashed a crop to bring in wood and building supplies. I'll get started on the sod house tomorrow. Now let's get the stock and the wagon settled. That'll be camp home until the dugout is ready to move in."

Golden shadow crept across the land office floor. The clerk stretched. He pulled the watch from his vest pocket and flipped the cover open. Five minutes of five—time to close up. He let himself out through the gate in the counter and was about to turn over the "Closed" sign when a tall, dark silhouette appeared at the door.

Titus Thorne flashed a smile meant to disarm the unsuspecting. Those who knew him knew better than to approach the man unarmed. He wore a tailored, dark suit over a long, lithe frame. A handsome rake, he had sloe-dark eyes fit to wilt a lady, with impeccably barbered hair and moustache.

"I was just about to close, Mr. Thorne. Perhaps you could come back in the morning."

"I shan't keep you, Cletus. I'm planning to claim a parcel. I'd like to point it out to you and have you assess the tax bill for me."

The clerk withdrew to his counter, defeated. "Is the claim staked?"

Thorne paused. "It is."

He spread the map on the counter. "Where is it located?"

"South of the river, five miles west of town . . ."

"At the creek."

"Why, yes. How did you know?"

"That parcel was claimed only this morning by a young couple from Ohio."

Thorne darkened. "How . . . unfortunate."

"Sorry, Mr. Thorne. I registered the claim myself."

"Have the taxes been paid?"

"They have. All is in order."

"I see. I had my heart set on that section."

"Perhaps they might sell for the right price."

"Or something like that. Thank you, Cletus. Good evening."

The table lamp created an island of light. Flying insects danced in and out of the halo. Beyond the circle of light, night sounds serenaded the silence resting on the burbling creek. A gentle breeze ruffled the willow break, playing through the sycamore leaves overhead. Clare sat at the table, cleared of their evening meal, her pen lightly scratching the vellum page.

Lawrence, Kansas
September 2, 1854
Dear Ma, Pa, and all the Mason clan,

We've arrived. Micah promised we would write. He asked me if I would do it. The poor man turned in after supper. Our days are long, his burdened by heavy labor as we prepare to winter at our new homestead.

We staked our claim on three-hundred-sixty acres five miles west of Lawrence, Kansas. Lawrence is situated forty miles west of Kansas City. The property sits on a bluff overlooking the Kansas River on a lovely creek. A mighty sycamore stands sentinel over it to remind us of home. I think we may christen the farm Sycamore for it.

Micah is busy building a sod home into the side of our bluff, overlooking the river, to shelter us until we can build a proper house. I know it sounds primitive, but as it begins to take shape I can see we shall be comfortable there.

The land is good and rich, Pa. Micah plans to plant wheat in the spring. They've built a grist mill in Kansas City; and, while forty miles seems like a long way, shipping our crops to market by river barge makes the distance practical. Micah believes that in time a railroad will shorten even that distance. As we look at the autumn fields waving in sun-golden grasses, wheat promises a future filled with acres of gold.

We have found things to be much as we envisioned when we left Hudson. The journey was long, with some harrowing moments, but we managed them. I won't trouble you with any but one. We had what could have been a most unfortunate encounter with two ruffians in Indiana. We were spared any damage or inconvenience when Brother Brown's sons came along and ran the scalawags off. The Brown brothers were on their way to Kansas and are believed to be somewhere in the area here, though we have not encountered them again. Lawrence is very much in the free-soil camp, so the Brown boys must, as we, feel most comfortable here.

There is one more bit of news I should pass along before signing this off. Micah and I expect to begin our family late of next spring. God has given much to us in our new home, and now He brings us a child to share it with. Fondest blessings to you all.

Love,
Micah & Clare

Thorne drew rein at the crest of the ridge. Off to his right, the river wound her way toward Kansas City. Ahead, the sun filtered golden through the trees lining the creek bank. They'd parked their wagon there, likely still using it as a temporary home until something more permanent could be arranged. That appeared to be under way, with the scar of a digging just below the ridge line to the north. The young folk were wasting no time. How could he have been so foolish? This section had been part of his plan from the beginning. Now it would cost him more than taxes. *Damn.* His black stallion, Rogue, stomped, snorted, and tossed his head in agreement. He squeezed up a trot toward the wagon.

The woman bent over a washtub set beside the creek. Thorne let his gaze play over the round of her hips until his approach caught her attention, spoiling the view by bringing her upright. She squinted into the sun, the view not entirely spoiled. A comely thing for a sodbuster's wife.

"Good morning, ma'm." He tipped his hat, the picture of proper gentry.

"Yes?"

"Titus Thorne is my name. I own four sections south and west of here. Since we've become neighbors, as it were, I thought I'd drop by and introduce myself."

She fetched a bright smile. "Pleased to meet you, Mr. Thorne. I'm Clare, Clare Mason. Won't you step down?"

Thorne dismounted and gave the black his lead to crop.

"I'm afraid I don't have much to offer you. If you've the time, I could brew a pot of coffee."

"You're very kind. I only wished to introduce myself and have a word with your husband if he is about."

"He's working on a sod house, just there toward the river."

"I thought as much."

"Shall I fetch him?"

"No need. He shouldn't be hard to find."

"Come along. I'll show you." She set off for the river.

"Where are you folks from?"

"Hudson, Ohio."

"You've come a long way. What brings you to Kansas?"

"Why, this of course, though I don't suppose we had any more than a general notion of what to expect before we arrived. But our expectations have been far more than met." She started down the ridge bank toward the hollowed opening. "Micah, we've a caller."

He emerged from the cave-like opening, bare chested, sweat-slicked in muddy streaks. He wiped his hands on a rag.

"Micah, this is Mr. Thorne. He's our neighbor."

"Titus Thorne, Mr. Mason." He extended his hand.

"Pleased to meet you, Mr. Thorne."

"Mr. Thorne stopped to introduce himself and have a word with you, dear."

"Oh? What can I do for you then, sir?"

"More like, what I might do for you."

"And what might that be?"

"It's about your claim here. I've had my eye on this section for some time now. I'd every intention of claiming it myself. You can imagine my surprise when I discovered you'd done so. Well, what's done is done . . . my misfortune, but I mean to make it right by you."

"Right by me? I'm afraid I don't understand."

"Why, buy you out, of course. I'm prepared to pay a dollar an acre, as is, unimproved."

"I'm sure that's a very generous offer, Mr. Thorne, but my wife and I are comfortable here. We've no interest in selling."

"Comfortable? Come now, Mr. Mason, you've barely scratched a hole in the ground. I'm offering you three hundred-sixty dollars for your trouble to find a different place to feel comfortable."

"I understand. But we've only just completed a very long journey to find this home. We've no interest in moving on."

"Oh, all right. Drive a hard bargain if you must. A dollar-fifty an acre, but that's my final offer."

"It's not the money, Mr. Thorne. We're home. We're expecting our first child, and we intend to give that child a home here."

A vein throbbed in Thorne's temple. "I see. You're taking a great risk, you know. This is rough country. Carving a working farm out of raw land is no easy feat. Holding on to it if you succeed can be even more difficult. You'd be wise to reconsider the generosity of my offer—it's certain gain. Holding on to land is, shall we say, a far less certain proposition."

"We accepted that bargain when we left Hudson."

"When you left Hudson, you had no idea what you bargained for. Good day."

Chapter Thirteen

Jackson County, Missouri
October 1854

A bright harvest moon hung low on the eastern horizon. Golden light lay on the fields and filtered through the trees. Music and muted laughter floated down from the big house on a gentle night breeze. Caleb waited nervously in the shadow of an ancient oak at the end of a hedgerow bordering the southwest section. *What's keepin' that girl?* By the sound of it the harvest celebration had gotten into full swing. She needed to be along if they were sure enough to do this fool thing. They'd need every last minute away before they were discovered missing.

The light snap of a twig and a rustle of leaves set his heart to racing. She appeared out of the trees like a forest sprite 'til she fetched him that pearly smile.

"What took you your own sweet time?"

"Missa Morgan Walker had me truss up that corset fit to squeeze the breath out'a her. She ain't been that skinny since before she birthed that boy of hers."

"Well, let's don't be wastin' no more time. Dey'll have the dogs on us come mornin'."

Caleb set off north at a brisk pace, keeping to the shadows of the hedgerow. He turned west at the north end of the field and put the big house behind them. A half mile west they struck a creek. Caleb waded into the water and turned south. Miriam stopped at the bank, hands on hips.

"Hey, what you goin' that way for? Kansas is the other way."

"Them dogs don't smell you in water. The catcher man will 'spect we gone north. He and them dogs be lookin' along up there while we goes on down this way a spell. We find us a good spot to get out of the creek and circle back northwest."

"My, my, if I knowd you was so smart about this I'd a had us gone some long time ago."

"We ain't brought it off yet, girl. Now quits your jabberin', and let's be on our way."

"Mighty bossy there, Caleb . . . must be the smell of freedom." She waded into the creek and followed.

"It ain't freedom smell worries me. It's blood smell."

Thirty minutes later, Caleb paused. Moonlight filtered through the trees overhead, dancing on the surface of the water. He looked up and slowly let his eyes wander to the west bank and the tree lined shadows beyond.

"How's you at tree climbin'?"

"Tree climbin'? I ain't done much since I grew into my womanhood. What you got on your mind?"

"See that limb up there?"

"Uh huh."

"If I was to boost you up there, could you shinny across there, get around the trunk and get to the end of that far limb yonder?"

"I 'spect so, but why?"

"That way we leave the creek without leavin' no tracks and no scent where we do. Even if that catcher man figures out we come this way, he'll still have a hard time pickin' up our trail."

"Boost away."

Minutes later Caleb dropped out of the tree west of the stream beside Miriam.

"Now let's get us to Kansas."

Kansas

Caleb scrambled down from a tree the following evening in the gathering blue shadows.

"Somebody's comin'. Maybe a mile or so back. They ain't comin' fast, but they's comin'."

"You think it might be him?"

"Might be."

"But ain't we in Kansas now?"

"We are. Them fugitive slave laws lets 'em hunt us all the same. We need to find a place to hide."

"I'm cold and hungry."

"Cain't help for either of them right now. We gotta keep goin'."

"Goin' where?"

"Goin' there." He pointed to a thin wisp of smoke rising above the trees to the northwest. "They's folks there. Good Lord willin' maybe they help us."

"You gonna just walk in like Sunday company?"

"That's about the size of it."

"It ain't Sunday."

"Best we can do. Come on."

"Micah." Clare stood at the wagon gate, preparing to dish up supper. She lifted her chin down the tree line edging the wagon road.

Micah eased away from the table, watching them come as he moved to his wife's side, or more particularly to the Colt dragoon holstered at the bedside in back of the wagon. A large black man and a woman came out of the trees, walking toward them in thickening evening shadows. The man smiled, showing even white teeth.

"Evenin', folks. My name's Caleb. This here's Miriam. We could use a little help."

Micah eased off the Colt. "Come on in. My name's Micah Mason. This is my wife, Clare. What can we do for you folks?"

Caleb glanced around. "We bein' followed."

"You runaways?"

He nodded. "We be in Kansas now, but that don't mean nothin' to them slave catchers."

"It does to me. Are they close?"

"A mile, maybe a little less by now."

"Clare, give me some of that jerky and finish setting our supper table."

She nodded.

"Follow me." Micah took a candle and turned toward the river. He led the way beneath the shadow of the old tree, picking their way down the trodden path to the sod house.

"It ain't home yet, but you can hide safe enough here." He handed the man the candle, a couple of matches, and the jerky. "I wouldn't use the candle until we know it's safe. I'll come for you when they've gone, and we'll fix you a proper meal."

"We's much obliged for your kindness. It's more than we could hope for."

"No kindness. It's the right thing to do. Now get on in there and stay out of sight until I come for you."

Supper finished, they sat sipping coffee in the halo of lamplight. Micah turned to the sound of an approaching horse. His hand edged closer to the dragoon tucked in his waistband. The shadowed rider spoke.

"Evenin', folks. Mind if I step down?"

Micah rose, the pistol now visible by light of the lamp.

The rider dismounted. A tall, powerfully built man, he wore a heavy coat, his features hidden by a bushy beard and the wide brim of a slouch hat. "I hope you'll excuse my stopping by unannounced. Name's Jacob Herd. I'm on the trail of runaway slaves, a man and a woman. Might you have seen them come this way?"

Micah shook his head. "If they come this way, likely they're headed for Lawrence. Lots of abolition sympathy there to take them in."

"That thought crossed my mind, though the last sign I had seemed like they was swingin' wider west. You sure you didn't see or hear anything?"

"No, sir. The wife and I been havin' a quiet supper since sundown. Not nary a soul come by until you come along. That wagon road there'll take you on into Lawrence."

The slave catcher fixed his gaze in thought. "I might a' misread that sign. It was gettin' dark."

"Lawrence will have more comforts to offer. All we got here is hard ground."

"You homesteadin'?"

"Staked our claim two months ago."

He glanced around. "Best get started on some more permanent shelter than that wagon. You wouldn't want to be caught out here with winter coming on."

"That's my plan and sound advice, too."

"You see any sign of them two, you hold 'em. There's a reward on both of 'em."

Micah patted the pistol butt. "Sure will."

Herd mounted and wheeled away down the road.

"You think he believed us?" Clare said.

Micah took his seat at the table. "Let's have some more coffee until we're sure he's gone."

Miriam and Caleb huddled in the pitch-dark dugout. They'd eaten the jerky in silence. It took the edge off their hunger. They heard faint voices and held each other's eyes in the dark.

"You think them white folks truly will hide us?" Miriam whispered.

"Got to."

"They ain't got to. That's the point."

"Uh-uh, I got to think they's goin' to. Why'd they do this much for us if they wasn't gonna hide us?"

"They puts rewards on runaways."

"They do. These folks seems God-fearin'. I don't see 'em bein' takin' for thirty pieces of silver."

"You got all that from him puttin' us up in this hole?"

"No. I got it from him sayin' bein' in Kansas means somethin' to him."

"I hopes you're right."

Time passed. Someone climbed down the ridge. A man and a woman appeared at the dugout entrance.

"He's gone. You can light that candle now."

A match flared acrid sulfur smoke to candle glow.

Micah and Clare each carried a plate of food. Micah had a blanket tucked under one arm. They sat around the candle, shadows dancing on the dugout walls as Caleb and Miriam ate.

"We sure are much obliged to you folks," Caleb said.

"Where you headed?" Micah asked.

"Kansas."

Micah chuckled. "You're in Kansas. Now where?"

Caleb shrugged. "Far away from that man as we can get."

"Well, you'll be safe enough here for the night. You can figure the rest of it out in the morning."

Chapter Fourteen

A chill blanket of mist hung over the river, gray in first morning light. She stretched her limbs to the chill breeze as though embracing the coming of a new season. Change began with the coming of the young folk, preparing to dwell in the hillside above the river. This morning something more had come to the promise. They came in the night. She sensed fear. She sensed hope. The coming seasons would play out to new purpose, marked out in the boundaries now raised on her land.

Micah and Clare rolled out of the wagon bed. Clare stirred the fire to light and set the coffee to boil. Spectral figures emerged from the mist carrying a folded blanket and the stub of a candle.

"Mornin'," Micah said.

"Mornin'," they said.

"Coffee will be ready presently."

"We best be on our way," Caleb said. "You folks been too kind, and we been way too much trouble to you already."

"Nonsense," Clare said. "I'll not hear of you leaving until you've had a proper breakfast. Micah, fetch that guest bench out of the wagon and put it beside the table."

In a matter of minutes Clare laid out bacon, eggs, fresh bread, and strawberry preserves. They sat down to eat.

"Where will you go?" Micah asked.

Caleb shrugged.

"You'll need a place to winter before long."

"I reckon so."

Micah looked at Clare. She nodded. "You know," he said, "I could use a little help around here. I can't afford to pay until we bring in a crop next year; but at least you'd have a place to stay and food for the winter."

"We couldn't impose."

Miriam cut her eyes to her husband. "He didn't say impose, Caleb. He said we could earn our keep. We knows how to do that."

"That's it," Clare said. "We generally need to talk sense to these men."

"What needs doin'?" Caleb asked.

"We need to finish the dugout house. We need a split-rail corral for them mules to call home. I suspect with the two of us workin' at it, we could dig a second dugout, too."

"Three of us workin'," Miriam said. She turned to Clare. "I can help. You shouldn't be doin' no heavy work in your condition."

"What condition?"

"You in a family way, ain't you?"

"Why, yes; but how did you know?"

"Miriam know things. You be needin' some help birthin' that baby come spring."

"I s'pose I will."

"Then it sounds like it's settled," Micah said.

Caleb looked from one to the next and nodded. "Looks like you got a couple of hands, Mr. Mason."

"Good. And it's Micah, Caleb." He held out his hand.

November, 1854

Dear Ma and Pa,

We hope this letter finds you and all the Mason clan in good spirits and health. We are doing well as we continue to settle our new home. We have made considerable progress in the short weeks since our arrival. Much of that is owed to a couple who have joined us in our endeavor. Caleb and Miriam arrived from Missouri not long after we did. They came to us one night in fear, pursued by an agent of their former masters. We did our Christian duty and hid them. We persuaded them to stay with us even though we can only pay them in a share of the fruits of our labors. They tell us a share is more than ever their labors have earned. We are grateful for their help.

Kansas shines a free beacon to those held in bondage in Missouri. Freedom stands in stark contrast to the dark practice that casts its shadow over our border. We heard Brother Brown preach against the evil in Hudson. We thought we understood it. We could not fully appreciate the barbarity. We saw it firsthand the night Caleb and Miriam arrived. The slavery dispute runs deep here. Beliefs strongly opposed on both sides. Let us pray the divisions can be healed peaceably.

Caleb and Miriam escaped Missouri in the hope of beginning a new life. It is a beginning we build together, starting with simple dugout dwellings to shelter us for the winter. I take comfort from having Miriam to assist me when it is time to bring forth the new life growing within me. With Caleb's help we should have full use of our fields in the shortest possible time. I cannot help but feel the Lord smiled on us by their coming.

Clare

Washington City
February 1855

Cold late afternoon light colored the office dull gray. Senator Douglas closed the war department report and laid it on his desk. He shook his head, removed his spectacles, and rubbed the bridge of his nose between thumb and forefinger. The report didn't help. He chided himself for not seeing this coming; he should have expected it. The question now: what to do about it?

He rose from his desk and crossed the office to the window. Hands clasped behind his back, he looked out over brown lawn and gusty, wind-blown cobbled streets toward the Potomac and a rumpled felt sky. The war department had completed its survey of rail routes to the Pacific. Secretary of War Davis put forward his recommendation of the southern route. It stuck in Douglas's craw in several places. The recommendation clearly reflected transparent regional bias. Republican interests in the north would have nothing to do with it. Even by popular sovereignty such a routing favored formation of slave states. They could expect fierce opposition in both houses. Then there was the matter of his own preference for a central route favoring Chicago. Winning that prize for his beloved home state motivated his purpose from the start. The secretary's recommendation now stood foursquare in the face of his ambition.

That the secretary should have chosen to favor his own regional allegiances should not have come as a surprise. The question now was how to oppose a fellow Democrat without alienating the southern caucus whose votes he would need to move the Pacific railroad forward. There'd be no difficulty in mounting an opposition. He could hear Senator Sumner from here. Hell, he could probably write the senator's speech for him. That would afford him the luxury of keeping his own opposition behind the scenes, hopefully conserving his credibility with southern Democrats. That much he could see. The unknown remained forging a coalition of sufficient strength to move the railroad forward and to do so on a central routing.

He returned to his desk and sat heavily, drumming his fingers on a blank page, awaiting his thoughts. Popular sovereignty had to be made acceptable to both sides. It worked once before; it would have to again. The southerners must be made to see their regional bias. Northerners must be made to see their regional bias. Northern regional bias . . . he paused. Hmm. That may be it. He needed a little northern regional bias to pit against the secretary's recommendation. If that might be inspired, then perhaps a compromise could be forged around a central route with the slavery issue determined by previously agreed provisions of the Kansas-Nebraska Act. It was worth a try. He dipped his pen in the ink pot and put pen to paper.

Senator Sumner,

Might I have a moment to discuss the war department report recommending a rail route to the Pacific?

Capitol Hill
March 1855

An invitation to dine with a Democrat rested uneasily on his mind. In the case of Senator Douglas, Sumner knew the business would involve the political equivalent of horse trading. The unknown was whose horse was to be traded and for what? The carriage rocked up Fourteenth Street to the soft *clop, clop* of a tall bay. The driver drew a halt in front of a Victorian brownstone known for fine dining, discreet rendezvous, and upper floors of dubious—though tasteful—repute. The cabby climbed down and opened the carriage door. Sumner stepped down, paid the man, and climbed the steps to an elegant front entry. There he was greeted by polished hardwood and an equally polished proprietress.

"Good evening, Senator."

A black man in starched white livery took his top hat and cloak.

"Senator Douglas is expecting you. If you'll follow me, please."

He was only too pleased to follow. She was stunning really. A light scent of lilac trailed an ample figure, matured by her years but fulsome with feminine promise none-the-less. She showed him to a private dining room appointed in more polished wood, red velvet, white linen, candlelit crystal, and silver. Douglas rose to full measure of his diminutive self.

"Charles, thank you for coming."

A familiar Democrat at that. He extended his hand. "Good evening, Senator. One could hardly refuse so kindly an offer."

"We're here to break bread. Please call me Stephen."

They took their seats.

"Would you care for a glass of claret, Senator? Or perhaps something of a stronger spirit?" the woman asked.

Deep green eyes . . . he imagined they came with a stronger spirit. "Claret will do."

She poured from a cut-crystal decanter and withdrew.

"I've taken the liberty of ordering steaks," Douglas said. "I hope you don't mind."

"I would have done so for myself. Thank you. Now, Stephen, what's on that fertile mind of yours this evening?"

"Ever the pragmatic New Englander, Charles—straight to the point. It's the Pacific railroad survey, as I mentioned in my note. More particularly, Secretary Davis's recommendation of the southern route."

"Yes, that. Totally unacceptable you must know. Breathtaking regional bias. A non-starter with my colleagues."

"I understand. Still you and I agree the railroad must be built. We've done business on that before."

"Your Kansas-Nebraska Act again. That bit of business has yet to be proven."

"Which is why you need to come out in support of the northern route."

"You'd have me take a position every bit as partisan as Davis's?"

"Of course. How else shall we draw the boundaries for a bargain?"

"Your central route."

Douglas smiled.

"Perhaps you didn't hear me. Your popular sovereignty compromise has yet to prove itself. Until it does, I hope you will forgive me; I remain somewhat the skeptic."

A waiter arrived with a platter of raw oysters.

"Fresh from the tidewater," Douglas said. He paused for the waiter to withdraw.

"Now, Charles, let us put our political differences aside for the moment to discuss a matter of personal interest on which we both can agree. Inevitably the railroad will be built. When it is, investors prudently positioned in the railroad line favored by government contract will be handsomely rewarded."

Sumner hunched forward, eyebrow lifted with interest, a forkful of blue-point poised at his chin. "Handsomely? Bloody fortune is more like it."

"There. You see. My point exactly—we do agree. And that is precisely why we should work to compromise on the central route."

"You have the advantage over me, Stephen. Is there something you know that I don't?"

"Not yet, but you and I both know we are in position to make prudent investments when the time comes."

Sumner washed down the oyster with claret. Douglas refilled his glass.

"Yes, I suppose we are."

"Now, the way to advance our cause, if I might return our politics to the table, is for you to draw the northern boundary to our upcoming debate so that we might strike our bargain for the central route."

"And you believe such a proposal would bring your southern delegation to compromise."

"I do. Both proposals are regionally biased. Both sides admit the railroad must be built. Popular sovereignty was enacted to bridge regional differences. A central route through Kansas and Nebraska is perfectly suited to strike such a balance."

"As always, Stephen, the devil is in the details."

"So is the money, Senator. A central route is a perfectly reasonable compromise."

"Once again, Stephen, you prove the shrewd, ever clever bastard."

The waiter arrived, carrying platters sizzling with steak.

Chapter Fifteen

Jackson County, Missouri

Former Senator David Rice Atchison drew on his cigar, waiting for Morgan Walker to greet his guests. Walker selected his lavishly appointed personal library to hold the meeting Atchison had requested. Senator Douglas successfully engineered his popular sovereignty compromise to obtain passage of the Kansas-Nebraska Act. As always, the devil was in the details, and this devil's details could not be left to chance. Atchison hurried home following passage to personally attend to the vital matter at hand.

Boot heels on the polished foyer beyond the library double entry announced the arrival of Walker and his guests.

"Senator, I believe you know Ruben Wright."

"Indeed. Ruben, good to see you, and thank you for coming."

"May I present Sheriff Sam Jones and Franklin Coleman?" Walker said. "Gentlemen, Senator Atchison." They shook hands. "Please, have a seat. Hannibal, brandy and cigars."

A white-haired black man in a starched jacket circulated among the men with a silver tray laden with cigars and crystal brandy snifters. With the guests served, he shuffled out.

Walker lifted his glass. "Senator, you have our undivided attention."

"Gentlemen, let me first thank Morgan for hosting this meeting tonight and thank you all for coming. A matter vital to your interests is about to be decided by the voters of Kansas. As you are aware, I supported passage of the Kansas-Nebraska Act for the inclusion of its popular sovereignty provision. I did so with some reservation. That provision of the law will determine whether those territories enter the union as slave or free-soil states. Control of the Senate hangs in the balance, and with it the future of our slaveholding rights. We all know northern interests, particularly radical Republicans, exhibit growing hostility to our rightful practice. Abolitionist influence in the northeast has organized something they call the New England Emigrant Aid Society to finance and foster the emigration of free-state minded men to the Kansas Territory. For the moment, they remain fairly confined to the Lawrence area, but more are on the way to spread the contagion of their views. Given the opportunity, it is certain they would abolish our property rights." He paused for a draw on his cigar to let the import of his words settle upon them. "We must make a meaningful response to the threat they pose."

A murmur of concern rippled through those assembled.

"What do you propose, David?" Walker said.

"Organize a resistance to counter the abolitionists. I propose we form a society dedicated to the preservation of our rights in Missouri."

"Our rights in Missouri are secure," Coleman said. "Kansas is the problem."

"Indeed it is. If Kansas enters the Union as a free state, the balance of power in the Senate will be brought to the side of their sentiment. We must not allow that to happen."

"But how?"

"As we speak, Kansas is preparing to bring the right to hold slaves to a vote. We cannot allow the northern abolitionist sentiment that runs rampant in Lawrence to determine the outcome of that election."

"Certainly we all agree with that, Senator," Walker said. "But what is to be done about it?"

"It is up to us to make sure enough votes are cast to win victory for our rights."

"We're Missouri men. We're not even eligible to vote in a Kansas election."

"We're Missouri men only so long as we stay in Missouri."

"Are you suggesting that we cross the border and vote as Kansans?"

"I am. And to do so in sufficient number to elect a legislature sympathetic to our cause."

"But isn't that illegal?" Coleman said.

"Only if you're caught," Sheriff Jones said.

Atchison smiled. "Precisely."

The room broke into a babble of conversation. Atchison let them have their say while they digested his message.

"Gentlemen . . . Gentlemen! Please. All of you assembled here this evening are leaders in your respective communities. You can organize the effort. You can spread the word. You can set forces in motion certain to secure our victory. I propose we drink to the south and the advance of our state's rights in Kansas."

"Hannibal! Refill our glasses."

Lawrence, Kansas
March 30, 1855

A March lion roared out of the northwest on a blustery, chill wind. Mud ruts stood stiff in the street, patched here and there by traces of dirt-stained snow. Wagons, buckboards, and saddle mounts clogged Massachusetts Street, making for unusual congestion considering the size of the community. Micah drew rein and stepped down at the Eldridge House rail. He tethered Sampson at the end of a long line of sleepy eyed, hip-shot horses. People moved in and out of the hotel front entrance at a brisk pace, anxious, it seemed, to do their business and get on to warmer pursuits. In this case, their business was to cast a vote for the territorial legislators who would decide the future of slavery in Kansas. It was election day, an important election at that, but the crowd—where did all these people come from?

He joined the line waiting in turn to enter the hotel, now serving as a temporary polling place. He hunched inside his coat against the wind. They hadn't been in Lawrence long enough to know that many people, and, apart from occasional shopping trips to town, they couldn't be expected to know many. Still, the size of the crowd, with so many unfamiliar faces, struck him as unusual.

The line crept across the boardwalk. He entered the hotel sheltered from the wind. The lobby spread out with tables to serve as polling stations. Micah picked up his ballot from the county clerk with a nod. He marked his *X*'s for the free-soil delegation represented largely by candidates of the new Republican party. He folded his ballot, returned it to the clerk, and started for the door.

"Micah."

He turned to Salmon Brown. He extended his hand. "Salmon . . . we heard you were in the area. Where have you settled?"

"We've established a compound we call Brown's Station near Osawatomie. And you?"

"We've claimed a farm five miles southwest of town. You'll have to come by some time."

"How's Clare?"

"She's doing well, thank you. We're expecting in a few weeks."

"My, my, Kansas must agree with you two. I trust you had no further difficulty along the rest of your journey here."

"No trouble after your timely aid. Has your father arrived as yet?"

"Not yet. He's attending to matters in the east. I expect he will be along directly after this."

"After the election?"

"Yes. I fear we are not going to approve of the outcome."

"Why is that? Free-soil sentiment runs strong in Kansas."

"It does, but not in Missouri."

"Missouri? Missouri men have no part in this election."

"I've been here since the polls opened, along with Mr. James Lane and a few others. We're keeping an eye on things. I, for one, don't like what I see."

"You think Missouri men account for the large voter turnout."

"I do. Mr. Lane challenged one or two earlier this morning. They became belligerent and called him a damn northern abolitionist. Their sentiments were plain to behold."

"Who is James Lane?"

"That gentleman over there."

He lifted his chin toward a tall man with wild, wind-blown hair standing by the county clerk's table. Micah hadn't paid him much mind when he picked up his ballot. He had a grimly set, square jaw with lively eyes that flicked over the crowd and up and down the voters claiming their ballots. "Is he here in some official capacity?"

"Only so far as free-soil men look to him as a leader. He's been building to a boil all morning. We know what's happening; if we could prove it, we'd stop it."

"You there." Lane pointed an accusing finger at a man claiming a ballot. "What's your name?"

"Franklin Coleman, not that it's any business of yours."

"You're voting in a Kansas election, Mr. Coleman. That makes it my business."

"And who might you be?"

"James Lane."

"Never heard of you."

"You will. Where you from, Mr. Coleman?"

"East Kansas."

"Missouri's east of Kansas."

"East Kansas," he repeated.

The next man in line spoke up. "You're a Missouri-man. Ain't never seen you before in these parts."

"And who might you be?"

"Charles Dow. I'm a Kansan, and you're not. Your Kansas is east of the Missouri border."

"The hell it is. I got as much right to vote in this election as any of you. What makes you so all fired righteous? You're nothing but a damned abolitionist."

"Well, we know where you stand," Lane said. "You cross that line back to Missouri, Mr. Coleman, you'll pay for this."

"Is that a threat, Mr. Lane?"

"It's a promise, Mr. Coleman."

Osawatomie, Kansas Territory
April, 1855

Fire crackled softly on the hearth. Warm light danced across the cabin's dirt floor. Salmon folded the *Free State Herald* and handed the paper to his brother, Frederick. Young Owen eyed his older brother expectantly across the wooden table.

"They stole the election," Salmon said. "You could see them Missouri men a mile off. You just couldn't prove it 'til they counted the votes."

"What's to be done about it?" Owen said.

"James Lane says there's going to be a fight."

"Father said as much before we left Hudson," Frederick said, tossing the paper on the table. "We had best send for him. He'll know what to do."

"I will write him this evening." Salmon scratched his beard. "If there's to be a fight, we'll need more than Father. We'll need guns; we'll need powder and ball."

"Father has wealthy, sympathetic friends in the northeast," Frederick said. "Be sure you tell him what we need. He may be able to send help even before he arrives."

Salmon nodded solemnly. "Much depends on what we do next."

Chapter Sixteen

Washington City
Capitol Hill

"Senator Sumner to see you, sir."

Douglas massaged the bridge of his nose between thumb and forefinger. Bright morning light fresh with the promise of spring did little to lighten the mood. He'd been expecting this since the first reports of election results came in by wire from Kansas.

"Show him in, Robert."

Charles Sumner crossed the office floor with the purposeful stride of an angry man.

"Charles."

"Save the amenities, Stephen. What have you and your Democrat colleagues done?"

"I assure you, Charles, I had nothing to do with it."

"Tell that to my caucus. 'Deal with the devil and what do you expect,' they tell me and rightfully so, it would appear. Popular sovereignty, my ass. I look like a fool for allowing your people to steal that election."

"I didn't do that, and neither did you."

"We allowed it to happen with your ill-considered 'perfectly reasonable' nonsense."

"One election certainly doesn't invalidate the law."

"It does for me. It may not change the law, but there is one thing that election will do."

"What's that?"

"You can kiss your Pacific railroad good-bye. That's what it will do."

"Now, now, don't be hasty. The Pacific railroad must be built. Remember what's at stake. The national interest must be served to be sure, along with a feather or two for the home nest. The positions from which we might draw our compromise are still in place."

"You might like to think so, but I have news for you. That Kansas election will serve only to embolden your southern Democrat colleagues. They will hold firm on the war department recommendation for a southern route. That has no more chance of passing my caucus than a snowflake passing through Hades. Face it, Stephen, you've made a mess of this, prospects for personal fortune notwithstanding."

Sumner turned on his heel and stormed out.

The White House

Warm sun bathed the south lawn. The scents of spring flowers and new grass floated on a gentle breeze. President Franklin Pierce stood on a crushed stone path admiring the flower beds while soaking up relief from memories of chill, gray winter days. Stone crunched on the path behind him, announcing his guest.

"Good morning, Mr. President. Escaping the confines of your office?"

"Good morning, Jefferson. As a matter of fact, I am. Thank you for indulging me out here."

"On a day such as this, the pleasure is all mine. What can I do for you, sir?"

"Walk along with me. I've a matter or two I'd like to discuss." Pierce led the way along the path at a leisurely pace. He paused. "Smell the lilacs. They are absolutely glorious when they bloom. Pity they last such a short time. Most good things do."

"This wouldn't be about your re-nomination, would it?"

Pierce cocked an eye. "Very perceptive, Jefferson."

"Not really. You'll need the support of the southern caucus. You assume I can influence them."

"That's it, in part."

"There's more then?"

Pierce clasped his hands behind his back and continued up the path. "Gaining southern support will benefit if our recently enacted popular sovereignty law works to everyone's satisfaction."

"Everyone's?"

"Everyone who counts for the purposes of this discussion."

"I see."

"We've had our first success with the vote in Kansas. Now it is up to us to see the will of the people followed through."

"Not everyone was happy with the outcome of that election. Accusations of vote fraud have been widespread and strident in Kansas, not to mention the rest of the north."

"Yes . . . well, there's not much we can do about northern abolitionists. There is somewhat more we can do out in Kansas. That's the other matter on which I need your counsel. I intend to appoint Wilson Shannon as Kansas's territorial governor."

"Shannon is a good man, a reliable Democrat with known southern sympathies. I should think my southern colleagues would look favorably on such an appointment."

"It's more than the matter of his appointment. We must ensure he succeeds in establishing Kansas as a slave state. Our friends out there faced more than token free-soil opposition. If those interests oppose him in carrying out his mission, we may need to assist him with federal resources."

"You mean troops?"

"If need be."

"I don't have to tell you, Mr. President, using federal troops in a matter of domestic jurisdiction is constitutionally dicey."

"I'm well aware of that, Jefferson. On the other hand, Kansas is too important to our cause to risk failure."

The cause being our re-nomination. "I see that, sir."

"I've chosen my man Shannon. Now, who have you to offer me, Mr. Secretary?"

"Bull Sumner."

"Sumner? There's a name not certain to inspire confidence. He's not related to that abolitionist senator from Massachusetts, is he?"

"Actually I believe he is, but don't let that trouble you. Colonel Edwin 'Bull' Sumner commands the 1st Cavalry at Fort Leavenworth. He's a fine officer. He'll accept his orders and do his duty, regardless of any personal feelings he may harbor on the matter."

"You're sure."

"Of that I am sure, Mr. President. It is only the prospect of ordering federal troops to a domestic police action that gives me pause."

"So you've said. I think our lilac blooms may outlast the cherry trees this spring. Don't you agree?"

Chapter Seventeen

Sycamore
April, 1855

Gray clouds hung thick with morning mist. Micah watched as Caleb guided Sampson down the field, cutting an even furrow. The man had a knack for it. Micah followed along, sowing what would be the first crop from their first field. His mind traced back over all they'd accomplished since Caleb and Miriam arrived that dark night the previous fall. They'd finished the sod house and dug a second smaller one along with building a lean-to and corral for the mules. Over the winter, they cleared this field of brush and grass as the weather permitted. He'd traded the wagon for a smaller buckboard they used to clear fieldstone in preparation for planting. The stone they gathered would one day find a place in the house they planned to build on the creek bank.

Miriam came out to the field at midday with a lunch basket. She stood at the end of the row they worked until they neared the end.

"Time for lunch." She smiled.

Caleb drew Sampson to a halt and wiped his forehead on a red bandanna. "What you got there, girl?"

"Ham sandwiches, pickles, sweet tea, and canned peaches for dessert."

"Um-um. That sounds mighty good. You go on and lay that out while I take this mule to water." He unhitched the mule and led him to the creek while Micah finished seeding the row.

"Where's Clare?"

"I told her to lie down and rest a bit. That baby gettin' heavy for her to carry around all day. It won't be long now. With all this plowin' and plantin' don't forget your stock needs."

"Stock needs?"

"You need a milk cow. Sooner or later that baby comin' gonna need more than mama's milk."

Micah and Caleb settled down to lunch under the shade of a tree at the end of the field. Morning cloud cleared off to a bright, sunny day.

"When you finish, just leave the basket," Miriam said, returning to the house. "I'll come back to fetch it later."

The men nodded around mouths full.

"I reckon we finish this field by evenin'. What be next?"

Micah glanced south. "We start clearin' the next field."

"How many fields you figure?"

"Eight, by the time we finish. We won't get crop in all of them this year. Maybe this one and the next. If the weather's good, we should have all eight in crop by next spring."

"That'll make for a powerful lot of wheat."

Micah smiled. "Cash crop, cash money. That's how we get paid."

How we get paid. "I likes the sound of that."

Fields carved in rows, planted in seed. Seed nourished as a mother sustains her unborn child. Sycamore fluttered spring leaves with new purpose. Life on her land served more than the seasons. The work satisfied. Promise swelled in a woman's belly. Another conceived fertilized seed deep in her furrows.

May, 1855

Lamplight flickered on the sod-house wall. Dark shadow surrounded an island of light, encircling the bed. The air hung heavy and still. Miriam poured water from a kettle, heating on the hearth.

"Ah! Ahhh!" Clare's breath came hard, ragged. The pain passed, closer this time.

Miriam picked up the lamp to more closely inspect her progress. "Won't be long now. Hurts bad, don't it?"

Clare nodded, her eyes clenched tight.

Miriam replaced the lamp and took her hand. "I wisht there was somethin' more I could do for you. Babies and the good Lord takes their own sweet time by and by."

Clare lifted an eyelid, her voice a raspy whisper. "There on the table. The Bible . . . perhaps you could read some. The word of God is a comfort."

"I's sorry, Miss Clare. I . . . I cain't read. We never was taught. Massa Morgan Walker say readin' don't do no good 'cept cause us negrahs uppity ideas."

Clare squeezed her hand. "We shall put that to right . . . Agh, ah!"

Miriam wet a towel in warm water to clean up a bit of blood. "It looks like that baby be along right quick now. You really think I can learn to read?"

"I'm . . . sure of it. You have the ability. You must be given . . . the opportunity."

"Now, push, Miss Clare. There. Now, harder. There, there. There she is. It's a girl!"

"It's a girl." Clare sank back to sweat-soaked bedclothes, listening to the song of her daughter's sweet wail.

The baby suckled contentedly at Clare's breast. Dark circles rimmed her eyes, undiminished by a fitful night's sleep. Miriam sat at her bedside just beyond the circle of candlelight from the nightstand.

"What will you name her?"

"Elizabeth."

"That be a pretty name."

"Elizabeth was John the Baptist's mother."

"Miriam is a Bible name they told me. I don't know the story."

"Miriam was Moses's sister. First Exodus, as I recall. You should read the story."

She shook her head. "Remember, Miss Clare. I cain't read."

"I remember. I mean we should start your reading lessons with First Exodus. Here, I think she's done. She's gone to sleep. Put her in her cradle and bring me the Bible."

Miriam took little Elizabeth and laid her in her cradle. She brought Clare the Bible. Clare patted the bedside.

"Sit here." She thumbed well-worn pages. "Yes, here it is. Exodus 15:20." She ran her finger over the words as she read.

"And Miriam the prophetess, the sister of Aaron, took a timbrel in her hand; and all the women went out after her with timbrels and with dances."

"What is a prophetess?"

"A prophet speaks God's word. Some prophets foretell the future. A prophetess is a woman prophet."

"Miriam was a prophet?"

"She was; and she was a leader. All the women followed her with timbrels and dancing."

"That's what the words say?"

"That's what they say. That one's your name." She tapped the word *Miriam*. "It's spelled *M-I-R-I-A-M*. We'll start with the alphabet."

"Afabit?"

"The *A, B, C*'s. You make words with letters that combine to make sounds. Once you know the letters and sounds, you can read anything."

"Anything?"

"Anything. You'll see."

Lawrence
June 1855

They commandeered the Eldridge House dining room. It had sufficient seating to accommodate their purpose. The bar remained open. James Lane sat at a corner table with two like-minded men, James Montgomery and Charles "Doc" Jennison. Like Lane, both were staunch free-soil men. All three knew the slavery issue would not be resolved without a fight. Tall and lean, of rugged conformation, Jennison was ruthless by nature with a mean streak that granted no quarter. Montgomery, a former school teacher and Methodist minister, took moral high ground where slavery was concerned—a position more common to abolitionists than purely pragmatic free-soil men. His followers regarded him a fearless though principled leader given to moral restraint that little troubled a man like Jennison. Charles Robinson held the floor.

"We've no choice but to organize our opposition to the fraudulent usurpation of power by pro-slavery Missouri men. They must not be allowed to subvert the rightful will of Kansans in a matter as morally vital as the holding of slaves. I ask you to join me now in forming a Free State party to put forward a slate of legislative candidates to recall and replace those intent on forming a legislature in Lecompton."

"Here, here!" The assembly pounded the table in accord.

"And with no less than you, Charles, to lead it!" cried a man near the door to another thunderous round of approval.

Lane rose at his seat. "Let me second that, Charles; but before I do, a word if I might?"

Robinson nodded. "Please, James. The floor is yours."

"We can organize our opposition party as Charles proposes.

We can—and we should—pursue our electoral recourse. But let us not delude ourselves in that. Our neighbors to the east and those among us who think as they do will resist our opposition and not just at the ballot box. Know the stakes, gentlemen; our opponents do. If we succeed, they will meet our opposition with force. We stand here today committed to peaceful purpose. But mark my word, those who resort to stealing elections will not stop at peaceful discourse. As we act here today, we are committing to a course that may lead to violence and bloodshed. Do not doubt me. Act accordingly. And, now, I second Charles Robinson to lead the Kansas Free State party, and may God have mercy on us all."

He took his seat to stunned silence. Somewhere someone clapped a tabletop. First two, then three, grew to a roar. "Here, here!"

They shuffled out of Eldridge House in small groups talking among themselves, variously assessing prospects for the enterprise they'd set in motion.

Lane, Jennison, and Montgomery lingered at their table. "I've received a telegram from Brother Brown by way of his son," Lane said. "He tells Salmon we should expect our first shipment from Reverend Beecher any day now. The shipments will be crated as canned tomatoes and farm implements. Salmon interprets that to mean small arms and perhaps cannon. Once they arrive, we shall be equipped to arm a militia. Those who listened today will be ready to join us. Spread the word quietly. We must keep these preparations discreet lest the border men take similar measures."

"How will we distribute the arms?" Jennison asked.

"When they arrive, we'll store them here in Eldridge House. I'll put out the word to the two of you. You can instruct your recruits to come in and claim their 'Beecher's Bibles' at times we shall appoint. We should have our men armed before our new party mounts an effective political opposition."

The wagons arrived two weeks later. Lane and two of his men unloaded the shipment to the Eldridge House storeroom. "Farm implements" included Sharp's carbines, Model 1842 .54 caliber smooth-bore muskets, and a light cannon. "Canned goods" included Model 1848 .44 caliber cap and ball Colt Dragoons.

CHAPTER EIGHTEEN

Sycamore
June, 1855

Dear Ma and Pa,

The joyous news can wait no longer. You have a beautiful new granddaughter, Elizabeth. She was born last month. With Miriam's help we came through it fine. Some say she looks like me, but I see Micah's eyes in her. She is a good baby. Fusses when she's hungry, satisfied when she's not.

Micah and Caleb got our crop in the ground this spring. Our growing season is well under way. The fields wave green-gold in the sun. They promise a fruitful harvest, a proper house in due time, and, dare I say it, a stove. Sycamore truly abounds in God's beauty and blessings.

You have undoubtedly read news accounts of our territorial election. Missouri men saw fit to tamper with our ballot, producing an election of dubious result. By nefarious means they managed to elect a pro-slavery legislature representative of few people living in Kansas. Micah says the community leaders in Lawrence are already calling for a second and this time fair election. How they mean to prevent a repeat of the last outcome is unclear to me. Who will say which legislature truly represents Kansas? I can't say. I only pray the outcome is not to be decided by violent means, though we hear blood strong sentiment on both sides of the issue.

I must close now as Elizabeth is calling for her lunch. In that, I am the only one to satisfy her.

Clare

August 1855

The rider, clad in a black frock coat and broad-brimmed pancake hat, drew rein on the road east of the creek. Golden wheat fields glimmered in heat waves beyond the trees lining the creek bank. They'd be ready for harvest in another month or so. The crop would fetch a fair price. The Masons' might indeed hold their claim. Thorne scowled in frustration. *How had he let such choice acreage slip through his fingers? Careless, just plain careless.* He made out young Mason in the field furthest south, accompanied by a black man. *Curious that . . .* he smoothed his moustache. He'd taken Mason for an abolitionist. *Could he be keeping a slave? No. More likely harboring a runaway. Hmm, if that were true, something might be made of it.*

She came up from the sod house, carrying a bucket to draw water from the creek. She bent to fill the bucket. A gentle breeze ruffled the skirt about her hips. Thorne shifted in his saddle. Fine figure of a woman. Mason had that, too. The land and the woman goaded him. She paused at the creek bank to look his way. Spotted, he gave a casual wave and rode on.

October, 1855

New life came forth in spring to suckle at a mother's breast, sprinkled in rooting rain. It grew tall and green the long summer through, ripening a golden grain in the long last of summer sun. Cut and gathered, threshed and carried, she grew drowsy with her labors, awaiting her coming rest.

Crisp autumn air swirled through sunlit golden-orange sycamore leaves, fluttering above the creek banks, or falling to its surface to be swept along in ripples to the river. Caleb spotted Micah returning from town astride Sampson. He smiled at the milk cow plodding along in tow. He glanced at the sun. Time enough to do a little hunting.

Micah drew rein and stepped down. He handed Caleb the lead to a brown-eyed Guernsey.

"She right pretty, this one."

Micah smiled. "Mostly she'll do for Elizabeth's needs."

"Along with a bit of butter maybe?"

"Along with a bit of butter, I reckon." Micah smiled. Caleb's thoughts never strayed too far from his stomach. "She gives us good reason to finish that pole barn before the snow flies."

"We still goin' huntin'?"

"You put her and Sampson up while I get my musket."

They set off across the harvested fields, the musket cradled in Micah's left forearm.

"What we huntin' for?" Caleb said.

"Deer would be a good choice. Buffalo if we get lucky. Either way, we can jerk a supply in for the winter."

Caleb lifted his chin to the musket. "You pretty good with that thing?"

"Grew up shootin' squirrel with a piece uglier than this. I expect I can hit a deer or a buffalo. How about you?"

"I didn't never shoot nothin'. Guns ain't for us folks, you know."

"Oh, that. Well, then, we best teach you how to shoot. No tellin' when we might have to defend this place."

"What about that?" He directed his gaze to the Colt Dragoon in the holster at Micah's hip.

"We'll start with the long gun. Pistols take a bit more work."

Caleb smiled. His big white grin crossed the fields they'd cut and baled the last three weeks. The land, delivered of its fruits, stretched out at rest beneath the warmth of a golden October sky. They shipped the crop by flatboat down river to the grist mill at Kansas City. They got a good price for it, too. This winter promised a sight more comfort than last.

Open country lay beyond the wheat fields to the west, broad rolling plains awash in browned prairie grass. Here and there tree stands marked the likelihood of a stream. Micah angled northwest toward the river.

"We'll find us a grove of trees to cover in. If we get a good spot we may see game come down to the river to water."

They found a likely spot among a grove of cottonwoods. Trail sign west of the stand said deer passed nearby heading down to the river. They settled in among the trees to watch and wait.

"How long you figure we have to wait?"

Micah shrugged. "Hard to say. That's the thing about huntin'. This should be a good spot, though. We know they pass this way. That west breeze keeps us downwind of 'em."

"Downwind?"

"The west wind blows our scent away from the trail so they don't smell us and spook. Now, the first thing you need to know about shooting is how to load your gun. Watch." He stood and drew a brass tube from his pocket. "This is your powder measure. You want to use the same amount of powder for each shot." He took the powder horn slung over his shoulder and pulled the quill stopper with his teeth. He poured powder into the tube and replaced the quill in the horn. "Now you pour the charge into the muzzle." He stood the musket on its butt plate and poured the charge into the muzzle. He drew a small oilcloth patch from a pouch at his belt. He spread it over the bore and placed a lead bullet in the center. He pushed patch and ball into the barrel, drew the ramrod from the rifle stock, and smoothly rammed the load down the barrel. "See here?" He held his thumbnail to a band etched in the rod. "When the rod seats the bullet to this position, you know it is seated properly to the charge."

Caleb nodded.

Micah raised the musket. "Watch this procedure carefully. You cock the hammer to this position and fit this cap to the nipple here. See?"

Caleb nodded.

"That primes the charge. Now hold the hammer and squeeze the trigger until the hammer releases. Lower the hammer gently, release the trigger, and set the hammer at half-cock; now the rifle is ready. You can cock and fire it when game presents the opportunity. Do you think you can do that?"

He knit his brow in thought. "Yes, sir."

"You'll get to show me once we've had a shot."

They settled in to wait. Time passed. Caleb dozed.

"Look there." Micah nudged him.

A small herd of brown shaggy buffalo trotted over a rise off to the south. At the scent of water, they picked up a trot down a gentle draw toward the river. Micah rose to a knee, watching them come.

"The lead cow is the matriarch. See the young bull trailing behind? That's the one I mean to take." The herd drew closer and passed. Micah leveled aim at the straggler bull. He pictured the shoulder just behind the bobbing head. Exhale. Squeeze. The musket charged a plume of blue smoke. The bull bellowed, stumbled, and went down. The herd bolted to the river.

"That good shootin', Massa Micah."

Micah handed Caleb the musket, powder tube, and powder horn. "Reload this and you'll be shootin' just as good in no time."

It took a reminder or two, but Caleb managed to reload the musket, correctly using the ramrod to confirm the load. Micah stopped him short of priming the cap, but made him demonstrate manipulating hammer and trigger to the half-cock positon.

"Well done."

Caleb grinned. "How we gonna get that bull back to the house?"

"You go hitch up the wagon and drive on out here. I'll keep watch on our kill so scavengers don't spoil it."

Caleb set off for the farm through the trees. He ambled across the field, prairie grass rising to his knees. He'd gone no more than a hundred yards when an Indian hunting party, tracking the buffalo, rode over the rise to the south. They spotted him and swung to the attack.

Micah hadn't expected to encounter a hunting party. He'd been told Arapaho sometimes hunted these plains, though this was his first encounter with them. He counted six, magnificently mounted on three paints, a white, a palomino, and a roan. Each brave was clad in buckskin and feathers and armed with bow and lance. They would ride down Caleb in short order; he had no time to think. They didn't know he was here. He primed the musket and shouldered it to full cock. He pictured the lead warrior on a sturdy paint, exhaled slowly, and squeezed.

The musket charged. The pony dropped its nose and rolled over a shattered shoulder, the rider pitched into the tall grass. The shot brought the rest of the party to a sharp stop. Rearing and prancing, they danced in a circle, searching for the shooter's smoke sign.

Caleb froze at the sound of the shot. He turned wide-eyed to the threat and dropped into the tall grass. *Now what?*

Micah laid the musket aside. *Five shots in the Colt. Each one might have to count.* He knew the gun's accuracy to be poor in his unsteady hand. The warrior fallen from his pony swung up behind one of his brothers. The band wheeled on him and charged the cottonwoods. Micah let them close. At fifty yards, he risked a shot at the lead horse. The paint buried his heels and bucked, sending his rider skyward. The attack dissolved into a melee of riders fighting to control their mounts. The fallen brave charged the thicket, brandishing a tomahawk with an ear-splitting cry. Micah held his fire until he could make out hot coals burning in the man's eyes. He fired. The heavy ball lifted the attacker from his feet and dropped him in his tracks. That seemed to settle the issue for the five remaining warriors. They recovered their mounts and galloped off up the ridge the way they'd come.

Caleb ran back to the cottonwoods. "Thought I was a goner there for a spell. Thank the Almighty you that good a shot. What do we do now?"

Micah handed him the musket. "First you help me reload. Then you go for the wagon. We've still got that bull to bring in."

"What if they comes back?"

"That bunch won't come back without some of their friends. No sense leavin' good meat to them."

Caleb reloaded the musket to half-cock and set off for the farm.

Chapter Nineteen

Hickory Point
Kansas Territory
November 21, 1855

What in blazes is this? Charles Dow inspected the scene. Fresh cut stumps told the story. Someone had cut two mature hickory trees, recently, by the moist feel of the stumps. They cut them up and trimmed them, too, judging by the sawdust and branches left behind. They'd loaded the logs on a wagon. He shrugged deeper into his coat against a sharp northwesterly wind cutting out of gray, cloud-rumpled sky. He let his eye follow the frosted ruts leading away from his property. He stepped into his saddle and eased his horse out after the wagon track. The trail went lost once it joined the well-traveled main road. By then, Dow had a pretty good idea where his trees were headed. He squeezed up a lope for the sawmill.

He found the wagon parked in front of the mill. Four men busied themselves unloading it. Dow didn't recognize any but one of them—the Missouri man he and James Lane confronted at Eldridge House the day of the fraudulent election. He rode in and stepped down.

"Them's my trees you stole."

Coleman lifted a bushy brow under the brim of his slouch hat. "I don't know what you're talkin' about."

"I'm talkin' about them trees there you cut off my property. That's stealin' in Kansas."

Coleman dropped his hands to his side, clenching and unclenching his fists. "You best climb back on that horse and get the hell out of here before I lose my good humor."

"Oh, I mean to climb on that horse and ride straight to the sheriff. Then we'll see about your humor." Dow turned on his heel and started for his horse.

Coleman reached up in the wagon box, drew a 10-gauge shotgun, leveled it, and fired.

The charge at close range pitched Dow face forward, dead before he hit the ground.

"Now you done it," one of the other men said.

"Shut-up, Sparks."

"Cuttin' a couple of trees is one thing. I didn't sign on for no cold-blooded murder."

"What're you gonna do, Franklin?" another said. "You can't just wait here for a posse to come out of Lawrence and hang you."

"Get the rest of these logs unloaded. I'll take the wagon and drive on over to Jackson County and turn myself in to Sheriff Jones. If anyone asks, Dow there attacked me. I shot him in self-defense."

Lawrence

James Lane paced the lamp-lit Eldridge House storeroom. Titus Thorne sat on a crate of "farm implement" muskets while Salmon Brown and his brothers followed Lane with their eyes.

"Son-of-a-bitch shoots poor Charles in the back and claims it was self-defense. Turns himself in to that two-bit Jackson County tin star, and some Missouri judge turns the son-of-a-bitch loose. That's about as much justice as a free-soil man can expect from them damn slavers."

"What's to be done about it?" Salmon asked.

Lane stopped his pacing, clasped his hands behind his back,

and let his gaze wander the darkness beyond the storeroom window. "I say we pay Franklin Coleman a little visit."

Jackson County, Missouri
November 24, 1855

Coleman huffed out the lamp, preparing to leave the barn. The sound of horses approaching fast stopped him in the shadows. They rode into the yard, five or six otherworldly apparitions, faces and features masked in shadow and blue steam from their horses' breath. Red-orange firebrands danced while their mounts pranced and pawed frost-hardened ground.

"Torch the house and barn!" someone said.

Coleman ran to the back of the darkened barn and slipped out the stock door. He crossed the corral, hopped the fence, and disappeared into the woods. Hidden from view, he watched the raiders set his house ablaze. Flames climbed the walls, licking the eaves. He watched them crawl across the roof. Two riders broke away to the barn. A blazing brand arced through the barn doors in a shower of sparks. Flames spread across the straw-strewn floor, igniting timbers reaching the loft. Hay went up in a ball of intense heat, slicing through the roof, leaping for the cold night sky. A second rider circled the barn. Coleman recognized him in the instant before he set his torch to the barn.

Salmon Brown.

"They burned my place to the ground, Sam." Lamplight flickered over grim-set, shadow-masked features.

Sheriff Sam Jones stroked his beard and squinted. "Likely some of Dow's kin or friends. You recognize any of 'em?"

"Just one. Salmon Brown."

"Him . . . I 'spect they was all free-soil abolition men. All right . . . nothin' more to be done about it tonight. You can sleep in the jail. There's bunks and bedding in the cells. I'll raise a posse in the morning, and we'll pay Mr. Brown a social call."

Osawatomie
Kansas Territory

They rode out of a lingering morning mist, horses blowing clouds of steam over heavily armed, dark, nondescript riders. Jones signaled a halt.

"Yo, the cabin! Salmon Brown, come out with your hands up. This is Jackson County Sheriff Samuel Jones. I've a warrant for your arrest."

Salmon caught his brother Owen's eye. "You make sure James knows what's goin' on here." He crossed the cabin to the door and stepped into the cold morning air. Jones sat across the yard flanked by a dozen posse men. "What's the charge, Sheriff?"

"Burnin' Franklin Coleman's place to the ground."

"I don't know what you're talkin' about."

" 'Course you don't. You got a horse to ride, or would you prefer to walk?"

"Horse is in the corral."

"We'll be pleased to help you saddle it. Give him a careful hand, boys."

Three men dismounted to escort Salmon to the corral.

The road to Lecompton wound through a wooded defile. Cold sun filtered through limbs bare but for a few brown leaves lingering in loss of color. A blanket of fallen leaves covered the path, ruffled by a gusty breeze. The posse strung out to near single file, with Sheriff Jones in the lead.

"Halt there!"

The command echoed down from the hillside. Jones reined up and drew his gun.

"I'd put that gun away if I were you, Jones. You're surrounded."

He scanned the hills. A forest of rifle and pistol muzzles peeked out from the trees above his position on both sides of the road.

"We'll be relieving you of your prisoner here and now."

"I have a warrant for his arrest."

"Your warrant ain't worth the paper it's writ on here in Kansas."

"Says who?"

"Says me."

"And who might you be?"

"Just one of them little ol' Kansas Jayhawks."

"I don't know nothin' about Kansas Jayhawks. I know jays for noisy thiefs."

"I wouldn't go too far with that if I was you. You're talking to the hawk wing of us Jayhawks. Now, turn your prisoner loose, and we'll let you by all nice and peaceful like."

"He burned Franklin Coleman's house and barn to the ground. Likely with the help of some of all you hidin' in them trees up there."

"Coleman lived to tell about it. That's a sight more chance than he give poor Charles Dow. Charles wasn't doin' no more than protecting his property."

"That was self-defense. Judge Tucker ruled it that way."

"Not much defendin' yourself needed when you shoot a man in the back. We got no interest in the opinion of your slaveholder judge. Now, pull out of that line, Salmon, and ride on up here. Sheriff, you or any of your men make a move to stop him, we gonna rain lead on your head."

Salmon swung out of the column and fast climbed his horse into the hills through the trees.

"Now, Sheriff, you and your men are welcome to be on your

way back to Missouri."

"You haven't heard the last of this, Jayhawk. We'll be back."

"We'll be waitin'."

Chapter Twenty

Franklin, Missouri

Jones stood hat in hand in the midst of a two-story entry foyer dominated by a candlelit crystal chandelier. The white-haired black butler's footsteps echoed down the polished wood corridor, his white coat an apparition floating in the darkness.

"The senator will see you now."

Jones followed the white coat to large double doors opening to a lavish library salon.

"Sheriff Jones," the black man announced at the door.

Former Senator David Atchison rose from a dark-green velvet settee set beside a cheery fire. A light scent of wood smoke flavored the air to the occasional snap and pop of a log. He set the book he'd been reading on a side table and nodded.

"Thank you for seeing me, Senator."

"Nonsense, Sheriff. Always a pleasure. Would you care for a whiskey to take the chill off this evening?"

"That would go mighty good."

"Joachim, two please." The black man disappeared.

"Have a seat, Sam." He indicated a pair of matching wing chairs opposite the settee. "Now what's on your mind?"

"Lawrence. Them abolitionists is turnin' it into an armed camp. I took a posse out after the men who burnt Franklin Coleman's place. We was takin' one of 'em to Lecompton when we was jumped by a bunch of them. Claimed they was Jayhawks, whatever the hell that is. Threatened to shoot us all if we didn't give up our prisoner. We can't let 'em get away with the likes of that, Senator."

"No, we can't."

Joachim arrived with the drinks. He set them on the table and withdrew.

"That ain't the whole of it, either. Them abolitionists has organized a Free State party. They's fixin' to nominate candidates for a legislature and hold themselves another election."

"We've overcome that before."

"Maybe so, last time. Back then we kinda put it over on 'em before they really knew what happened. That was before they knew what to look for. Now they've turned out an armed militia. It won't be so easy next time."

Atchison swirled his whiskey in the firelight and took a swallow. "So, you think they might succeed in holding a free-soil election then."

"I do."

"We can't allow that to happen."

"I figured you'd see it that way. That's why I come to see you. I just don't know what's to be done about it."

"How many men you figure they raised?"

Jones shrugged. "Hard to say . . . couple hundred maybe."

Atchison smiled. "There's your answer."

"What answer?"

"They raise a couple of hundred men, we raise a thousand and more."

"To do what?"

"March on Lawrence. I'll put out the call. We'll put fear of the righteous Almighty before them."

★ ★ ★ ★ ★

Lawrence

They sat around a scarred table amid the munitions cases in the Eldridge House storeroom. Late afternoon light muted by a thick blanket of cloud seeped through window grime, casting those gathered in somber gray to match the gravity of the mood.

"Atchison's got a call out to raise a Missouri militia," Doc Jennison said. "He's not just recruitin' landed men, either. He's takin' all manner of riffraff, river men, and ruffians. Some say he means to raise a force over a thousand."

"What does he propose to do with a force so large?" Montgomery asked.

"He plans to march on Lawrence."

"What the hell for?" Lane said. "We ain't done nothin' 'cept pull brother Brown out of that little scrape with Sheriff Jones."

Montgomery folded his hands circumspectly. "There's more to it than that, James. Atchison has undoubtedly heard of our effort to advance a free-state legislature. Men who resort to stealing elections are certainly capable of resorting to force should peaceful means fail them."

"Then there is little else to be done but to raise our own force and prepare to defend ourselves. If you'll recall, I said from the founding of the party this might well be the outcome."

Montgomery nodded. "We knew it could come to this. You said as much in this very hotel last spring."

"It's time to rally our fellow Kansans. If Missouri men are prepared to do battle, we must rise in opposition."

"Where do we begin?" Doc said.

"First, the defense of Lawrence—an earthworks perimeter from which to defend the town. We can move the six-pounder to the upper floor of the hotel rampart. We'll see how Atchison's ruffians care for a taste of ball and grape."

"Surely we can mount a defense, but how are we to sustain it?" Montgomery posed the pragmatic question.

Lane smiled. "We sustain our resistance at Missouri's expense. Like the mythical jayhawk—part bird of prey, part noisy thief."

Territorial Governor's Office
Lecompton, Kansas

Wilson Shannon wrung his hands. He resorted to the habitual gesture under duress. These days he had duress aplenty.

Atchison sat across the desk watching the man fret. President Pierce thought the man suited to territorial governance; Atchison had his doubts. He was a reliable Democrat committed to the cause of slavery, but governing a territory as divided as Kansas took mettle. Shannon might be over-matched governing a girls' boarding school.

"Thank you for coming, Senator. I'm afraid I am sorely in need of good counsel. I simply didn't know where else to turn. The reports out of Lawrence are most disturbing. They are organizing a political opposition to our legislature which would be trouble enough; but, worse still, they are assembling some sort of militia. The president expects me to uphold the results of the election, but I'm at a loss as to what to do with these stiff-necked people."

"I'm aware of the problems in Lawrence, Wilson. What you describe has the ring of rebellion about it."

"It hasn't come to that yet, but the kettle is certainly heating to boil."

"If the free-state faction means to usurp your authority by force, it seems to me you have no choice but to raise a territorial militia to put down the threat of rebellion."

"I can see that. But, face it: do you seriously believe we could raise a sufficient force like-minded to our cause to oppose them?"

"I can see how that might be a problem. Perhaps I can help you there. We've had some problems spill across the border into Missouri. Jackson County sheriff Samuel Jones has been obstructed in his duties by the Lawrence free-soil faction. He's raising a rather large posse to deal with the problem. I suspect he and his men might find common cause with your need of a territorial militia."

"Missouri men in a Kansas militia? That seems a bit irregular."

"A territorial militia need only be sanctioned by the territory. You have the power to do that. Who is to say if a few Missouri men rise to a just cause? Trying times call for stern measures."

"Yes, I suppose they do."

"Sheriff Jones should be ready to march by the first of the month. Should you approve it, I'll speak to him on your behalf."

Shannon pursed his lips, wringing his hands. "Yes, yes, please do."

Chapter Twenty-One

Sycamore

Titus Thorne trotted up the lane on the black stallion he called Rogue. Smoke from the sod house flattened out in the winter chill. Someone was home. He stepped down at the crest of the ridge and dropped rein. They'd put in a flight of crude wooden steps down to the entrance level. He rapped at the door. Mason answered.

"Mr. Thorne, what can I do for you?"

"A word if I might?"

"Come in."

Inside, the dugout was comfortably warm and dry. A thread-worn carpet covered the dirt floor. The single room was large enough to hold a bed, table and chairs, and a stove in one corner. A single window spilled grayish light. The woman sat beside the bed holding an infant. She was lovely even in these spare surroundings. Mason was a fortunate man. Too fortunate in many respects. She nodded, nervous at his attention.

"We don't have many comforts to offer," Mason said. "A seat at the table is the best we can do."

"Thank you. This shouldn't take long."

"This isn't about the farm again, is it?"

"Not unless you've changed your mind about selling."

"I've not. So, then what is it?"

"We're organizing a militia to defend Lawrence."

"Defend Lawrence from what?"

"Missouri men are raising a large force. They're calling it a posse under Sheriff Jones. Whoever heard of a posse approaching a thousand men?"

"A thousand?"

"We believe. Worse still, our dithering governor may give it the legitimacy of calling it a territorial militia."

"Why attack Lawrence?"

"The governor considers our free-state opposition to his proslavery legislature a rebellion. He feels compelled to put it down in the name of law and order."

"But we've only chosen to express our rights."

"It would appear one man's right is another man's rebellion. Unfortunately, the man in power comes down on the side of rebellion. He can't raise enough opposition to our cause in Kansas, so he turns to Atchison and his Missouri ruffians. We expect them to march any day now. Will you join us?"

Micah drummed the table with his fingers. "I suppose I must."

Clare gasped.

"What about my man, Caleb?"

"The runaway? You'd arm a black man?"

"Caleb is free. And, yes, I'd arm him."

"It's not for me to say, but I'd advise against it. There'd be plenty on our side who'd not take kindly to the idea. Opposition to slavery is one thing. Arming them is a mite more equality than most folks are inclined to condone."

"They're wrong about that."

"It'd only make trouble; we've got enough of that already. Are you with us or not?"

"I am."

"Good." He rose. "We'll see you in Lawrence as soon as you can get there." He turned to the door, giving Clare a slight bow. "Ma'am."

Clare waited for the door to close and Thorne's footsteps to climb up the ridge.

"You're going?"

"I must."

"But, Micah, it will be dangerous."

"Clare, sooner or later the slavery question must be settled for Kansas and the rest of the country. We have a duty to stand for high moral purpose."

"What will you tell Caleb?"

"The truth."

"You are going to defend his right to freedom, but he is not welcome to join you."

"He's welcome to join me. It's others that don't welcome him. I don't agree with it, but that's the truth. The good book says there's a season: 'A time to every purpose under heaven.' " He crossed the room and took her in his arms.

"I don't like that man. He looks at me."

"What red-blooded man wouldn't?"

"That's not what I mean."

"I know." He kissed her.

Lawrence
December 2, 1855

Micah walked to Lawrence on a cold, blustery day. Snow snakes skittered along the rutted road on a gusty wind, gathering drifts. The fortifications he found surprised him. Between Lane, Jennison, and Montgomery, they'd recruited a force of some five hundred men. They'd built a defensive perimeter of mounded barriers linked by a network of trenches and rifle pits. Eldridge House stood at the center of the defense with the six-pounder prominent in her upper turret. Micah found Thorne in the hotel lobby with Lane.

"Micah, glad you've come." Lane extended his hand. "The

festivities should begin any day now. Jones's column was last seen a day's march east of here. We've prepared a nice reception for them."

"It seems so. Where do I report?"

"Doc Jennison has the east flank; Montgomery holds the heights on Mount Oread to the west. My men man the center to our south. I'm keeping a reserve to reinforce any breach or defend to the north should they attempt an envelopment. You may join Mr. Thorne's reserves."

"The men are camped behind the hotel," Thorne said. "We've taken over the stable for shelter. I see you've brought your own weapons. Are you equipped with powder and shot?"

"I've some. If it comes to a fight, I shall need more."

"The hotel storeroom serves as an armory. Come this way."

A thick blanket of rumpled-felt cloud rolled off the western plains, laden with the heavy scent of snow. Jones led a column some twelve hundred strong north along the wagon road to Lawrence. He drew a halt as two horsemen galloped down the road from the west. The scouts drew rein to report.

"I'd say they're fixin' to fight, Sheriff. We got 'em outnumbered, but they're dug in around that Eldridge House. Three, maybe four, rings of earthworks. Looks to be a cannon in the top turret of the hotel."

"They built the damn thing with the intent of a fortification. Very good then. Stay by in case I am in need of a messenger." He rode on.

They reached Lawrence as dusk fell. Jones centered his line on Eldridge House southeast of town. He sent two hundred men east and west under the command of two of his most experienced deputies. They made camp and lit fires for warmth and to show the strength of their numbers.

★ ★ ★ ★ ★

Night came with a cold, hard wind and light swirl of snow. Micah found Salmon Brown sheltered with the reserves in the stable. The men huddled together for warmth, unwilling to risk fire in the flammable confines of a stable. Word spread on light clouds of steam. The governor's Missouri men had arrived.

"Rumors say they's a lot of 'em," Salmon said.

"Let's go out front and have us a look." Micah rose.

"Owen, you stay by and keep us a place. This barn's pretty near full-up."

Owen needed no encouragement to stay out of the cold. Micah led the way around to the front of the hotel. Campfires too numerous to count half-ringed the town from the river to the dark peak of Mount Oread.

"Makes you wonder if they's anyone left in Missouri," Salmon said in a whisper of steam.

"They rush us come morning, it's gonna make for one powerful fight."

"Father said it must come to this—it's God's will."

"Sure looks like it. You scared, Salmon?"

"Fool not to be."

Up Massachusetts, the jangle of harness chain announced the approach of a carriage. The driver drew rein in front of Eldridge House. Charles Robinson stepped down from the driver's seat beside a black-cloaked figure. They mounted the boardwalk step. Caught in pale window light, the dark-cloaked figure revealed himself—Governor Wilson Shannon.

"What's he doin' here?" Salmon said.

Micah shrugged.

Robinson led Shannon inside. James Lane greeted them.

"We've a room upstairs where we can talk." Lane led the way up the stairs.

Jennison and Montgomery eyed the governor suspiciously.

The room was furnished with a small table, chairs, and a sideboard laid with a crystal decanter and glasses.

"Brandy?" Robinson offered.

"On a night such as this? It's a must."

Robinson poured. He handed glasses to Shannon and Lane.

"Have a seat, gentlemen." He set the decanter on the table at his elbow. "Governor, thank you for coming. We have a situation here cool heads must resolve before blood is shed."

December 3, 1855

Dawn brought more snow. Jones passed his glass over the earthworks. Men could be seen moving among the trenches. Rifle pits bristled with sharpshooters. Lane had put up a stout defense. *We try to march on that town, a lot a' men gonna die.* He snapped the glass closed. "Messenger!"

"Rider comin'. Looks like a flag of truce. Hard to tell in the snow."

Lane moved up the trench to his forward position. A gray specter resolved out of the swirling snow. The rider drew rein at the perimeter wreathed in steam.

"Got a message for James Lane from Sheriff Jones."

"You found him."

"The sheriff says there's no need of sheddin' a lot of innocent blood here. Hand over those responsible for the Coleman cabin raid, and he'll take his prisoners and depart with his posse."

"Like he done justice to the man who killed Charles Dow? You tell Jones—"

"That will be enough, James," Robinson said. "Governor?"

"This is Governor Shannon. I have a note for Sheriff Jones."

★ ★ ★ ★ ★

The wind roared out of the west, driving blinding white torrents of snow. Visibility deteriorated to the point the messenger had difficulty finding his way back to Jones.

"I have a note from Governor Shannon."

"Shannon? What's he doin' there?" Jones read the note.

"What's the governor want us to do?" a man nearby asked. "Die on them earthworks or die out here in the snow?"

"Man's right," the messenger said. "You cain't fight nature like this and expect to win."

"Mount up, boys. The Governor says we're headed back to Franklin."

Sycamore

Candlelight flickered on the frosted window. Outside the wind howled; snow swirled white devils in a wild winter dance. Miriam held the book toward the halo of light, moving her finger across the page as the words came to her.

"You goin' read that book all night, girl?"

She glanced toward the sleeping pallet in the darkened far corner.

"I got a spot's all warm for you here."

"You do, do you?"

"I do."

"I seem to recall you said that once before."

"I did. I seem to recall you findin' no fault in my warm."

"Hmm. I didn't, did I?"

"No fault a'tall."

"Wellst if you's to put it like that, there's a little somethin's been on my mind."

He chuckled. "Oh, what that be?"

She closed the book and stood. She lifted her night shift over her head and smiled into the darkness behind her. She snuffed out the candle and crossed the room, her promises frosted in gray window light and orange ember glow. He pulled back the quilt to receive her. She wriggled into hard-muscled warmth and was gathered into his arms.

"Mmm. That is warm."

"See what I told you? Now what might you have on your . . . mind you said?"

"I been thinkin'."

"Uh oh."

"What 'uh oh'?"

"When you be thinkin', it usually end up begettin' big things."

"No, I been thinkin' 'bout begettin' a little thing."

Caleb propped himself on an elbow and caught a dark glimmer in her eyes in the low light. "What sort a' little thing you begettin' to think about?"

"A little thing like Elizabeth." She kissed him soft and sweet. "It'd be so nice and easy to." She kissed him hard.

"There you go again, begettin big ideas."

"Um hmm."

Chapter Twenty-Two

Lawrence
January, 1856
The Eldridge House polling station did a brisk business this election day monitored by Lane and a few of his men. They came in orderly lines, placed their ballots, and left. Charles Robinson, head of the Free State party, stood by, an intent observer. They'd dispatched Montgomery to the east and Jennison to the west to set up similar monitoring at polling places across the territory. This time they meant to aggressively ensure the votes taken were the votes of Kansans. The precautions proved unnecessary. Both Governor Shannon and Atchison had satisfied themselves that the legitimate territorial legislature had been chosen by the previous election. The election being conducted by the free-staters was both unnecessary and illegal.

The votes were counted and consolidated over the course of the next two weeks. When all the votes were tallied, Kansans elected a free-state legislature by a wide margin. That legislative body would elect Charles Robinson governor. Kansas would now have two legislatures and two opposing governors.

The White House
Washington City
January 20, 1856
A snow storm boiled out of the Blue Ridge, swirling down the Potomac, snarling street traffic in the city. Pierce gazed at a

white wonderland beyond his office window as he pondered the problem at hand.

"Secretary Davis is here, sir."

"Send him in." Pierce stood to greet his secretary of war. "Jefferson, thank you for coming on short notice and under such difficult conditions."

"A good soldier gets an urgent summons from the commander in chief; what more is there to do? Let me guess: it's about that election in Kansas."

"It is. Have a seat." He handed Davis a telegram. "Governor Shannon's report."

Davis read the cryptic communique. "What do you propose to do about it?"

"I'll address Congress, of course. We have a state of rebellion on our hands. I'll make the case to Congress and the people that such lawlessness is not to be condoned. It is incumbent upon us to ensure the exercise of lawful authority. Governor Shannon will doubtlessly need the assistance of your department to maintain order."

"I was afraid that's where this was headed. As we've discussed, Mr. President, the use of federal troops in domestic matters raises serious constitutional questions."

"Yes, I've heard that speech before. Unfortunately, we can't spare the luxury of indulging it in this case."

"Can't the governor raise a local militia to enforce the law?"

"Not in sufficient force."

"You'd think a territory with sufficient popular support to elect a legitimate legislature would be able to raise a militia to enforce the will of the people on the losing side."

"Come now, Jefferson. You're a southerner. Don't be naive."

"If my observation seems naive, perhaps we have a different problem."

"You know the problem as well as I. You'll make the Fort

Leavenworth command available to Governor Shannon as we discussed."

Davis confined his misgivings to a scowl. "Yes, Mr. President."

Capitol Hill
Washington City
January 24, 1856

The chamber rose, dark-suited legislators framed in the tawny, wood-paneled glow of soft light spilling from tall, even rows of windows. Applause died out to the echoes of the speaker's gavel.

"Honorable gentlemen, I give you the president of the United States."

Pierce climbed the podium to another round of restrained applause. He acknowledged the pro-forma enthusiasm with a smile and wave. The appearance of such popularity, dutifully reported by the press, could do no harm to his bid for re-nomination.

"Please, please." He held up his hands in a feeble appeal for quiet that served only to encourage his side of the aisle to carry on. At last, members began to take their seats. Order spread over the chamber as the starched convocation settled in their chairs.

"Gentlemen, I come before you today on a matter of grave concern. There exists today in our Kansas Territory no less than a state of open rebellion. By now you have heard the reports. Certain factions in Kansas have sought by unlawful election to establish legislative and executive offices in opposition to the territory's duly elected legislature and duly appointed governor."

Some restless muttering and uneasy postures could be heard in the northern and northeastern delegations. Pierce continued in seeming disregard.

"Kansas now claims two territorial governments with opposing governors and capitals: one established by the rule of law, the other asserted as a platform for insurrection against lawful governing authority. These lawless usurpers and assemblies must disband and disperse. Should they fail to resign their fraudulent claims, the legitimate territorial governor shall be within the right of law to call out local militias to put down their rebellion."

An undercurrent of disagreement rippled through the assembly.

"Radical extremists have seized the controversy as an opportunity to advance their cause by lawless means. Governor Shannon has asked for our support in putting down this rebellion and restoring order. I have asked the secretary of war to make sufficient federal troops available to the governor and his appointed magistrates and militias so as to restore the rule of law and bring this uprising to a swift and just end."

Southern Democrats rose to applaud. Their northern colleagues followed in somewhat restrained support. Northern representatives affiliated with other party interests sat in stunned silence.

He means to use federal troops buzzed from incredulous mouth to ear.

Fort Leavenworth
Kansas Territory
January 28, 1856

Strong winter wind howled around post command, driving drifting and snow snakes before it. It rattled the windows and whined in the eaves, challenging the potbelly stove in the commandant's office to beat back the chill. A knock at the door brought Colonel Edwin "Bull" Sumner up from the warmth of his coffee cup.

"Telegram, sir." The fresh-faced trooper with a German accent snapped off his salute and extended the transcribed message.

Sumner accepted the foolscap and returned a resigned salute. "That will be all, Corporal."

The trooper turned on his heel and left the cramped office.

Sumner lifted a brow at the war department sender line. He cut to the bottom of the page—J. Davis's signature had his attention. He scanned the cryptic lines, closed heavy lidded eyes, and let the meaning sink in. He read the lines a second time, jaw muscles bunched behind a full-face beard shot through with gray. A cousin to abolitionist Senator Charles Sumner, Bull Sumner had his own sympathies. They had no standing in this. The orders were clear: support Pierce's pro-slavery governor no matter the will of the people, much less the sentiments of his own conscience. They intended to use federal troops to uphold and defend the ill-gotten result of a corrupt election. He was but a simple soldier, no constitutional lawyer. Still, he'd learned enough of the separation between civil and military authority to know right from wrong. He inhaled deeply and exhaled slowly, the barest hint of steam tracing his breath. The orders were clear. He re-read a phrase: *'unlawful insurgency.'* Unlawful indeed. Who here is on the wrong side of the law? He had his orders.

Sycamore
April, 1856

The buckboard rocked along the dirt road through bright sunshine, returning from Sunday services in Lawrence. Redbud splashed purple mist on budding early spring green. Clare sat beside Micah in the box, holding little Elizabeth. Caleb and Miriam sat in the bed, Miriam holding the gentle swell of her belly. Micah turned up the lane to the farm. The bones of a spacious frame house stretched out to greet the midday sky.

"Look there," Clare said.

Micah drew rein. He followed her gaze to the old sycamore. A blue carpet spread spring flowers beneath its branches, spilling down the ridge toward the river.

"Isn't it beautiful?"

"It's bluebonnet," Miriam said.

"We might gather a bouquet for the table."

Micah clucked to Sampson, continuing up the lane.

"We gonna work on the house some today?" Caleb asked.

"Sunday's a day of rest," Micah said over his shoulder. "Tell you what. Let's take the musket out past the fields and let you have some target practice."

Caleb grinned.

Clare and Miriam fixed lunch while Micah and Caleb unhitched the team and turned them out to graze. After lunch Micah shouldered the musket, powder horn, and bullet pouch. He and Caleb set off down the cart path between fields one and two, where the summer wheat crop sprouted green. This year they had six fields planted. With good weather, they should take in a bountiful harvest. As they walked, Caleb cast a far gaze across the fields to the horizon.

"What be comin' of it, Micah?"

"Coming of what?"

"Slavery in Kansas. Me and Miriam hear folks talk at church. They say that slavery governor and them legis-lawyers of his is fixin' to pass a slavery law."

"The Lecompton legislature election was illegal. That's why we had a new election. Our legislature will adopt a constitution that prohibits slavery. Governor Robinson will see to that."

"So, between two governors and two legis-lawyers, who decide who be right?"

"Right decides who's right."

"I sees trouble comin'."

Micah eyed his friend. "I hope you're wrong, but you could be right." They walked on together.

"Maybe we should move on. There's free land further west."

"Free soil or free land?"

"Both."

"Kansas will be free, Caleb, and so will you."

"You cain't know that."

"I do know, 'cause free is right. Look, Clare and I have been talkin'. We couldn't have worked this place alone. We were plain lucky you and Miriam came along the way you did. We work good together. We want you to stay. What would you say if we sold you fields five and six? We could build you your own place. You'd have your own crop. We'd still pay you shares for workin' ours."

"You'd do that?"

"We would."

"We don't have the money to buy that land."

"You got a dollar?"

"You'd sell them acres for a dollar?"

Micah nodded. "And we'd work the fields same as we do now."

Caleb walked on in thought. "I'd pay you shares on my crop."

"Seems fair."

They paused at the end of the field.

"A man's land be worth takin' a stand for. You sure about this, Micah?"

"I'm sure."

"Could be trouble."

"Could be. I hope not; but if there is, we'll be ready."

"Best then you get on with teachin' me how to shoot."

Promises. Men walked her fields between rows of her offspring, side by side at leisure as they did at work. The bones of a more permanent home arose along her creek bank. They planted. They built. They brought new life. An island of tranquility amid powerful forces, some seen, others as yet unseen. She could feel them. Seasons to come would test these promises and her guardianship of the land and those who dwelt there.

Chapter Twenty-Three

Constitution Hall
Lecompton, Kansas
May 1856

The gavel banged adjournment. Governor Shannon smiled, self-satisfied as the legislators filed for the door in the fading light of late afternoon. Officially they'd adopted a pro-slavery constitution. His next measures would be taken up by the courts. He'd selected a few legislators to impanel a grand jury. They would meet in the morning to take up certain matters with respect to sedition offenses in Lawrence. He'd personally overseen the attorney general's work in drawing up the charges. The jury should make short work of the necessary indictments. Serving those indictments should sever the head of the serpent.

Morning sun slanted through tall courthouse windows, bathing the somber, dark-suited men seated at a long, polished table in an otherworldly glow. It had taken less than an hour to present the charges and no more than that for the jury to return the foregone conclusion.

"Has the jury reached a verdict?"

A tall man at the far end of the table rose. "We have, Your Honor."

"Then I shall ask the bailiff to read it."

A short, stocky figure stepped out of the shadows and approached the table. The tall man handed him a single sheet. He adjusted his spectacles.

"We, the jury, find sufficient grievance in the matters of evidence presented to charge Charles Robinson with the crime of treason. We similarly find sufficient grievance to charge James H. Lane with the crime of treason. In the matter of the *Kansas Free State Herald* and its editor, we find sufficient grievance for a charge of sedition. Lastly, we, the jury, recommend that Eldridge House be condemned as a public nuisance and obstruction to maintaining civil order."

"The court hereby orders the issue of bench warrants accordingly."

Governor Shannon rose. "Thank you, gentlemen. The court's orders will be served by US Marshal Israel Donelson as soon as the warrants are issued."

The judge's gavel banged. "Court stands adjourned."

Franklin, Missouri

Atchison stood in the double library doors open to the gardens. A soft evening breeze ruffled the curtains framing the door and the tail of his coat. He drew on his evening cigar, savoring wisps of blue smoke. Once set in motion, they had little choice but to see it through. There was nothing to be done for it. The inner door clicked open behind him.

"Sheriff Jones, Senator."

"Thank you, Joachim." The white-jacketed black man bobbed his whitened head and backed out the library door, ushering in Sheriff Samuel Jones.

"You sent for me, Senator?"

"I did, Sam. Thank you for coming. Have a seat." Atchison indicated a wing chair across from his desk.

"What can I do for you?"

"Governor Shannon needs our help. The Kansas grand jury has indicted Charles Robinson for treason. They've condemned

Eldridge House and the Kansas free-state newspaper as public nuisances. The governor has asked us to raise a posse to support the US marshal in serving the orders on Lawrence."

"You mean finish the job we started last December."

"Yes . . . well, hopefully with a more favorable result. This time we need to be a little less bellicose in our preparations so as not to alert the free-soil faction to our intentions. Do you understand?"

"Keep it quiet and surprise them."

"That's it. If you're agreed, I'll tell the governor to have his marshal contact you directly. The two of you can plan the enterprise."

"My office is at your disposal, Senator."

"Good. Keep me informed, Sam. I'd like to ride along, just to make sure that nest of vipers is stomped out once and for all this time."

"Very good, sir."

Washington City
Capitol Hill
May 19, 1856

Wood polish and damp wool scented the air. The Senate assembly waited in anticipation.

"The Chair recognizes our gentle friend from Massachusetts."

Senator Sumner rose from his desk and strode purposefully across the floor to mount the rostrum at the head of the chamber. He turned to the assembly, jaw hardened, resolute.

"Distinguished colleagues and gentle friends, I come before you today to expose the greatest swindle ever perpetrated on the people of this nation. We in this assembly, myself regrettably included, have been duped to enact into law a swindle. A swindle, swaddled in the sheepskin known as 'popular sovereignty,' was thus enacted to enable territorial expansion into Kansas and Nebraska. Today with the masquerade stripped away, we bear sad witness to the subjection of Kansas to the practice of slavery previously prohibited by the Missouri Compromise." The chamber divided—grumbles of agreement from the north, stone silence to the south.

"Proponents of this swindle have sought to deny sovereignty to the citizens of Kansas, asserting slave-holder rights by force and fraudulent ballot. Having committed fraud, perpetrators of this evil now seek to institutionalize and shelter the holding of slaves under the pretense of a territorial constitution. This crime against Kansas is a monster which could not be birthed by free and fair exercise of the citizen franchise. Injustice will now impose by force the sinful stain of slavery on free soil.

"Forces of evil opportunism have seized on the Kansas-Nebraska swindle to drive out the voices of freedom, deny settlement to those who oppose slavery, and usurp the sovereign power of the territory to legislate its future. Thankfully, the first two have failed. Righteous voices of those opposed to evil have been heard. Sadly, the latter battle for the future remains in doubt. Violent men bent on disenfranchising good citizens enabled malicious interlopers to steal their verdict at the ballot box.

"Having thus fraudulently obtained the levers of government, they have served to enact evil measures once again disguised in the cloak of law. In Kansas, they now represent that anyone who speaks or writes against the right to hold slaves shall be deemed a felon subject to imprisonment at hard labor. These villains would treat as criminals those who uphold the law of nature by exercise of free speech under our constitutional protections. By yet a second act, they assert that an applicant for the right to practice law in the territory must acknowledge, uphold, and defend in addition to the constitution, the Territorial Act establishing slavery in the territory and provisions of the

Fugitive Slave Act. Thereby, they countenance the admission of no legal opposition at the bar. Further, by yet a third tyrannical decree, they seek to disqualify from jury any man who does not acknowledge the right to hold slaves. In governance, they go on to appoint magistrates and court officers to uphold the laws of the territory. Thus they impose the tyranny of their usurped authority on good citizens who have no say in local matters.

"Thus stands the Kansas-Nebraska crime complete. A crime perpetrated in the name of popular sovereignty. This is not legitimate sovereignty, let alone popular. This is not government by the people. This is piracy in halls protected by an overarching constitution. It cannot stand. And yet it does stand, in insult to righteous providence. The result is civil unrest of the sort we witness in Kansas.

"We now know who among us condones such deceit. We know the charlatan from Illinois and his slave-holding puppet master from Virginia. We here must resolve to repeal this travesty and set the territorial direction on a righteous path to emancipation and freedom!"

The southern delegation rose in outrage, shaking fists and decrying the very suggestion. They stomped out of the chamber in symbolic defiance. The northern delegation rose to drown them out with support.

Lecompton, Kansas

US Marshal Israel Donelson stood on the steps of Constitution Hall. A ragged column of Missouri posse men clogged the road, raising dun dust to a bright spring morning. There must be seven or eight hundred in all, he thought. None too savory, either, this lot of border ruffians. They look more like a mob than a posse. This is the support we need to serve an arrest warrant and condemn a couple of public nuisances? It looks like we're going to war with caisson and cannon in tow. Sheriff

Jones and a handsomely mounted gentleman detached from the column and rode up to the courthouse steps.

"Marshal Donelson, may I present Senator Atchison? Senator, Marshal Israel Donelson."

"Marshal, my pleasure."

"Senator, I see you've come in force."

"We'll make no mistake this time, Marshal. Nor shall we be driven off by a snow storm."

"I should think not." *A former Missouri senator with an armed militia called out to serve civil warrants in a neighboring territory. Such is the nature of the slavery dispute.*

"We stand ready to march on your order, Marshal," Jones said.

CHAPTER TWENTY-FOUR

Lawrence
May 21, 1856

Two horsemen galloped down the road from the northwest. Donelson signaled a halt as his advance scouts returning from Lawrence drew rein.

"What is the situation?"

"No sign of organized resistance, Marshal. The fortifications the sheriff here warned us about have fallen into disrepair over the winter and do not appear to be manned at this time."

Donelson nodded. "Good."

They rode on until Lawrence came into view along the west bank of the Kansas River. Donelson again called a halt.

"How do you plan to play this, Marshal?" Jones asked.

"Since they do not appear prepared to mount a resistance, we shall keep this peaceable as far as possible."

Jones glanced at Atchison. He sat his horse impassive.

"I shall take my men into town to serve the arrest warrants. Sheriff, take your men south of town and center your position on Eldridge House. Do not advance on the town. I will summon you when I have secured my prisoners. You may then serve your orders. I urge you to use restraint, however, as we should endeavor to accomplish this without bloodshed."

"We've experience with the likes of Lane, Montgomery, and Jennison. They're not likely to take our orders lying down."

"You heard the scouting report, Sheriff. There is no sign of resistance. We are not spoiling to provoke a fight here. Now, please, proceed to your position and hold for further instructions."

Jones looked to Atchison. Atchison wheeled his horse west toward Eldridge House on a line south of town.

Donelson led his party of eighteen deputies into town, turning north along Massachusetts. Here and there someone on the street paused to stare at the heavily armed posse, unsure what it might mean. The posse crossed Main Street to Eldridge House and drew rein. Donelson was about to dismount when the desk clerk appeared at the hotel door. He wrung his hands nervously.

"May I be of service?"

"I'm US Marshal Israel Donelson out of Lecompton. I have warrants for the arrest of Charles Robinson and James Lane."

At that, a sober, bearded figure with a balding pate stepped out of the hotel onto the boardwalk.

"I'm Charles Robinson. A warrant on what account?"

"The charge is treason, Mr. Robinson. I'm afraid I must ask you to come with us."

"And who, pray tell, has issued this charge?"

"The Kansas territorial grand jury."

"You mean a jury called by the fraudulent body asserting itself to be the territorial government in Kansas."

"Duly constituted and appointed by the territorial governor. Take him into custody." Two men dismounted and secured the prisoner. With the prisoner in custody, Donelson summoned Sheriff Jones.

"Now, Mr. Robinson, where might I find Mr. Lane?"

"He has a house just north of here, though, to my knowledge, he is away at this time."

"Would you be kind enough to show it to us on our way out of town?"

Robinson nodded as Jones and twenty of his men drew rein.

"Sheriff, you may proceed." Donelson mounted his horse, prepared to leave with his prisoner.

"Marshal, if you please," Robinson said confidentially at Donelson's side.

"Sir?"

Robinson directed his gaze up and down the street, where a crowd had begun to gather. "If you might spare a moment, I may be of service here."

The marshal nodded.

Jones stepped down and climbed the Eldridge House boardwalk. "By order of the district court, these premises are hereby declared a public nuisance, condemned, and shall be demolished in the interest of public safety. You are further ordered to surrender all weapons and munitions stored upon the premises."

The crowd closed in on the posse, grumbling among themselves.

"Turn over our guns? Hell, no!" someone shouted.

Robinson raised his arms. "Gentlemen, gentlemen, please! Let us make no more trouble here than these border ruffians. The law is on our side, and we shall be vindicated." He turned to the desk clerk. "Show these men to the storeroom, William."

The clerk disappeared, followed by a half dozen of Jones's men. Within the half hour they'd extracted a howitzer and six cases of small arms crated as farm implements.

"Procure a wagon to haul the contraband," Jones said. "Remove all the furniture from the building!"

Donelson caught Robinson's eye. "May we?"

He shook his head in resignation at what was to come and nodded.

"Now, if you would, please direct us to Mr. Lane's residence."

When Lane's house indeed proved empty, the marshal led his deputies and prisoner northwest out of town.

With the marshal's departure, Atchison marched on Lawrence with the main body of Missouri men.

"Sheriff, what is the situation?" Atchison asked.

"We are clearing this pest house for destruction, Senator. We've encountered no resistance to this point."

"Very good. Dispatch some men to dismantle the *Free State* printing press and offices while we await demolition of this atrocity."

Jones issued his orders. Men stormed down the street and smashed in the door and windows of the newspaper office. Someone produced an axe and proceeded to hack the printing press to bent steel and splinters. Drawers of printer's type were torn from their cabinets, carried out, and thrown in the river. Barrels of printer's ink were opened by axe and spilled on the floor. The last man to leave the premises set a torch to it.

With the hotel cleared of its furnishings, the Missouri men opened the stores to plunder, including contents of the wine and whiskey cellars. These passed among the men, fuelling the mob mentality. As liquid jocularity spread among the rioters, Jones ordered the cannon brought into line.

Atchison looked on in approval as Jones prepared to level Eldridge house at point-blank range by ball and grape. With matches burning sulfur smoke to a celebratory row, Jones commenced.

"Fire at will!"

The Eldridge took volley after volley. Doors and windows blew through. Brick gouged and pocked, yet she stood defiant, her structure strong and true.

" 'Tis a waste of shot and powder, Sam," Atchison said. "Mine her with powder charges and blow the damn thing up."

"Aye, sir." Jones rallied his men. They rolled kegs of powder into the lower floors and armed them with fuses. Torches set fuses alight. The mob pulled back away from the impending destruction. Explosions burst one after the other, finishing windows spared the cannonade, and still she stood firm against assault.

"Burn the damn thing down!" Jones vented frustration. "Burn the town!"

The mob broke and ran to plunder. Torches flared to light.

Atchison watched Lawrence looted and burned. "Carry on, Sheriff." He mounted his horse and rode east into descending twilight.

Smoke still hung thick as morning fog as Micah and Caleb rode the buckboard toward town. Charles Robinson's house atop Mount Oread and the burnt-out ruins of Eldridge House epitomized the devastation. Lawrence was laid waste, a smoldering black scar on the land.

"Trouble be more than comin'," Caleb said. "Trouble be here."

"It sure looks that way."

Wood smoke and charred remains colored the air as they drove up Main Street toward the center of a once vibrant town. A crowd gathered at the Eldridge House ruin. Micah recognized Owen Brown among them along with the familiar figure of his father. He drew rein and climbed down. Caleb rounded the buckboard at his shoulder.

"What happened?"

"We only arrived this morning, so we are still trying to piece the story together," Owen said. "Best we can tell, the district court in Lecompton issued a warrant for Charles Robinson's arrest and condemned Eldridge House and the *Free State Herald* for public nuisances. Sheriff Jones showed up with a posse the size of an army. They arrested Charles and took him off to jail before looting the town and burning it to the ground."

Off to the south, two riders galloped up Massachusetts stirrup to stirrup. James Lane and Doc Jennison drew their mounts to a halt and leaped down. The crowd cleared a path for Lane with Jennison in tow.

"Who is responsible for this?" Lane demanded.

"Sheriff Jones," John Brown said. "Sheriff Jones and an army of Missouri men burned the town. They are but the agents of evil. Who is responsible? That raises a deeper question."

"That may be so, Brother Brown, but deeper questions can't pay for what has been done here," Lane said.

"All may be redressed, but the evil here runs deeper than a drunken mob of border ruffians. They are but instruments of unlawfully elected usurpers of Kansas's rightful sovereignty. They embody the evil of slavery in the Lecompton legislature. They are led by no less than the illicit governance of President Pierce's appointed puppet, Wilson Shannon. The wrongs done Lawrence cannot be assuaged by the blood of a few border ruffians. To redress the wrongs done Lawrence we must root out the evil at its source and wherever that evil finds nourishment. The evil is slavery and the institutions of government that sustain it. It is that evil we must root out, in its every form, wherever we find it. Redress it we shall by blood and by fire. By blood and by fire, so help us a righteous God!"

The crowd roared approval. Lane glanced at Jennison.

"Me? I'm startin' with Missouri blood."

CHAPTER TWENTY-FIVE

Capitol Hill
Washington City

South Carolina Representative Preston Brooks seethed at the back of the deserted Senate chamber. He'd had enough of the self-righteous abolitionists' moralizing rhetoric. Senator Charles Sumner sat at his desk alone near the front of the chamber. Sumner had given a speech condemning the Kansas-Nebraska Act as whoremaster to the southern house of slavery. He'd maligned Douglas for it; he berated James Mason of Virginia; but worst of all he'd slandered the good name of Brooks's home state and his infirm uncle, Andrew Butler, senior senator from South Carolina. Such insult to the family honor and home could not be allowed without redress.

Brooks started down the aisle, silver-headed cane in hand. His pace quickened along with his rage as he advanced on the unsuspecting Sumner.

"Harlot's spawn to slavery, are we?" He brought the silver-knobbed hickory down hard across Sumner's hunched back and head with a sickening crack.

Sumner twisted in his seat, wide-eyed with surprise and pain. He raised his arms in feeble defense of his head, a failed attempt to fend off the blows falling upon him like a rain squall. He struggled to rise from his desk. His lanky frame caught in a too-tight space. The beating poured on.

Sumner shuttered his eyes against red gouts of pain. Light

grew dark at the margins, fading darker still. He lurched free of his desk, managing to stagger into the aisle.

Brooks pressed his attack. The cane head broke off. Still he rendered retribution with what remained of the hickory until he spent himself and his rage.

Sumner sank to his knees and slumped to the floor senseless and bleeding.

Brooks dropped the cane. He strode up the aisle to the back of the chamber, vindicated by light of his honor.

The White House
May 23, 1856

Jefferson Davis paced the polished floor of the reception secretary's office, waiting to see the president. Colonel Sumner's report on the incident in Lawrence was disturbing to say the least. The situation in Kansas was deteriorating rapidly.

"The president will see you now, Mr. Secretary." Pierce's assistant backed away from the open office door, allowing Davis to pass. The door closed behind him.

"Good morning, Jefferson. What's on your mind this fine morning?"

"Not such fine news, I'm afraid, Mr. President."

"Oh? Have a seat."

He took a chair across from the president's desk. "I received a report from Colonel Sumner last night. Colonel Sumner, you may recall, is commandant at Fort Leavenworth, Kansas."

"One could hardly forget the name. Dreadful business about the senator. I don't often agree with his politics, but caning him with such brutality on the floor of the Senate is not to be condoned. What does the colonel have on his mind?"

"Lawrence was sacked two days ago."

"Sacked?"

"Burned to the ground."

"By whom?"

"A so-called sheriff's posse, dispatched by Governor Shannon's Lecompton district court to arrest the leader of the Free State party for treason and condemn two properties the court judged public nuisances."

"And that precipitated sacking the town? Was there armed resistance?"

"None."

"I'm afraid I don't understand."

"The sheriff's posse more closely resembled a vigilante mob composed primarily of Missouri men. Colonel Sumner advises that former senator Atchison was involved. It's the same faction that had a hand in electing a pro-slavery legislature. Lawrence has become the center of free-state opposition."

"Hence the treason charge."

"It would appear. The question is: what is to be done about it?"

"Yes. Couldn't have come at a worse time with my renomination hanging in the balance. Unfortunately, the Douglas popular sovereignty provision seems to have unraveled from some people's perspective. It may be Douglas's doing, but the disaffected will lay responsibility at my doorstep."

"I appreciate the political delicacy of the matter, Mr. President, but what's to be done about civil unrest? The free-state adherents cannot be expected to take this lying down. Colonel Sumner believes we may be on the brink of all-out war between Kansas and Missouri."

"That would be altogether too dire. We can't allow that to happen." He drummed his fingers on the desk in thought. "I will wire Governor Shannon and order him to disband the sheriff's posse. If he needs force to maintain peace and order, I will instruct him to call on Colonel Sumner. I suggest you remind Colonel Sumner of the possibility and instruct him to support Governor Shannon as the governor sees fit."

Davis sat silent, composing his thoughts. "As we have discussed, sir, the use of federal troops in a civil matter is dicey constitutional policy."

"I've heard your reservations on that before, Jefferson. In this case the constitution be damned. I must maintain law and order on that border. Everything depends on it."

His re-nomination depends on it.

Pottawatomie Creek, Missouri
May 24, 1856

The cabin stood at the center of a small clearing mottled in moonlight by the passing of broken clouds. Somewhere inside a lamp illuminated the front window. A single outbuilding stood shadowed beside a corral. John Brown and his sons drew rein under cover of trees surrounding the clearing.

"Light the fire of righteous wrath," Elder Brown said.

Matches and torches flickered to light along the irregular file of horsemen. Satisfied they were ready, Brown spurred his horse into the clearing. At the sound of riders fast approaching, someone inside huffed out the lamp. The raiders circled the cabin and outbuildings, setting them ablaze. Brown and sons Salmon and Owen dismounted and advanced to either side of the cabin door. Orange firelight danced over the shadows, gleaming on drawn short swords.

The cabin door burst open to a billow of smoke. A muzzle flash exploded inside. The gunman stumbled out, choking and blindly firing a dragoon at shadows. Brown leveled his pistol and fired. Muzzle flash and smoke staggered the man. He fell still.

Four more men left the cabin. Brown and his sons met them with swords, hacking them to unspeakable gore. Save the fire, it ended as suddenly as it had begun.

"Now, God's righteous wrath hath smote this first of the evil doers! In the days ahead we shall mete out still more blood and fire." Brown wheeled his horse to the ride back to Kansas.

Franklin, Missouri
May 25, 1856

Sheriff Jones stood in Atchison's library, hat in hand, ashen with horror and rage.

Atchison considered the news. "Who's responsible for this?"

"Jayhawkers, Bindly said. He thought the leader might be John Brown, but he couldn't be sure. He called 'em Jayhawkers before he succumbed to his wounds."

"This Bindly died, then."

"Yes, sir. They must'a took him for dead where he fell. Them others was hacked to pieces somethin' terrible."

"Jayhawkers . . . what do you make of that?"

"Them Kansans that freed young Brown from my posse after they burnt out Franklin Coleman last year called themselves that. Some Irish say it's a mythical bird, part hawk and part jay."

"Part bird of prey and part noisy thief. I guess we know what we're up against." Atchison tapped forefinger to lips in thought. "John Brown, he said."

Jones nodded.

"It appears the old brimstone preacher has decided preaching blood and fire isn't enough. He's decided to mete out his own brand of blood and fire. Clearly, we didn't eliminate public nuisance when we rooted the vipers out of Lawrence."

"You want the governor to call up a posse to go after Brown, Senator?"

"No, Sam. Not this time. Shannon won't do things our way on this one. President Pierce has authorized him to call on the army. They might make some arrests, but they won't inflict the brand of justice these fanatics deserve. I intend to make an example of Brown and his people. We'll show them they can't get away with this. Captain Pate has raised an irregular militia. Let's turn this one over to him. He can pursue the culprits without need to maintain the pretense of law enforcement you're obliged to carry. I'll send for the captain. Your work is done for the moment, Sam."

Brown's Station
Osawatomie, Kansas
May 31, 1856

Dark clouds spit rain on a chill breeze. Owen Brown galloped into the compound, his coat billowing in the wind. Chickens and pigs scattered in his path. He drew rein at the cabin and leaped down.

"They's comin', Pa!"

John Brown appeared in the cabin door. "Who's comin'?"

"Missouri men. An army of 'em."

"Where?"

"Day's march from Black Jack Springs."

"They'll likely camp there. Salmon, get yourself a fresh horse and ride to Lawrence. Tell James Lane we need his men, Doc Jennison, too, and that Methodist preacher."

"Montgomery?"

"That's him. Tell them to meet us in the hills north of Black Jack Springs tomorrow. Now, ride!"

Chapter Twenty-Six

Black Jack Springs
June 1, 1856

Cook fires dotted the banks of Captain's Creek, suggesting a camp of some fifty border ruffians. Captain Henry Clay Pate walked the camp seeing to the readiness of his men. The muted conversation of men anticipating battle spread over the usual night sounds punctuated by the snap and pop of the cook fires.

"Evenin', Cap'n."

"Evenin', Smythe."

"You figure them Jayhawks for a fight, or we gonna have to chase 'em clear to Lawrence?"

Pate shrugged. "Your guess is as good as mine. I can't see Brown and his wild-eyed clan putting up much of a fight against these odds. We should be on them before they know what hit them."

"I s'pect you're right, Cap'n. These boys'll be disappointed if they don't see some action, though. What do you figure to do with the old firebrand hell-hound?"

"Hang him."

June 2, 1856

The camp began to rouse at the first hint of pre-dawn. Cook fires stirred to light, heating coffee. Men wandered into the trees lining the creek bank to relieve themselves. The man called Smythe scratched his beard and yawned as he watered a bush beside a beech tree. The crack of a branch across the creek cut his eyes to the gloom, searching for some critter come down to the creek to water. Someone somewhere shouted something indistinguishable. The far creek bank exploded in a wall of muzzle flash and blue smoke advancing a rolling volley of small-arms reports. Smythe staggered back against the tree, his gaze drawn to the dark stains spreading across his chest as darkness closed in on him.

Up and down the near shore, Missouri men fell, seized their weapons, or dove for cover behind whatever they could find. Pate rallied his men behind three wagons. They turned them over to form a makeshift barricade. They returned fire in sporadic bursts in response to measured volleys lashing the campsite from across the creek. A veil of powder smoke floated over the still morning air.

The sun slowly crept over the gently rolling hills to the northeast where Brown and the Jayhawkers held the high ground. Midday burned off morning haze. The air hung heavy and moist. Little disturbed the scene, save fat buzzing flies and occasional exchanges of fire. Back and forth across the creek shots lashed out at targets of opportunity or suspected targets, with neither side inflicting decisive injury following the initial fusillade.

Brown felt justified. They'd caught the Missouri men unawares. He summoned Lane and Jennison to parley behind the lines.

"We've got them pinned down," Brown said.

Lane nodded. "We have the advantage to strike a decisive blow."

Brown measured their resolve. "Doc, take your men across the creek on the right flank. Mr. Lane will cross on the left. Set a line on the high ground and train your fire on their horses and mules. Doc, you flank their wagons and advance from the right. When they pull back from your advance, they will come under Mr. Lane's guns. That should put them to flight."

Jennison flashed a yellow-stained grin.

Brown raised his arms in blessing. "The Almighty bears a swift sword. Now, go."

Heat rose thick and wet along the creek bank. Sweat burned Pate's eyes as he searched the tree line across the creek for movement. His linen soaked in perspiration. A man hunched low ran toward him through the trees from his left flank. An errant shot followed him, biting tree trunk to no ill effect. The man dropped to his belly beside Pate.

"We've got movement on the left. Some of 'em's crossing the creek. We can hear 'em."

"Have you deployed a line to hold them?"

"We have, though there's no tellin' how many they is."

The Jayhawks circle. They have the initiative. Pate toyed with the idea of a counter advance from his right flank. Dividing his command without knowing the enemy strength troubled him. He waited. Time passed.

Word passed up the line from his right. *Jayhawks are crossing the creek further upstream.* Movement on both flanks. The news gathered sour in Pate's gut. They could be enveloped. They might be overrun. Shooting from the hillock on the right rained on the picket lines. Squeals of death rose from horses and mules as they fell defenseless before a winnowing fire. Pate rummaged in his kit for a kerchief, fastening a white flag to his saber. He lifted the flag and waved it to signal a truce.

"Pa, they's showin' a white flag," Salmon said.

Brown stood. "Cover me. Be ready on my mark." He stood, taking a few steps down the slope toward the creek bank, folded his arms, and squinted at the flag. The man carrying it rose and came forward to the water's edge.

"May we discuss terms?"

"Terms of what?"

"Terms to bring this standoff to a close without further bloodshed."

"You may cross."

Pate eyed the man. Could the old firebrand be trusted? Given his position, he felt he had little choice. He waded into the creek and crossed.

"How do you want to settle this affair?" Pate asked.

"Your surrender, if it please. Order your men to lay down their arms."

"I have no such intention. We shall withdraw peaceably."

"Indeed you shall." Brown drew his pistol and cocked it. "Now order your men to lay down their arms."

"We are under a flag of truce!"

"You may be. You are also under arrest."

"You intend to hold me?"

"I do."

"I've never heard of such a breach of military protocol."

"And I've never encountered a band of border hooligans deserving of military courtesy. You may dismiss your men as soon as they lay down their arms. Boys!"

Salmon and Owen stepped over the rise, pistols leveled at Pate.

Fort Leavenworth
June 3, 1856
Bull Sumner read the governor's order.

> *By authority of President Franklin Pierce, you are to establish a military constabulary to serve at my request. You are hereby requested to dispatch troops for the purpose of suppressing certain guerrilla factions operating in and about the vicinity of*

Lawrence and Osawatomie, Kansas Territory, under the command of one John Brown. Said guerrilla groups, also known as Jayhawkers, have precipitated border provocations and hostilities.

Wilson Shannon,
Governor, Kansas Territory

He'd been warned. Now they meant to do it. The request suggested Kansans are the problem; Missouri, men have no part in it. The president's order on its face grated on the constitution. To make matters worse, the governor intended to use the army to enforce partisan pro-slavery policies of dubious legal standing. Undoubtedly, he did so with the president's full support. He had his orders. As a military man, he could only put his personal reservations aside.

Brown's Station
Osawatomie, Kansas
June 5, 1856

The Brown compound consisted of cabins occupied by the clan. While not exactly fortified, it created a highly defensible position in a clearing that afforded ample fields of fire. Colonel Sumner drew his column to a halt a hundred yards east. He drew his glass from its case, fitted it to his eye, and inspected the place. Hot summer sun shimmered in a dusty yard pecked by a handful of chickens. He handed the glass to his aide, 1st Lieutenant James E. B. Stuart, more commonly known by the initials, J.E.B.

"Short of the gun ports I see no obvious signs of resistance."

Stuart swept the glass across the property. "I don't see anything, either, sir. Still, knowing what these people are capable of argues for caution."

"Do you refer to the Pottawatomie incident or Black Jack Springs?"

"Both. I doubt the old man will give up Captain Pate without a fight."

"Likely not; though I believe we should try reason first. Put up a white pennant."

Stuart lifted a brow. "Sergeant." Sufficed to relay the order. "May I remind you, sir, that didn't work out too well for Captain Pate?"

"I'm aware of that, Lieutenant. We'll respect our flag and retain our arms. Hold the troops here, Lieutenant. Sergeant." He nudged his horse forward.

"Company comin'!" Owen called.

John Brown stepped out on the porch of Salmon's cabin and followed Owen's attention east. Salmon appeared at his side.

"Looks like regular army," Brown said.

"Wonder what's on their mind."

"Likely them border ruffians we run off."

"What's their call on the army?"

"By the look of that flag, we're about to find out."

Two riders, one gold braided and a standard bearer, drew rein at the compound perimeter.

"Yo, John Brown!"

"You found him. Who's askin'?"

"Colonel Edwin Sumner, first cavalry out of Fort Leavenworth."

"State your business."

"I've come to secure the release of Captain Henry Clay Pate. I understand you have him in your possession."

"By whose authority?"

"Governor Wilson Shannon on the authority of President Pierce."

"What's Pierce and the army got to do with a civil matter?"

"Treason is no civilian matter."

"Treason?"

"The president has determined that trespass against territorial law is a treasonous offense."

"Territorial law! Do you speak of that kangaroo courthouse in Lecompton?"

"That is the duly elected territorial government in Kansas."

" 'Duly elected.' Surely a man of your pedigree, Colonel Sumner, knows the falsehood in that."

"I understand your frustration, sir. Still, I have my orders. May I ask by whose authority you hold Captain Pate?"

"By authority of the duly elected free-state legislature."

"I'm afraid, sir, that claim of authority has been determined to be invalid. Lecompton is the recognized territorial authority, and Governor Shannon is its duly appointed administrator. Now, I must ask that you hand over the prisoner at once."

"And, should I, what do you propose be done with the leader of the ruthless mob who invaded our land?"

"That will be for the governor to decide."

"The governor." Brown shook his head in disgust. "And if I refuse?"

"I should hope we'd not come to that."

"He hopes." Brown shook his head again.

"He means to take the man by force, Father," Owen said.

"I can see that."

"We've made our point. We sent the Missouri men packing at Black Jack. Surely, they will think twice about marching on us again. Trying Pate won't amount to much. If the army tries to take him by force, we have wives and children in danger."

"There is that. All right; it's against my better judgment, but release him."

Salmon scurried off. Brown turned to the expectant Sumner.

"We'll not oppose the army here this day, Colonel, though I deeply regret as you must, seeing the army used as the partisan instrument of immoral slave-holders. It is a crime against God, nature, and the very founding principles of this country."

Sumner held his peace.

Chapter Twenty-Seven

Lecompton
Convention Hall
June 23, 1856

Governor Wilson Shannon stood, hands clasped behind his back, silhouetted in golden light streaming through tall windows near the head of the cavernous hall. The sound of boot heels signaled the approach of a new arrival. He glanced over his shoulder.

"Colonel Sumner, thank you for coming."

"I'm under orders, Governor. What's on your mind?"

Shannon overlooked the edge on the question. "Straight to the point, then. You are aware, I presume, the Free State party plans a convention in Topeka on the eve of convening their so called free-state legislature on Independence Day."

"I have heard that."

"Then you must know that rogue assembly is not legally constituted under Kansas law. Such an assemblage can only serve to foment mischief or, at worst, rebellion. These malicious agitators must be stopped. As the duly appointed governor of Kansas, I hereby request that you disperse that illicit body, peacefully if possible, or by harsher means should they be required."

Sumner rubbed his chin in thought. "Are you not concerned at the prospect such action may violate the participants' rights to free association and freedom of expression?"

"Such rights do not extend to impersonating a lawful legislative assembly."

"They are a legislative body elected by Kansans to represent them."

"Elected, if you will, by unlawful ballot."

"Elected, they would charge, in response to a fraudulent ballot stolen by ineligible votes."

"Colonel, those election results have been certified by appropriate authorities. Our opinions and the opinions of those disgruntled by defeat are of no consequence. You and I have but one duty and that is to uphold the law. Now, have I made my instructions sufficiently clear?"

"You have, sir." Sumner turned on his heel and strode to the back of the hall.

Sycamore

They finished the house by the end of June. Micah, Clare, and little Elizabeth moved in. Caleb tunneled a passage between the smaller dugout he and Miriam shared to the adjoining larger one Micah and Clare left behind. The addition would make room for the baby budding in Miriam's belly. They gathered around the supper table in the house to celebrate the new arrangement.

"My, my, it sure do look fine in here." Caleb admired the spacious, comfortable room for his part in building it.

"It does, thanks to you," Micah said. "After this crop is in next spring, we'll build one for you up the creek on your section."

Miriam smiled a faraway thought. "A house of our own . . . think of it. Pinch me, Caleb, so I know I ain't dreamin'. Things sure be lookin' up by then if the free-state legislature do right by us."

"The legislature plans to hold its first session on Independence Day," Micah said.

"Them Lecompton Missouri men gonna let 'em?" Caleb asked.

"The free-state legislature was elected by a fair ballot of Kansans."

"Ain't stopped them Missouri men from makin' mischief before."

"I suppose you can't rule out trouble, but I haven't heard any talk of Missouri opposition."

"Them scallywags ain't nothin' but trouble. I don't trust 'em no how."

"Can't say I blame you for that."

"Are you men going to talk politics through the whole of a Sunday supper?" Clare asked. "There's apple pie for dessert. Perhaps that will sweeten the two of you up."

"Amen, sister." Miriam rose. "Let me help you clear them dishes."

Dear Ma and Pa,

Much has happened since last I took pen in hand. The house is finished. It is a luxury and a blessing. The dugout sheltered our needs along with all manner of burrowing creatures. I shall not miss sharing our home with nature. As if a house with a roof weren't enough, I now have a stove to make light work of the cooking.

Hard as it is to believe, your granddaughter is a year old and toddling about the house with a curiosity to everything. Ma, you well understand the pleasures and pandemonium attendant to that. She is a delight as she threatens to utter her first words. Still more news, our Miriam is expecting a child in fall. Our days are filled with promise.

The border hostilities with Missouri continue. Micah was

called to serve in the defense of Lawrence this past winter. Fortunately, that incident ended without bloodshed. We've not been so fortunate in recent months, though the fighting thus far has not affected us here at Sycamore.

We think of all of you often and with fondness. Know that we miss you but know, too, our purposes in moving west have indeed been rewarded. Until next time then I remain,

Clare

Thorne passing by on his way to Topeka and drew rein at the cart path leading to the Mason place. A fine new house stood in the trees by the creek. The fields beyond grew golden lush with the season's wheat waving on a sunny summer breeze. The crop would fetch a handsome price. Mason would prosper. His property would only increase in value. *How had he been so foolish as to let it slip through his fingers?* Rogue stomped, impatient. *All in good time.* He'd have his opportunity *all in good time.* He let out the black at a jog.

The black-clad rider astride a prancing, black stallion passed beneath her shade. A chill storm cloud of a man ruffled her leaves at his passing. No good attended this one. He coveted close to home. A larger storm gathered beyond her horizon in the east. Which might pose the greater danger? She couldn't say. Hers was but to watch and, in her own way, pray. Time would tell in seasons to come. For now, the house was a home. More life budded in her small brood. Her fields grew ripe as her days passed in peace.

Constitution Hall, Topeka
July 4, 1856

Thorne joined the sweating throng on the Constitution Hall steps. A holiday atmosphere buoyed spirits in spite of oppressive midsummer heat. The free-state legislature convened in commemoration of the nation's founding. As he took in the crowd a lone horseman trotted down Kansas Street and drew rein at the hall. He tethered his horse and made his way through the crowd, climbing the steps to the entrance. Thorne followed. He entered the chamber and found Lane and Montgomery observing the proceedings. Lane lifted his chin to the man making his way down the central aisle to the dais.

"Marshal Donelson," he said as much to himself as his companions.

Recently released, Charles Robinson looked down on the new arrival.

"Mr. Chairman."

"Marshal Donelson. Am I to be arrested again?"

"Let us hope not, sir. I request permission to address this assembly for the purpose of reading an official proclamation by the president of the United States and the territorial governor of Kansas."

"You are addressing the duly elected governor of Kansas Territory."

"Your assertion; the president wishes to express his opinion on the matter."

Robinson made a gesture of welcome. Donelson climbed the podium and addressed the free-state assembly.

"By order of the president of the United States and the governor of the Territory of Kansas, this body is hereby notified that it is not lawfully constituted to enact legislation under the laws of the Territory of Kansas."

The chamber erupted in jeering and cat calls. Donelson reddened. He let the outburst die down.

"This assembly is hereby ordered to disperse and give no further appearance as to legislative pretense."

The crowd grew louder and more strident.

"Very well, then. You leave me no choice." He glanced at

Robinson. "I suggest you persuade these men to comply."

"That sounds like a threat."

"Think it more a warning." He descended the podium and marched up the aisle to the shouts and jeers of those assembled.

"What do you suppose happens next?" Thorne asked.

"I reckon we'll find out soon enough," Lane said.

Donelson retreated south on Kansas. Colonel Sumner waited with a force of some two-hundred-fifty men and artillery near the Garvey Hotel.

"It's in your hands, Colonel," Donelson said.

"Very well." Sumner mounted.

"Column of twos."

"Forward, ho!"

The column marched north on Kansas to Constitution Hall. Sumner deployed his cavalry left and right anchored by artillery, giving enfilade cover to Kansas Street. Three platoons of infantry held the center, with the centermost platoon slightly withdrawn. The crowd gathered around Constitution Hall grew progressively more uneasy and angry at the show of force.

Sumner dismounted and crossed the street. The crowd parted, allowing him to climb the steps to the entry. Inside, the assembly instinctively sensed his presence. Conversation quieted as he strode down the center aisle under the expectant eye of Charles Robinson.

"Good morning, Colonel. Would you care to join us?"

"If I might."

"Please, sir, have a seat."

Sumner took the offered chair on the dais.

Robinson turned to the assembly. "Gentlemen, the assembly will come to order for the purpose—"

Sumner rose. "I'm sorry, gentlemen, I'm afraid I must object."

A murmur rippled through the hall to silence. Attention

riveted to the speaker.

"It is my duty today to enforce the proclamations of the president and governor that you have previously heard read by duly authorized civilian authority. I am ordered to disperse this unlawful assembly as decreed under Kansas law."

"Unlawful, or contrary to the wishes of our federal overlords?" someone shouted.

"I have no partisan feeling in the matter. I am merely a soldier under orders."

"Orders under what constitutional authority?" Robinson asked.

"By authority of the president of the United States and his appointed representative, the territorial governor of Kansas."

"The Constitution assures us the right of free assembly."

"The Constitution assures your right to assemble; it does not convey the right to act as an unlawfully constituted legislative body."

"In this case, that right has been granted to a legislative body established as the result of a fraudulent election."

"I have no knowledge of such allegation. Now I must insist this assembly disperse with no further pretense to the purposes that brought you here."

"Are we then to assume this order is backed by the threat of force?"

"It is, though I pray that should not be necessary." He resumed his seat.

Unintelligible babble washed through the hall, gradually dying away as the representatives began to leave, one by one or in small groups.

When the hall was clear, Sumner followed Robinson up the aisle. Outside they were greeted by an angry crowd, frustrated by the dismissal of their representatives. Robinson took in the scene. He read the mood of the crowd and the threat implied by federal troops. He raised his hands for quiet.

"My friends."

"My friends . . . please." The murmur subsided. "We have agreed to resolve this dispute peaceably. Your representatives and I will pursue all available legal remedies to secure your rights in this matter. I urge you to entrust the dispute to our care and disperse peacefully to your homes."

They began to drift away, wagging tongues and shaking heads.

"Thank you, sir," Sumner said.

He descended the hall steps and remounted his horse.

Franklin, Missouri
July 15, 1856

Atchison sat in a rocking chair on the broad porch fronting his palatial home. He sipped a cool glass of lemonade. He'd forsaken his coat and loosened his cravat against the summer heat. He used a small fan to encourage a cooling breeze. A rider appeared on the road beyond the white fences and lawns spilling down the slope of his estate. The rider wheeled in at the gate. *Now who might this be?*

Captain Henry Clay Pate drew rein and stepped down. He climbed the porch.

"Captain Pate." Atchison smiled. "I'm pleased to see you've been released."

"My thanks for Governor Shannon's intervention. I'm sure you had a hand in it."

"His authority to call on the army is useful in certain matters. Have a seat. Care for some lemonade?"

"Anything to staunch this heat."

"Joachim!"

He appeared in the doorway. "Suh?"

"A glass for Captain Pate."

"Yes, suh." He disappeared.

"But now to unfinished business," Atchison said.

"I thought we might get back to that."

"The Browns continue to agitate against our cause in Kansas. The old man must be stopped."

"I consider it my duty to complete the work we were denied at Black Jack."

"Splendid. I thought you might."

Joachim appeared with a chilled glass, set it at Pate's elbow, and withdrew.

"Now tell me of your plans. How do you propose to root out that particular nest of vipers?"

Pate took a swallow. "I should think we might draw them out with a surprise advance on Osawatomie."

"Two birds with one stone as it were. The Browns and another breeding ground of free-state sedition."

"Exactly."

"When do you propose to strike?"

"Need to reassemble my command . . . see them properly equipped and trained. Perhaps by fall."

"So long as that? You're talking experienced men. Assembly and training can't take as long as that."

"Properly equipped requires horses, weapons, powder, and ball."

"You mean properly equipped requires money."

"It does."

"Step into my study, and I shall write you a draft good for a result next month."

"As you wish, Senator."

Chapter Twenty-Eight

Osawatomie, Kansas
August 25, 1856

Frederick Brown waited anxiously in the misty light of an early summer morning. The Colt Dragoon stuffed in his waistband testified to the gravity of the situation. With father and brothers away, the best he could do was send word to James Montgomery and pray his Jayhawkers arrived in time. He paced, his attention riveted on the road to the south shrouded in morning mist. He heard it first. Horses galloping toward him in some number. Could it be the Missouri men already? He looked for the nearest place to take cover. Horses and riders resolved out of the fog, shadows at first. He watched them pound up the road. He reached for the Colt. Then he saw it—Jayhawk signature red flannel. He began to relax.

Montgomery raised a gauntleted hand to signal a halt as the Jayhawkers drew rein.

"What's the trouble?" The preacher leaped down from his horse. Droplets glistened on his black beard and cheeks.

"Border ruffians is comin'. They's fixin' to sack the town out a' revenge for Black Jack Springs."

"Where are they now?"

"Not rightly sure. Southeast, I reckon."

"How strong in number?"

Franklin shrugged and ran his gaze over Montgomery's men. "Ain't one of them armies like hit Lawrence, though, I'm toldt more'n a hundred. You surprise 'em you might make a fair fight of it."

"I'm not interested in fighting fair. I'm interested in winning. Come on, boys. With luck, we can cut 'em off at Middle Creek."

Middle Creek

The scout returned at mid-morning, his horse lathered by thick summer heat.

"Pate's brigade be ridin' toward Middle Creek."

"How many?"

"By the look of it don't count more'n seventy."

Montgomery nodded. "Then we strike on their flank."

The scout led the way south. The column swung east, bearing down on Pate's column. The Missouri men opened fire on sight.

"Give 'em the Almighty's hell fire!" Montgomery spurred to a charge.

The Jayhawkers bore down on Pate's column, pistols and carbines blazing a powder smoke trail the like of a highballing locomotive. Pate's advance broke in the confused flurry of mounted combat. Montgomery's onslaught sent the Missouri men spinning in a melee of spooked horses and thrown riders dashing for cover. The Jayhawk charge overran the Missourians, scattering border ruffians like chickens in a barnyard.

Montgomery wheeled his men and charged again. The dehorsed fell. Those who could, rode to safety in every direction. The raiding party dissipated and disappeared.

Frederick Brown watched them go with a smile. They'd put the devil to flight as righteous justice should prevail. Father would be pleased.

Montgomery reformed his column and rode west.

Franklin, Missouri
August 27, 1856

Pate tethered his horse and climbed the porch steps. He crossed to the imposing double entry and rapped the ornate brass knocker. The old black man, Joachim, opened the door.

"Senatah Atchison be s'pectin' you, suh. This way."

Of course he is. He sent for me. Pate followed the old man's shuffle down the corridor.

"Captain Pate," he announced at the library door.

Atchison summoned him to his desk with a wave.

Pate took a seat.

"Damn poor return on my investment wouldn't you say, Captain?"

"Yes, sir. No one is more disappointed than I."

"I should think not. A second defeat at the hands of that rabble leaves one to wonder about your fitness for command. What the hell happened?"

"Somehow they found out we were coming with enough time to organize opposition."

"Opposition that surprised you in the field. The question still remains: what is to be done about Brown and his miscreant spawn?"

"I am re-forming my men. They believe they've routed us."

"They have routed you twice."

"With this last, I should think their guard will come down if we strike again swiftly."

"When?"

"Two days' time."

"Third time charm, is it?"

"Yes, sir."

"See to it."

Osawatomie, Kansas
August 30, 1856
With the Missourians routed at Middle Creek, Fredrick Brown relaxed. He should have remained vigilant. Four days later a second band of ruffian raiders swept out of the south to sack the town. Free-state townsfolk resistance melted in a blaze of powder flash, smoke, ball, and burning buildings. Frederick Brown stood tall. Colt in hand he met the charge, taking a fatal bullet in the chest.

Sycamore
September, 1856
Miriam clenched her jaw, her eyes shut tight against feeble candle glow in the very dugout bed in which she'd midwifed Clare the previous year. She'd attended birth pain. She knew what to expect. Not really. Clare sat at her side, holding her hand, the pains and pleasures of Elizabeth's birth brought back in the moment. Miriam's breath came in ragged gasps as a pain subsided. Clare wiped her forehead with a cool cloth. A new wave clutched at her belly and back.

"They're coming faster," Clare said. "It won't be long now."

"She takin' her own sweet time by my account."

"She? You think it's a girl."

"I know it. Agh!"

"Hang on, girl."

She did.

"I never heard of such a thing," Clare said.

"Knowin' it?"

She nodded.

"I know lots a things."

"Things like what?"

"Things I just know when I's right. Like marryin' Caleb.

Like runnin' away when we did. Like stoppin' here when we did."

"I'm glad you knew that one."

"Oh, oh!" Eyes clamped shut, features contorted.

Clare moved the lamp. "I believe it's time. You can push with the next one."

Miriam furrowed her brow, eyes closed, jaw bunched in knots, cheeks puffed. A sweat slicked vein bulged over the bridge of her nose. Guttural sound—part growl, part grunt—escaped clenched teeth, and then it was gone.

"Why, it's a beautiful girl!"

"Ahhh." Miriam sank back in the sweat-soaked bedding. "See, I knew."

"Since you knew, you must have a name in mind."

She smiled, exhausted. "Rebecca."

October

Fields, crops, a house, and babies. New purpose spread out around her. The fields grew rich, golden, and ripe with offspring. Gathered, the crop would give rest to the land for the long slumber of another season. The tree spread her red-gold blanket along the creek bank. Chill nip bit the breeze arranging her cover over the ground. The sun drifted west and south as the days grew shorter. Quiet, cold slumber beckoned.

Backbreaking long days up before the sun and fighting to use the last of its rays—that's the harvest. Micah and Caleb divided their time between cutting, raking, and loading bundles on the wagon. Clare and Miriam took their turns at bundling the cuttings and minding the little ones. They cut, bundled, and loaded until a wagon was full. That made for a break while Micah and Caleb drove the wagon down to the riverbank to unload. The harvest gathered there, awaiting the river barge that would take the crop to the grist mill in Kansas City. So passed fall harvest days, morning to midday to cool, crisp evening. Day after day. Field by field.

They'd taken the first wagon load from field three to the river. Clare and Miriam took the girls to the house to prepare lunch. Micah and Caleb were driving the empty wagon up from the river when an arrow struck the buckboard dash with a quavering *thunk*. Both men stared at the arrow wide-eyed for an instant before war whoops called them back to their peril. They leaped down from the wagon, abandoning it in the yard as they raced to the house. Caleb followed Micah as he bounded up the porch step amid arrows falling like silent bolts in their wake.

Inside, Micah grabbed the carbine and tossed it to Caleb. He crouched in the doorway, rifle ready, as the war party flashed through the trees. Micah drew the Colt Dragoon from its holster on a peg by the door, silently cursing his foolishness at not having taken weapons to the fields while giving thanks for the fact they hadn't been caught in the open with the women and girls. He handed Caleb powder and shot.

"Here they come. It looks like they mean to circle us. Cover the back, but hold your fire unless they try to rush us. I'll come runin' if I hear a shot."

Caleb dashed to the back of house as an arrow struck the door frame.

Micah leveled the Colt at the lead warrior and fired. The Arapaho swept by, a second brave, then a third. Another pulled his pony up to leap on Sampson's back in an attempt to drive off with their mules. Micah's shot pitched him off the mule as the remainder of the war party circled the house. The carbine exploded behind him. He ran to the back of the house.

"Take the front and reload."

Caleb ran off at a crouch. Micah took his position beside the shattered kitchen window. A baby cried from the bedroom. The war party raced by with no further attempt to breach the house. He ran back to the front door.

"You reloaded?"

Caleb nodded.

"Take the back then."

Something heavy hit the roof. Something that ran. Micah looked up at the sound. It offered no target, only the uneasy sense of an unseen threat. Three shots left. He'd never have time to reload.

The bright, clear call of a bugle split the tension.

"Halleluiah!" Caleb shouted. "The Lord done sent us a band a' angels wearin' blue coats!"

The Arapaho broke off the attack, racing away to the south as fast as they'd come.

The brave on the roof dropped to the ground and ran to collect his pony. His body jerked, pitched, and toppled to the ground under a hail of cavalry bullets.

The troop drew to a halt as Micah and Caleb stepped out on the porch.

"Lieutenant James E. B. Stuart, G Company 1st Cavalry out of Fort Leavenworth at your service, sir. Is everyone all right?"

"We are, sir, and in your debt."

"Then we shall see the heathen think twice before returning this way. My compliments." He doffed his plumed hat and spurred away in pursuit of the war party.

Clare, Miriam, and the girls peeked out of the bedroom.

Tension drained out of the men.

"They're gone," Micah said.

Thorne tucked up his cloak against a cutting wind. Gray, rumpled cloud scudded downriver. He watched from the ridge as they loaded the last of the harvest on the barge that would take it to the grist mill. It was a fine crop that would provide a worthy return on the season . . . profit that should have been his.

The barge cast off, poled into the current, and turned downstream. Mason stood on the deck and waved to the black man they called Caleb. He returned the wave, climbed aboard the wagon, and wheeled the mule team to the climb up the ridge.

The black man was something of a curiosity to Thorne. Was he a freed man hired hand or runaway slave? The latter might hold the prospect of opportunity. With Mason away it seemed a good time to find out his answer. He eased the black down the slope.

"Gee there, Sampson." Caleb slapped lines. The dark rider, Titus Thorne, drew rein, blocking his path.

"Fine looking crop you harvested this season."

"Yes, sir. Mighty fine."

"Your master must be pleased."

Caleb turned cautious at the comment. "Micah ain't my master."

"You're a freed man then."

Caleb nodded.

"Does he pay you a fair wage? I can always use a good man. Of course, I'd need to check your papers first."

"Micah and I is partners."

"Partners is it? Well, that is a matter of a different color."

"It is, Mr. Thorne. Good day to you." Caleb clucked to the team.

Partner and uppity, too. Thorne knit his brows. *Partner.*

Chapter Twenty-Nine

Kansas City
October 1856

Micah trudged up the wharf from the dock to the mill intent on consigning their crop with the miller. He noticed a portly man in a baggy suit and bowler hat, standing in the yard beside some sort of an odd looking machine. He gave it no thought.

"Micah." The miller extended his hand. "I saw the barge pull in. Looks like a fine crop this year."

"It is that." Micah smiled. "I'm mighty glad it's in, too."

"Harvest can be backbreaking with a crop that size. Do you hire help?"

"Caleb and I do most of it ourselves, though we've had to hire help to bring in fields three and four. I hate to do it for the expense, but you have to get it out of the field when it's time."

"I understand. We should have it threshed in a week's time. We can settle up then. Market rate for the bushel, same as last year."

"I'll be back then."

"Say, while you're here you may want to talk to that drummer outside."

"You mean the fellow with the funny lookin' sledge? What for?"

"That's no sledge he's sellin'. They call it the McCormick Reaper. It's a harvesting machine."

"I recall reading something about that. Does it work?"

"Seems to. Talk to him."

"Much obliged. See you next week."

Micah stepped into the yard. The man wiped his shiny, red face and bald pate with a handkerchief. He replaced his bowler with a smile. "Kirby Delabrough, sir, may I be of service?" He extended a pudgy hand.

"Micah Mason." He eyed the ungainly contraption.

"This here machine is the latest in industrial farming, the McCormick Reaper."

"How does it work?"

"Step right around here and I'll show you."

The drummer led the way toward what must be taken for the front of the thing.

"You hitch your team here. They pull the reaper through your field. That turns this wheel here. The wheel gathers wheat to these blades down here. That's where you get your cutting. The wheat comes off this platform ready for raking and binding."

"And all that works?"

"Sure does. With a good team, you should expect to cut twelve acres a day. How does that compare with what you do now?"

Micah shrugged. "Two of us, three to four acres."

"Makes for long days, don't it?"

"It does. How much does this thing cost?"

"One hundred-twenty dollars."

Micah shook his head. "Too expensive."

"Tell you what we can do. You put thirty dollars down, and we'll sell you the reaper. You can pay the balance off at thirty-five dollars a year for the next three years. If you're hiring hands to help you bring in the harvest, this machine will more than pay for itself."

Micah scratched his chin. "It might at that. I need to come

back next week to settle with the mill. Can you show us how it works then?"

"Show us?"

"My partner and me."

"Sure . . . sure. I'll arrange for a team and a field to cut. Take this leaflet along to show him. It's got a drawing and all the particulars explained."

Micah nodded.

Sycamore

"A harvesting machine?" Caleb said around a mouthful of roast buffalo.

Micah passed the leaflet across the Sunday supper table.

Caleb studied it and passed it to Miriam.

"Must cost a fright," Miriam said.

"It's not cheap, but I think it can pay for itself."

"How so?"

"That machine with a good team can cut twelve acres a day. At that rate, we can harvest all four fields in two weeks. We still have to rake and bind, but I believe the two of us can harvest our whole crop in a month."

"We don't have to hire no help," Caleb said.

"That's right."

"So how much do it cost?"

"More than we can afford all at once, but if we put down thirty dollars, we can pay the balance over the next three crops at thirty-five dollars a year. We can pay for it in shares."

"What you think, Miriam?" Caleb said.

"It's a lot of money. After them three crops, though, seems like we come out ahead."

"That's the way I got it figured," Micah said.

Caleb nodded. "Let's go into Kansas City next week and have us a look at this magical machine."

Kansas City
A Week Later

A brisk wind blew out of the northwest, chasing cotton-ball clouds across a bright blue sky. Micah and Caleb stood side by side, watching the reaper glide along behind a sturdy matched pair of bay horses. Neat rows of cut wheat ready for raking spilled out behind.

Kirby Delabrough looked on curious. He hadn't expected the black man and wasn't sure what to make of it. They seemed to be partners as Mason suggested. Most unusual, really.

"Isn't she everything I said she'd be?" Delabrough said.

Both men nodded.

"What do you think, Caleb?" Micah said.

"Just like you said."

"Is it worth it to your share?"

"Uhum."

"I believe we are ready to proceed, Mr. Delabrough."

"Step over to the carriage. I have the papers we need right here. That'll be thirty dollars."

Micah counted the money as Caleb continued to watch the reaper, far away in some thought.

"Sign here."

Micah dipped the offered pen in an ink pot and signed on the carriage seat. He handed the pen to Caleb, who made his mark.

"Very well, gentlemen. Congratulations. You are now the proud owners of a McCormick Reaper. Your reaper will be delivered in time for spring planting."

Caleb glanced over his shoulder. "You mean that thing do planting, too?"

The drummer smiled. "Not yet."

"You 'spose they could make one of them pick cotton?"

"One never knows what the inventor's mind might bring

forth. Why do you ask?"

"You got a machine like that to do the work of twenty men, it wouldn't pay to even feed slaves."

Delabrough and Micah exchanged surprised glances.

Chapter Thirty

Lawrence
March, 1857

Eldridge House rose defiant from the ashes of the Jones raid. The lobby and a few rooms reopened, affording small shelter from a freezing rain. Micah ducked into the dimly lit lobby, littered with building materials making their way to the work crews rebuilding the upper floors. A cheery fire danced in the lobby fireplace. James Lane, Charles Robinson, and a handful of prominent free-state men clustered around the fire, intent in conversation. Micah crossed the lobby, curious.

"You're a lawyer, James," Robinson said. "How do you read the Supreme Court's finding in the Scott case?"

Lane shook his head. "I'm not sure juris prudence much enters into the majority opinion as rendered by Justice Taney. The rambling rhetoric of a self-serving southern Democrat better suits the contorted logic of his opinion than any finding rooted in the constitutional principles intended to guide the court in such matters. Justice Taney, along with his six southern colleagues, holds that Mr. Scott has no rights of federal citizenship by virtue of the color of his skin, state or territorial law to the contrary notwithstanding. He asserts on behalf of the majority that Congress exceeded its authority in permitting states to determine the matter of slavery by popular sovereignty. He goes on to claim the federal government has a constitutional obligation to protect slaveholder rights, thereby establishing the right to hold slaves in perpetuity. I must say, though, that is no more than my reading of the opinion. I am at a loss to follow the legal precedents to his argument, let alone any citable constitutional provision."

"So we are then to believe that Mr. Scott, who lived as a free man, has no rights of citizenship including rights to own property or vote. Are we also to conclude the Kansas-Nebraska act is now void, and slavery is the law of the land?"

"That's my reading of it, Charles," Lane said.

The crowd burst into a babble of incredulous conversation. Micah couldn't believe what he'd just heard. He excused his way through the crowd in the direction of the fire, pausing at Lane's elbow.

"Excuse me, Mr. Lane. I only just came in and heard your explanation. What case is this?"

"Micah, good to see you. A rather bad bit of finding by the United States Supreme Court, I'm afraid. The case involved a civil suit brought by a former slave, a man named Dred Scott. He brought suit against a New York man named Sanford. The suit asserted Mr. Scott's freedom for having lived in a free state for some years. The court majority seized on the circumstances of the case to hand down a rather sweeping decision in favor of slaveholding."

"What does that mean for the freed man who owns a section of my land?"

"That would be up to a court to decide, should anyone challenge his rights of ownership. If you ask my opinion, based on this finding I would expect a court would invalidate his claim."

"Thank you, sir." Injustice warmed his blood quicker than fire. He re-crossed the lobby and stormed out to cold rain. He lifted Sampson's tether and climbed to the buckboard seat. He wheeled away home, his thoughts coming furiously. *What to do?*

Sycamore

They gathered in the parlor. Micah recounted all he'd heard in Lawrence as best he could.

"What we gonna do now?" Miriam spoke for all of them.

"Seems like them justices made law," Caleb said.

"Law maybe, not justice," Clare said.

Micah met Caleb's eye. "Law's been broken before."

"What's to break? We don't own the land."

"Yes, you do."

"The law says . . ."

"No. I say. The law is wrong, Caleb. It can't stay that way. Somehow, someway, someday it has to change."

"Maybe so; but we be here right now."

"So, here's what we're gonna do. The claim is still in my name. We sold you the section, but we've never recorded the sale. For now, it's a good thing we didn't. I sold you that section for a dollar. I'll give you your dollar back, and I'll hold the section for you until the law gets made right. Until that happens, we go about our business just like we always have. You work my land for a share, and I work your land for a share. That's what counts. Folks will be none the wiser."

"What if somebody find out?"

Micah looked from Clare to Miriam to Caleb. "Who's gonna say a word? We got to trust each other, Caleb."

Caleb bobbed his head in agreement. Titus Thorne and his black horse intruded at the back of his mind.

"Trust you, Micah Mason? I do. Never thought I'd say that to a white man, but after all we been through . . ." He nodded. "I do trust you."

Micah pulled a tattered dollar out of his pocket and slid it across the table to Miriam.

"Just for safe keepin' until you give it back."

Lecompton
September, 1857

Thorne jogged Rogue along Elmore Street at midday. White puffball clouds drifted east on a blue palette sky accompanied by a pleasant breeze. Ahead the whitewashed, two-story, clapboard Constitution Hall stood sentinel above the road on the side of a hill. He checked his mount to a walk, wheeled into the hitch rack, and stepped down.

He climbed the stairs to the territorial land office located on the first floor. The land office clerk, an officious scarecrow in a slack, black suit and starched collar, appeared dark and featureless in the dim glow of a large window. Thorne approached the counter separating clientele from a desk cluttered with piles of important looking documents. The clerk peered over the top of his spectacles at Thorne's approach. Annoyed by the interruption, he unfolded himself from his chair to greet his visitor.

"May I help . . . Mr.?" A prominent Adam's apple bobbed over his loose paper collar.

"Thorne, Titus Thorne. I'd like to protest a claim."

The clerk lifted his brows over the tall, handsome stranger. *A protest . . . most unusual.*

"What parcel and what grounds?"

"Four sections, south of the river five miles west of Lawrence."

"And the grounds?"

"I believe the claim is jointly held by one Micah Mason and a black man known only as Caleb. By recent finding of the United States Supreme Court, the black man lacks the constitutional right to own property. Joint tenancy of a white man not withstanding I believe the court's decision invalidates the claim."

The clerk scratched a lean, lined chin. "You'll need a court to set aside such a claim, of course, but I believe you speak of the

Dred Scott decision. It would seem to render such a claim . . . awkward."

"Could you verify the registration so that I have the proper information to file suit?"

The clerk shuffled to a dusty cabinet at the back wall next to the window. A shower of dust mites billowed in a shaft of window light at the drawer opening. He fumbled through the records, pausing at one before drawing it into the light. He held it up, squinted, and turned to the counter.

"I believe this is the parcel you describe, Mr. Thorne, but you must be mistaken. This parcel is registered to one Micah Mason. It makes no mention of any joint tenant."

"May I see that?"

The clerk returned to the counter and handed him the record card.

Damn. What the hell is going on here?

"I see. Perhaps they've yet to file notice of their partnership interest."

"Well, if they apply, I shouldn't think the request would be granted in light of the court's decision, at least not on the authority of this office."

Thorne laid the card on the counter. "Thank you for your assistance." He started for the door, jaw clenched in frustration. As he reached the stairway to the second floor the sound of angry voices drifted out of the legislative chamber above. The constitutional convention was in session. Curiosity tugged at his sleeve. He climbed the stairs.

A great room occupied the whole of the second floor. Serving as district courtroom most times, it now hosted the territorial constitutional convention. The delegates here were charged to draft a territorial constitution under which Kansas might petition for admission to the union. Pro-slavery representatives chosen in the disputed territorial election dominated the body, with but a handful of free-state Kansans headed by Charles Robinson. As he slid into the gallery back row he recognized Robinson's familiar figure at the podium. He gestured to the chair using a sheaf of paper clenched in his fist for emphasis.

"You call this a constitution? This is nothing more than the practice of slavery codified in immoral law. By itself it is a disgrace. The fact this body proposes to adopt it on behalf of the people of Kansas is nothing short of criminal."

He shook the document at the seated legislators. "Most of you owe your seats in this body not to the people of Kansas but to the scallywag Missouri men who crossed our border to steal our deliberation of this issue. You cast your votes in fraudulent fashion. You committed fraud by your election, and now you would add to those crimes by perpetuating the morally repugnant and vile practice of slavery."

"Mr. Chairman!" The speaker, David Atchison, stood off to the side at the front of the spectator gallery, a dark silhouette in muted light. "Mr. Chairman, how much longer must we listen to these fallacious and reckless allegations? This body has a constitution before it. Exercise your authority and proceed."

"Here, here," someone called from the legislators' seats. "I move we call the question!"

"Second!" someone else shouted.

Robinson turned on Atchison. "Senator, if I may demean the office by addressing you so. You, sir, have no standing here. You are a Missouri man. Your part here is only to assure the fraud you instigated is seen to its final perpetration."

The chairman's gavel cracked like a pistol shot. "Yield the floor, Mr. Robinson. We have a motion to call the question and a second. All in favor?"

The pro-slavery delegates roared "Aye!"

"Opposed?"

"Nay," cried a smattering of free-state delegates.

"The question is called. For approval of the Lecompton constitution as presented."

"Aye!" the majority shouted.

"The ayes have it." The chair cracked his gavel.

"Nay!" Robinson resounded across the chamber. "Nay, I say, nay! So long as I have breath in these bones I say nay!" He led his free-state delegation out of the chamber.

Thorne shook his head. *Noble defeat? Nay, only defeat.*

Chapter Thirty-One

Washington City
February, 1858

Senator Douglas trimmed the desk lamp as early evening shadows crept across the office floor. He stepped to the sideboard and poured whiskey from a cut-glass decanter into a matching glass. He glanced out the window at street lamps winking to light across the capital. Horse drawn carriages moved among the shadows as Washington made its way home to supper. He selected a cigar, scratched a match to sulfur flash, and puffed his smoke to light. He sat in an oversize wing chair at his desk side, his diminutive frame fairly disappearing in comfort. He took a swallow of his drink. Quiet contemplation gave his thoughts to matters at hand.

Buchanan had bollocks, you had to give him that. While Pierce preferred to dither in half measures, Buchanan set a new tone with his partisan agenda. His proposed legislation would admit Kansas to the Union as a slave state based on ratification of the Lecompton constitution. The proposal fed red meat to his southern caucus. The question was, what to do about it? The moment Buchanan put forward his proposal, he'd felt pressure from his Democrat colleagues to support the bill. The southern caucus had no reservations about the checkered provenance of the legislature that adopted the Kansas territorial constitution. Douglas's personal ambition handed him a testy stake in the matter.

He let the whiskey warm his belly. He'd challenge that awkward bumpkin of a country lawyer to a series of debates sure to elevate his stature as a presidential candidate. Favoring free soil for economic reasons stopped well short of abolitionist equality. Such a position would resonate with the mood of the electorate north of the Mason-Dixon line far more than Lincoln's strident abolitionism. He'd mop the floor with the reedy-voiced scarecrow. That was reasonable. But now Buchanan had stuck him with this damnable piece of legislation. If he opposed it, he risked losing the south. If he backed it, he'd lose in the north even among moderate Democrats.

He drew on his cigar and let a veil of smoke color his thinking. Might there be some way to tangle the bill procedurally so as to avoid having to take a tough vote? Appealing as that notion might be, newly elected presidents enjoyed a honeymoon of sentiment that would be hard to overcome. No, the bill would come to a vote, a vote he did not relish. He might hold enough of the south with a states' rights position on slavery; but that came straight back to the damned Lecompton constitution. The odor of scandal permeated election of that legislative body and, so, fouled the aroma of the president's bill. One could scarcely endorse it without tainting oneself by association.

He swirled amber liquid in lamplight and drained the glass. His best chance of winning the White House started with opposing the admission of Kansas under the fraudulent cloud hanging over the territorial legislature that produced the Lecompton constitution. He'd paint Lincoln as a radical abolitionist and hope his moderate southern sympathies drew enough favor in the south to win a bitterly divided electorate. He might even argue that the Dred Scott decision secured the future of slavery, making the Kansas admission moot. But that was a conversation best had behind closed doors.

He flicked a long white ash into a crystal tray on his desk. He held up his glass, considering the last amber droplets spinning a rainbow of reflected color. Few things in politics ever are as they appear. Time for another.

Lawrence
April, 1858
Lane, Montgomery, and Jennison met in the rebuilt Eldridge House storeroom. A steady rain spattered the loading platform planks outside. Gray light filtered through the windows, rendering the men seated on crates in somber shadows.

"The territorial legislature adopted the Lecompton constitution, but Robinson convinced the governor to put it to a vote," Lane said.

"How'd he manage that?" Montgomery asked.

"He convinced the governor that the border violence is owed to election fraud. If they ram that constitution down the people's throats, the violence will only increase. So, we're gonna have another election in August overseen by federal troops this time."

"You think that'll keep it fair?" Jennison asked.

"It may, but I say we don't take no chances."

"What do you mean?"

"We got from now to August to run as many pro-slavers out of the territory as possible."

"The governor will call out the army," Montgomery said.

"Them bushwhackin' Missouri men won't sit by idle," Jennison said.

"You're both right. But we need to win that election. It starts with eliminating the opposition."

Both nodded.

"Doc, you take the southeast. James and I will take the northeast. We know who the slavers are. We give 'em fair warning. Slavery ain't welcome in Kansas. Get out or we burn you out."

"How we gonna do that?"

"I'll have notices printed. We post 'em, so as those they're meant for can't mistake the message. 'Bout the time they figure we mean it, we'll get our election."

Lecompton, Kansas
April 20, 1858

Three days of rain cleared out to the promise of a fine spring day. Campbell Carter stepped onto his cabin porch and stretched. He faced a good day to finish his spring planting. It would be a hard day. He smiled. With passing the Lecompton constitution, soon enough he'd ease his burdens with a field hand or two.

A flutter on the breeze caught his eye. It looked like someone had tacked a paper on the fence post. He crossed the yard, tore the flier off the fence, and read.

Notice: Slavery not welcome in Kansas.

Get out, or get burned out.

Carter glanced north and south along the wagon road for some sign of anyone who might be responsible for posting such a thing. He crumpled the paper in a calloused fist. No free-soiler was going to run off a former Tennessean. Sure as hell not when the law was on his side.

He stomped back to the house, shouldered his musket, patch, and powder, and headed for the field.

May 7, 1858

Lane and his men drew rein in the trees. Dark, running clouds muted the moon to an eerie glow. The cabin, corral, and outbuildings stood silhouetted in the clearing, marked only by the light of a single lamp shining from one cabin window. A whisper of smoke from the chimney floated on the breeze. Peaceful night sounds were mildly disturbed by the groan of saddle leather, stomp of a horse hoof, or a jangle of tack.

"Looks like Carter didn't get the message," Lane said as much to himself as to his second.

"What do you aim to do?"

"Burn it down—outbuilding, cabin, the whole place."

"What about Carter?"

"Leave him to me." He looked to his men. "Is that understood?"

A dozen dark figures nodded.

"Then get to it."

Matches flared. Torches bloomed in the darkness. Jayhawks stormed the clearing. Lane followed his men into the clearing. He held his horse off the cabin door.

The door threw open a shaft of light as the clearing grew orange in firelight. Carter stood framed in the door, musket in hand.

Lane cocked his colt and leveled it at the man's chest. "Drop the gun, Carter. You got but one chance now."

The man dropped his gun.

"You was warned, Carter. Now you got but one chance. Get out. Get out or you're next."

"Who are you?"

"A Jayhawk. A slaver's worst apparition. Now get out before I change my mind about letting you go."

Carter set off, walking down the road into town.

Lane's second rode up. "You let him go. Why?"

"So he spreads the word to his friends. It's time for slavers to leave."

Chapter Thirty-Two

Trading Post
Kansas Territory
May 19, 1858

William Clarke Quantrill came to see it as a duty. Southern interests were being unjustly persecuted in Kansas. The Jayhawk campaign to rid the territory of pro-slavery sentiment went too far. Guerrilla bands known as Bushwhackers rose to oppose them. A simple school teacher, he'd come to the ranks of a band, known as the north ferry men, by chance association. In time, he'd come to see their cause as righteous retribution by the lights of their leader, Jacob Herd.

A slender man of modest stature with light hair and a hint of a moustache beneath a prominent nose, his drab, shabby appearance would easily disappear in a crowd. One day, his reputation would not. He rode with the Bushwhackers when they took Trading Post by surprise.

They stormed the town and rounded up eleven Montgomery men known to be responsible for a recent raid in southeastern Kansas. They herded the men into a nearby ravine. Little more than a foot soldier in this band, Quantrill took his place in the rank of mounted executioners facing the accused. Herd, the infamous slave catcher, cocked his pistol. Realization dawned. These men were not merely accused; they were condemned. A man at the end of the rank turned toward Herd.

"You can't just shoot these men in cold blood."

"Shut up!"

"I'll not be party to murder." He wheeled his horse out of line.

"Get back in rank. Do your duty, you yellow-bellied coward!"

The man spurred away.

"Close rank," Herd said.

"If you shoot, shoot straight," one of the condemned said.

Herd leveled his pistol. "Fire!"

The Bushwhacker line exploded powder smoke. Quantrill did as ordered.

Two men fell dead. Eight more went down wounded. One blood-spattered man fell unscathed. As if by unspoken instinct, all the survivors feigned death.

Herd dismounted. He climbed down into the gully followed by Quantrill and another man. He kicked the first body he came to.

"Make sure they are dead."

The next man he kicked gave up a groan. He leveled his pistol at the man's head and scattered his brains at point-blank range.

Up the gully Quantrill's second shot finished another. Two more shots dispatched a third.

Satisfied their work was done, Herd climbed the ravine to his horse. He toed a stirrup, swung into the saddle, and swept his gaze over the dead and presumed dead. He wheeled his horse east. The band lined out for Missouri.

Washington City
June 19, 1858

Senator Douglas gathered the morning paper and settled in at his desk with a cup of coffee. A glorious summer day poured through the windows lighting his office. Lincoln's speech to the Republican state convention delegates promised an interesting read. According to reports he'd received, his opponent had gone to extremes on the slavery issue, turning the biblical phrase "A house divided against itself cannot stand" to his moralistic purpose.

The text wandered over the legal intricacies of the Kansas-Nebraska Act, Lecompton constitution, and the Supreme Court Dred Scott decision in an effort to taint Douglas with the perpetuation of slavery in the whole of the republic. It was a ridiculous notion at best. It did single out the gangly backwoods country lawyer for his abolitionist leanings, thus permitting Douglas the luxury of a more moderate free-state position, sympathetic to southern states' rights. The effect of the Dred Scott ruling might render all that moot, as it appeared to strike down a state's right to prohibit slavery; but that was a matter for the future to decide. The Illinois electorate would be comfortable with his views, while Lincoln could easily be painted the extremist.

Douglas scanned back to the top of the article, choosing his opponent's more inflammatory statements for his use. "The government cannot endure" half slave and half free. He claims not to see the Union dissolved, but only a house that ceases to be divided. He asserts that moral authority will ultimately sustain his position. One man's moral righteousness may impinge upon another man's civil rights. The house may indeed cease to be divided, but the finality of Dred Scott may not produce the resolution our dewy-eyed idealist envisions.

He took a swallow of coffee. No, there was more than enough here to secure his re-election to the senate. From there, the White House beckoned.

Lawrence
August 2, 1858
Eldridge House once more served as polling place on a swelter-

ing election day. Micah drew the team to a halt not far up the block. He climbed down and dropped the tie-down weight. He stepped up the boardwalk and started down the block to the hotel. Two blue-coated cavalry troopers stood by the front entrance. Micah nodded to them as he stepped inside. James Lane and Charles Robinson stood off to the side watching the parade of voters claim their ballots, mark them, and deposit them in locked boxes. They were accompanied by a familiar cavalry officer.

Micah took his place in line, signed for his ballot, marked his "No" vote to reject the Lecompton constitution, and deposited it in the ballot box. He nodded to Lane.

"How we doin' this time?"

"Nothin' but familiar faces."

"Good." He extended a hand to the officer. "Lieutenant Stuart, I believe."

He accepted the offered hand. "You have the advantage of me, sir."

"Micah Mason. I did have the advantage of you last fall when you ran that Arapaho war party off my place just west of here. You rode off in such a rush I never did get to properly thank you."

"Ah, yes, I remember now. Pleased we could be of service that day."

"Not half so pleased as we."

Stuart chuckled. "You think that little scrape might have ended badly?"

"I have no doubt of it. My thanks belatedly."

"Don't mention it. It's what we're paid to do."

When the votes were counted, Kansans rejected the Lecompton constitution by a wide margin. The newly elected free-state legislature would begin repealing the slave laws in the next session.

Wakarusa Creek
December 19, 1858

Minister Stewart's stockade stood in a clearing served by a creek. John Brown, accompanied by sons Salmon and Owen, drew rein at the gate amid a late afternoon swirl of snow.

"Yo, Brother Stewart!" Brown hailed.

A portal in the gate cracked open. The gate followed in recognition. Brown and his sons rode into the yard and stepped down at the house. John Stewart, also known as the fighting preacher, stepped out to the porch.

"Brother Brown, welcome." By way of benediction the sometime Methodist minister offered what passed for a smile. "Come in, come in out of the cold. See to their horses," he instructed the gatekeeper.

Stewart led the way into a comfortably spacious cabin warmed by a cheery fire on the hearth.

"Coffee?"

"That would be most welcome," Brown said.

"Have a seat." He gestured to a long, rough-cut table with benches where meals were served. A stout woman of severe demeanor with steel-gray hair emerged from the kitchen carrying a heavy steaming pot and cups. She passed the cups and poured.

"Will ye be stayin' for supper?"

"Of course, my dear," Stewart replied for his guests. "It's much too late to continue travels this day." He took his seat at the head of the table and blew steam off his cup. "Now what brings you all this way on a winter's day, Brother Brown?"

Brown and his boys warmed their hands on their cups.

"Emancipation, God willing," Brown said.

"Noble purpose, good friend. Might you be more specific?"

"Taylor Caldwell. His slaves cry for freedom."

"I'd not heard that."

"I have in prayer. Now will you and your men join us?"

"What do you propose?"

"We shall go to the farm and free them."

"Caldwell shall surely resist."

"Should we ride together, that would be a most unwise decision for his part. Still, you are likely right in your estimation. For that we should expect to add livestock and stores to our liberation."

"Useful in trade and sustenance. You can count on our support. When do you plan this divine emancipation?"

"Might you be prepared to ride in the morning?"

"I shall see to it."

The following afternoon the Caldwell farm came into view shortly before dusk. A wisp of smoke drifted to the sky darkening in the east. Sun slanting across an expanse of prairie at the raiders' back hid them from their quarry. Still, they could make out the main house, slave quarters, a barn, and a corral.

"Rest here until full darkness," Brown said.

They dismounted to take a cold supper. Darkness fell. Lights winked on in the house and slave quarters. The raiders mounted and rode in to circle the yard. Brown hailed the house. The door opened to the figure of a man silhouetted in light.

"Who goes?"

"The righteous have come to set your Negroes free."

Caldwell reached inside the door for a rifle. Stewart fired. Caldwell clutched his chest and fell at his own doorstep. A woman screamed.

"Salmon, see to the Negroes," Brown said.

Salmon and his brother rode off to the slave quarters.

Stewart turned to his men. "Tend the stock, while Brother Brown and I search the house."

Brown and Stewart stepped down, leaving their horses to browse in the yard. They climbed the porch to the grieving widow.

"Why? Why have you done this terrible deed?"

"It is just retribution for practicing the sin of slavery, madam," Brown said.

"Murder. You murdered him, and you speak righteously of sin? You'll see your vile self in hell one day."

"Not likely, madam, for it shall be overcrowded by slave holders."

They stepped over her and commenced searching the house. They stripped it of food, clothing, and blankets, which they distributed to eleven slaves Salmon and Owen liberated from their quarters. Stewart's men produced a wagon, mules to pull it, and a yoke of sturdy oxen.

Brown and Stewart appraised the booty from the porch.

"A fair night's work," Brown said.

"The stock shall fetch a fine price."

"To that you are welcome, Brother Stewart. My soul is satisfied by the faces of freedom I behold before me."

"Shall we burn the house and buildings?"

Brown cast an eye on the sobbing woman. "She has paid enough for her husband's sins. Leave it be."

They mounted their horses and rode into the night.

Chapter Thirty-Three

North Ferry Tavern

Quantrill read the notice printed in the latest edition of the *Missouri Democrat.*

$500 Reward
Offered by Order of the Governor of Missouri
Dead or Alive for the Murder and Plunder
of Taylor Caldwell

Reverend Stewart. It had to be. How best to collect? He folded the paper and stared into his tankard of beer. Lively conversation and jovial laughter surrounded him but were no distraction. *How to collect?* Stewart knew him. He had enjoyed the man's trust for his free-state sympathies on first arriving in Kansas. His sympathies had changed, though Stewart had no way of knowing that. He could trade on that. The man had a streak of greed he might use to entice him into a trap in Missouri. A slow smile tugged at the corners of his thin moustache. The germ of a plan sprouted in his mind's eye. He drained his tankard and scraped his chair away from the table.

Wakarusa Creek

Quantrill arrived at the Stewart compound confident in his plan. He gained admission to the stockade and invitation to sup with the fighting preacher. While putting up his horse in the stable, he was approached by a black man.

"Here, suh, let me help you wid dat."

"I shouldn't have thought Reverend Stewart would keep slaves."

"Oh, I ain't no slave no more. The Reverend an' Brother Brown freed us. I's waitin' on travel to Canada."

"Were you taken from the Taylor Caldwell farm?"

The question furrowed the black man's brow. "Let me get you some grain for that horse."

The man was clearly uncomfortable with the answer to his question—answer enough as far as Quantrill was concerned. It made for another enticement to add to his offer. With his horse put up for the night he made his way to the house. Reverend Stewart greeted him at the door.

"Come in, William. Have a seat. Supper will be served presently. Would you care for a cup of cider while we wait?"

"That would go down good on a parched throat."

Stewart poured two cups from a pitcher and took his place at the table.

"Now, William, to what do we owe the unexpected pleasure of your company?"

"A prize I find worthy of your consideration."

Stewart lifted a questioning brow. "My consideration? What sort of prize?"

"The Morgan Walker farm. The stock alone makes a grand prize, though some say he holds gold on the premises. Of course, there is the just cause of some thirty slaves we might free."

"Tempting as all that may be, Missouri has become somewhat inhospitable to me in recent days. I'm afraid I must decline. Perhaps Brother Brown would find merit in emancipating so large a number of the enslaved."

"He may. Then again, he may disapprove of taking livestock and gold."

"He may. One never knows his need at the moment. Perhaps Jennison then. You've only to say gold or stock to him."

"Hmm. Perhaps. Or perhaps I shall find it necessary to scale back my ambition."

"Well, William, if you find yourself in possession of stock you wish to sell, I might be of service to you there."

Quantrill smiled. "Why, yes, Reverend, I believe that might be arranged."

North Ferry Crossing

The ferry crossing provided the inn and tavern Jake Herd's border ruffians called home. Quantrill and Herd sat at a corner table in the dimly lit rough-hewn public room. Herd smoked his pipe and nursed a whiskey as he listened.

"Stewart's got 'em. All we got to do is take his compound and return 'em to the Caldwell family for the statutory reward. If they'll not stand for it, we sell 'em on the open market for their full value."

"How many did you say he has?"

"The reports say Caldwell's loss was eleven. I didn't count 'em but that number seems about right."

"And how many men does Stewart have?"

"That'll vary depending on if he's planning a raid or not. He ain't plannin' a raid anytime soon with that bounty hangin' over his head in Missouri."

"You sound pretty sure of that."

Quantrill smiled.

"So how many men?"

"Handful at most."

Herd nodded into a puff of pipe smoke. "Sounds like we might turn a profit on the opportunity."

"No doubt. You in?"

"We're in. When do we ride?"

"Two days."

Sycamore
January, 1859

The wagon clattered up the road to the house on a frosty, gray midday. Sampson and Delilah blew clouds of steam as a thin mist blanket rose off their backs from exertion in the cold. Micah hauled lines in the yard. He helped Clare down. Caleb came down the lane from their cabin to help with the unloading. Miriam stood on the porch of the Mason house with the two little girls in tow.

"You go along inside, dear, and get out of this cold. Caleb and I will bring in our supplies and take theirs on up to the cabin."

Clare climbed the porch and herded the girls inside to squeals of delight. Miriam followed, closing the door.

Micah and Caleb unloaded the Masons' supplies and carried the bundles into the house.

"What's the news up to Lawrence?" Miriam asked.

"I hear Brother Brown and Reverend John Stewart freed Taylor Caldwell's slaves," Micah said.

"Taylor Caldwell? Is you sure?"

"That's the talk. Why?"

"Massa Morgan Walker sold my mama an' baby sister to Taylor Caldwell. Mama's been gone fer a spell now, but my sister Liza might be with them still. Do you know where they are?"

"Stewart's compound," Micah said. "I saw Owen Brown at Eldridge House. He told me the Caldwell slaves are there waiting passage to Canada."

Miriam turned to Caleb. "We gotta go quick. We can bring her here with us."

"She be considered a runaway. She be better off in Canada."

"We be runaways, and we be here."

"That's different. Our trail went cold when Micah and Clare took us in."

"So? Liza's trail can go cold when we take her in."

"And if it don't, it could warm up our trail again."

"Liza's blood kin. I'm goin' to find her. Are you comin' with me?"

Micah suppressed a smile.

Caleb rolled his eyes and shrugged.

"She been this way since the day she proposed jumpin' the broom to me."

"She proposed?" Micah chuckled.

"She did," Caleb said.

Miriam bunched her fists on her hips. "You the one said yes. Don't you dare be takin' to regret now."

"Take the wagon," Micah said. He pulled the carbine down from its pegs along with powder and ball. "Best take this."

"We'll mind Rebecca," Clare said.

Wakarusa Creek

The Stewart compound gates opened to Caleb and Miriam. Caleb drove the wagon into the yard amid a scurry of chickens. Reverend Stewart came down to the yard from the house to greet them.

"Caleb, Miriam, what brings you by?"

Miriam climbed down from the box without waiting for Caleb to help her.

"We heard the Taylor Caldwell black folks is here."

Stewart knit his brows. "Who told you that?"

"Owen Brown toldt Micah Mason."

"I see." Stewart relaxed.

"My baby sister Liza might be with them."

"I'm afraid we don't have any babies here."

"Oh, she ain't no baby no more. That's what she was when Massa Morgan Walker sold her and my mama to Massa Caldwell."

A curious crowd had begun to gather, black folk drawn by two new arrivals. One spoke up.

"You lookin' fer Liza?"

"Yes! Is she here?"

The man shook his head. "She jumped the broom with a Morgan Walker field hand last spring. Massa Walker liked his man, so he bought her for him. Massa Caldwell said sompin' 'bout prime breeding stock."

Miriam drooped her head in disappointment, clenching her fists at her side. Caleb wrapped his arms around her.

"Seems like you gals is always marr'ing into some kind of trouble. At least she's happy."

"It's too late to head back to Sycamore tonight," Reverend Stewart said. "Put up your team and spend the night here. You can start back in the morning."

Bundled in blankets with Miriam on a bed of straw in the Stewart barn, Caleb woke with a start at the first shot.

"What is it?" Miriam sat up wide-eyed in total darkness.

"Bushwhackers I reckon. You stay here." He grabbed the carbine, powder, and ball.

"Where you goin'?"

"Somebody's got to defend this place." He ran out the door followed by a half-dozen former Taylor Caldwell slaves.

Moonlight splashed the yard in a chill glow. Reverend Stewart and a few of his men scrambled to the stockade portals on either side of the gate. Mounted raiders swarmed over the clearing marked in muzzle flash, powder charge, and the splatter of ball against timber. The Stewart men returned fire with carbine and shotguns. The raiders pulled back their charge.

"Caleb, mind the catwalk atop that back wall," Stewart shouted. "The rest of you come with me." He ran back to the house followed by the former slaves.

Caleb scrambled up a ladder at the back wall of the compound to a narrow walkway. He peered through the first portal he came to. Moonlight painted the trees beyond the clearing in shadow, a barren briar patchwork of branches held aloft on stout trunks. Something moved in the trees. Off to his right two men broke from the shadows and rushed toward the wall, a coiled rope in hand.

Stewart led the men to an armory at the back of the house.

"How many of you men know how to shoot?"

Three hands went up.

He handed each of them a rifle, powder, and ball. "Man the portals on the east wall. Two of you shoot. One reloads." They ran off the way they'd come. The reverend handed two of the remaining men shotguns. He took a third shotgun for himself. "We'll take the west wall."

"I don't know how to shoot this thing," one said.

"You're about to learn fast."

"Yes, suh."

Stewart led the way into darkness.

The rope snaked up to the top of the wall, the loop caught purchase, tugged tight. Rope and timbers strained under the weight of a climber. Caleb waited, crouched beside the rope. Someone grunted with exertion through the timbers. A slouch hat peeked over the wall, the shadow of a head inched into view.

Caleb struck. The carbine stock smashed the climber across

the bridge of his nose. He fell back with a scream, landing on the second man waiting to climb. Caleb swung the carbine over the top of the wall into the upturned face of a man struggling to regain his footing. He fired at near point-blank range. The face disappeared. He ducked back behind the wall as the trees lit in a volley of muzzle flash and ball.

Caleb worked to reload powder, wadding, and ball. *Finally hit something with this thing.* A second thought hit him. He reached for the rope, reeled it in, and dropped it inside the stockade. *Let's see if they got any more.*

Behind him, off to the right, shotguns gave out their throaty roar.

"Nothing to this!" The never-fired-before black man said over the muzzle smoking in his portal.

Reverend Stewart smiled. "Now reload!"

The man fell back from his portal replaced by another. He fumbled with shot and cartridge.

As long as they don't press us any faster than these boys can reload, chances are we can hold them off. Stewart felt a small measure of confidence return since the first shots being fired.

The raid settled into a battle of attrition. Both sides exchanged fruitless fire. Herd fumed. He turned an accusatory scowl on Quantrill.

"You said Stewart only had a handful of men."

"He does, if you only count white men."

"You think he armed the slaves?"

"What do you think? He got them walls manned somehow. We could try burnin' 'em out."

"Burnt black men don't fetch statutory reward money let alone full price on the block. I've lost three men so far. I ain't goin' in for no more. Come on. We're gettin' out of here before first light."

Chapter Thirty-Four

North Ferry Crossing
April, 1859

Thorne jogged Rogue through a dreary, cold drizzle up the muddy road to the North Ferry Inn. Rusty brown stained the black's belly and hocks as he splashed through mud to the rail. Thorne stepped down, his riding boots sinking into the ooze. He stepped up to the shelter of the boardwalk and shook rainwater from his cloak. He ducked inside and paused, allowing his eyes to adjust in dim, smoky light. He spied the object of his search seated at an inconspicuous table set off from the bar. The man arched a brow at his approach.

"Thorne, what brings you up here on a day like this?"

"Nice to see you too, Jake."

"Sorry, I didn't mean to sound inhospitable. It was merely surprise. Have a seat."

Thorne peeled off his wet gloves, dropped them on the table, and hung his cloak over a vacant chair. Herd motioned the waiter for a second glass.

"Thanks. I could use a little something to take the chill off." He settled into a hard, wooden chair.

Herd poured. Thorne took a swallow.

"Now then, what is it that brings you all the way up here?"

"A bit of business you may find of interest."

"I'm listening."

"You probably heard about the recent failed raid on the Stewart compound."

"I heard."

"I'm sure you did. One of the freed men who defended Stewart is a man who might be of interest to you."

"Who might that be?"

"The man works the Mason farm. He goes by the name Caleb."

"What's that got to do with me?"

"I believe the man and his woman ran away from Morgan Walker. The Caldwell folk might not have stood the reward for their runaways, but Walker surely will."

"Hmm. Walker did retain me to track a pair of runaways a few years ago. As I recall he owned the woman. The buck belonged to Ruben Wright. Their trail did dry up in the vicinity of the Mason farm. What's all that got to do with you? It can't be the paltry reward."

Thorne shook his head. "You're welcome to the reward should you choose to avail yourself of it. The runaway and the abolitionist Mason work that section in partnership. It's land that naturally complements my holdings. By rights it should have been mine. Mason jumped his claim before I could file. Together they resist me. Left alone, the holding is too much for one man to work. I mean to have that land. Mason cannot hold out. Are you interested?"

"It seems I already have an interest courtesy of Morgan Walker."

"Splendid."

Sycamore

Sun kissed the western horizon as Caleb finished the last row. They'd put in a long day since sunup. Even the normally resilient Delilah plodded at the end. He let her drink her fill at the creek bank. Cook smoke drifted to the evening sky, promising one of Miriam's fine suppers. Finished, the jenny blew her nose with a snort.

"All right, girl, let's get you along back to Sampson. He probably got a sack a' grain he holdin' with your name on it." He clucked at the lines, crossing the creek and turning north on the tree shadowed wagon lane toward the barn. Something moved. A dark figure stepped out of the trees in his path. *Who might this—*

He never completed the thought. A blow to the back of his head rendered him senseless.

A wagon emerged from the trees. They bound and gagged him. It took three men to load him into the wagon. Two men climbed into the box. Herd and Quantrill mounted horses hidden in the trees. They took the wagon road east.

"Micah! Micah!" She pounded on the door. Lamp light spilled through the door into her tears.

"Miriam, what is it?"

"Is Caleb here?"

"No, why?"

"He's hurt. I think they must'a took him."

"Who took him?"

"I don't know. Slave catchers maybe."

Clare put her arm around her sobbing friend.

"Tell me what happened," Micah said.

"He didn't come in for supper. I went out to find him. I found Delilah hitched to the plow on the lane to the barn. Caleb ain't nowhere around. It ain't like him to leave that mule hitched up. Then I seen dark spots on the ground. It's fresh blood."

"Show me." Micah took a lamp and led the way out the door and up the lane to where the jenny stood in her traces. He saw blood stains along with boot prints of three, maybe four, men, wagon tracks, and horse sign. The wagon turned up the road east.

"All right, here's what I want you to do. Put up Delilah. Miriam, I want you and Rebecca to hide out in the dugout house."

"You think they'll come back?" Miriam said.

"I don't know, but we're not takin' any chances."

"What are you going to do?" Clare asked.

"Ride into Lawrence to get help. Then we're going after Caleb."

Lawrence

Micah loped down Massachusetts to Eldridge House. He drew a halt and stepped down. He looped a rein over the rack and bounded up the steps. He found James Lane at his usual table playing cards with Doc Jennison and a few others. Lane took one look at Micah's face and the Colt at his hip and knew it meant trouble.

"Micah, what's the matter?"

"It's Caleb." The story spilled out.

"Where do you figure they're headed?"

"If it's slave catchers, they'd return him to Morgan Walker for the reward."

"Doc, can you and your boys help?"

Jennison nodded.

"Good. Then let's ride."

Thirty minutes later Lane, Jennison, Micah, and a dozen Jayhawkers rode south.

Jackson County, Missouri

Caleb's head hurt something fierce. If he'd had his supper he'd surely have lost it. The bumping and jouncing of the wagon did nothing to improve his lot. Dim light penetrated the canvas tarp they had covering him. They'd taken no chance of a free-soil man unraveling their plan. He could tell by the light and warmth that the new day was well along into morning when they splashed across a creek he remembered. They must be northwest of the Morgan Walker farm. The driver drew the wagon to a stop. He could still hear the creek. The change in light told him they must be stopped in the shade along the tree lined bank.

"Wait here," someone said, "while me and Quantrill have a talk with Walker."

Herd, it had to be. Horses galloped away. The wagon box groaned as his captors climbed down.

"How's our package doin'?"

Someone pulled back the tarp. Even the shaded light caused him to blink.

"He's awake and he's breathin'."

The canvas dropped back in place. They moved off somewhere talking quietly. Caleb tested the bonds on his hands. The ropes cut his wrists. Still he worked on them. There were two of them. Likely they were armed. Still, he might surprise them if he could free his bonds.

Herd drew rein at a main house with grassy lawns at the end of the stately drive entering the Morgan Walker farm. Quantrill took in the expanse of the place, the elegant house, quarters for thirty or forty slaves. Corrals and barns stocked with fine horseflesh, mules, and cattle. One pen held a powerfully built bull, certain to keep the herd plentiful with calves. It was a prize worth far more than a statutory slave price. Some of his friends on the other side would surely consider it prime opportunity. *All in good time. Today, he would learn.*

Herd stepped down with Quantrill at his side. They climbed a broad porch, fronting the house to elegant double doors. The brass knocker summoned a white-haired black man in starched, white coat.

"Is Master Walker in?"

"Who may I say is callin'?"

"Jacob Herd."

Recognition and fear flickered in the old man's eyes. He disappeared down a polished wood hallway bathed a tawny glow in midday day light spilling through lace curtains. He returned moments later.

"This way, Mr. Herd." He led them down the hall to a massive library.

The school teacher in Quantrill estimated it to be the envy of many a university.

"Jacob, it's been some time. To what do I owe the pleasure?"

"Unfinished business, Mr. Walker. It's good to see you, sir."

"And this gentleman is?"

"William Quantrill, Mr. Walker." He extended his hand.

"Pleased to meet you. Now, Jacob, what is this about unfinished business?"

"A few years ago, you hired me to track a couple of runaways. The buck's name was Caleb. I lost their trail and never recovered your property. By the happenstance of good fortune, I've come upon him and thought we might discuss your interest in recovering him."

"Ah, yes, I remember. He'd taken one of my house slaves. A young woman . . . Miriam, as I recall. So you've run across him after all this time. Actually, he belonged to Ruben Wright, so you may be talking to the wrong man. Is he servable?"

"If he weren't, I wouldn't trouble you with it."

"Then it's likely Ruben will stand the statutory reward. If not, I'm interested. He was a first-rate hand with a plow."

"Two hundred dollars is a paltry sum for a specimen like him. It took four of us to secure him. I should think a hundred a man would be more in keeping with his worth on the block."

"What of the woman? Do you know what became of her?"

"We don't have her, though I suspect we could find her."

"Then perhaps we might strike a bargain. I risk speaking for Ruben, but let's say five hundred for the pair? Two hundred now and the balance when you bring me the woman."

Herd scratched his chin. "In gold?"

"In gold."

Gold. Quantrill savored the sound. *He never batted an eye.*

Sweat from heat and exertion poured into his eyes and dampened his shirt. The day had worn past noon. *How much longer before Herd returned?* He had to make something happen soon, or he'd find himself back in bondage if he survived the punishment to be meted out after all these years. The ropes binding him proved stout. He'd rubbed his wrists slick with blood. Even that would not free him.

"Don't move!" Someone shouted beyond the wagon box.

"Drop your guns. Up with your hands."

Horses splashed across the stream.

"Where is he?"

"Where is Caleb?"

"I don't know what you're talkin' about."

Caleb recognized Micah's voice. He banged his boots on the wagon bed.

"Noisy cargo you got over there."

Someone grabbed the tarp and pulled it back.

Micah.

"Caleb!" He climbed into the box and untied the gag.

"You a sight." He choked on the words.

"Easy. Get me some water over here." He drew his knife and cut the ropes from wrists and ankles. Jennison rode up beside the wagon box with a canteen he handed to Caleb.

"Take it slow. You all right?"

Caleb nodded. "I is now." He sat up. His two captors stood

surrounded by heavily armed men.

"James, I suggest we make short work of this," Jennison said.

"Do as you think best, Doc," Lane said.

"You men are charged with abduction and assault. You are to be judged by a jury of your peers. How do you plead?"

"Plead? We ain't got nothin' to plead for. That man's a contraband fugitive."

"Not in Kansas."

"Fugitive slave laws cross that border."

"Gentlemen of the jury, how do you find?"

"Guilty!" the Jayhawkers cried as one.

"Then you are hereby sentenced to hang by the neck until dead."

They loped down the road to the creek as the sun began its westerly descent. The wagon stood parked as they left it. Little remained to the day. In the morning, they'd deliver the package to Walker and set about the business of returning to Sycamore for the woman. The first indication that something might be amiss struck Herd as they drew closer. *Where are they?*

They found the wagon empty. No sign of his men. Quantrill spotted movement among the trees. Shadows moving on a gentle breeze. He nudged Herd. His eyes pointed up. Purple, distorted, and still save for the gentle sway. Each body bore a scrap of paper pinned to its chest.

"Cut 'em down," Herd ordered.

Quantrill drove the wagon into position and lowered the bodies into the bed.

Herd tore off one note and read, "Slave catchers not welcome in Kansas."

Chapter Thirty-Five

Sycamore
May, 1859

Sunday, Caleb and Miriam took their turn at hosting supper. The neighbors had taken to sharing their main Sunday meal, alternating preparation and hosting chores. Micah and Caleb sat on the porch enjoying a bright spring day while watching the girls at play. Miriam bustled about the kitchen preparing cornbread, bucket beans, and her specialty, a thick, rich turtle soup. Clare assisted where she could.

"There's a meeting tonight in Lawrence. I believe we should go," Clare said.

"Meeting? What for?"

"It's a meeting of the Moneka Women's Rights Association."

"What's that?"

"It's a group of women working to see that women's rights are included in the Kansas constitution."

"What sort of rights?"

"The right to vote. The right to own property. Probably some more I don't know about yet."

"Them rights is for white folks."

"Some people think that. Some people don't think any woman deserves those rights. One thing is sure: we aren't gonna change anything unless we try."

"Maybe so for you white ladies. You go draggin' the likes of me along, you only gonna make your problems worse."

"Now you listen here, Miriam. That's what you said about learning to read. Well you did, and the world didn't come to an end. The vote is nothing more than your right to express an opinion and have it count. The United States Constitution guarantees the right to free speech. A vote is nothing more than official free speech."

"Free speech is for free folk. My folk ain't free. Didn't they tell Dred Scott he wasn't free? As I read it, he ain't free to own property, neither."

"That don't make it right. Laws are made, and laws can be changed. You just have to do something about it. Now are you coming with me or not?"

"You sure about this?"

"I am."

"You're the teacher."

"Absolutely not, Miriam," Caleb said. "Pass the beans. You ladies ain't driving into Lawrence an' drivin' home alone at night with them bushwhackin' Missouri mens be roamin' around."

"Caleb's right. It's too dangerous," Micah said.

"Fiddle-faddle! This meeting is too important for us not to go. Right, Miriam?"

"Right."

"What make it so important?" Caleb said.

"Women's rights," Miriam said.

"What rights?"

"The right to vote. The right to own property, to name two," Clare said.

Caleb shook his head at Miriam. "Girl, them's white folks' rights."

"I'm a woman."

"A black woman."

"I told Clare that, but she says denyin' folks the free speech of a vote don't make it right. Nothin' gonna change unless we change it."

"I'll tell you what changes. You show up at that meetin', and a whole lot of trouble is what changes."

"Nothin' good come easy. That's why I'm goin' to that meeting tonight. Now, pass the cornbread."

Caleb threw up his hands and passed her the bread. "What we gonna do with these two?"

Micah winked. "You stay with the girls. I'll ride shotgun for these two crusaders out to change the world."

Lawrence

They set the Eldridge House dining room in rows of chairs to accommodate the meeting. The room was full when Clare and Miriam arrived. The president of the Ladies Aid Society introduced the speaker, Clarina Nichols, editor of an abolitionist newspaper and a representative of the Moneka Women's Rights Association. A slight woman with long features of sober expression and severe bearing rose to address the assembly.

"Ladies, we gather here tonight to discuss the cause of women's rights. But more than that, we are here in the cause of equality." Her eyes roamed over the crowd, coming to rest on Clare and Miriam, standing at the back of the room.

"Ladies, we have two chairs here in the front. Please take a seat."

All eyes turned as they made their way toward the front of the room. A muted gasp rippled through the collective audience. Clare only imagined the room went chill. They found seats in the front row, nodded thanks to the speaker, and sat down.

A stir of petticoats from the back of the room suggested that some in the audience might be showing their displeasure by leaving. The speaker responded with practiced poise.

"The evils of inequality take many forms. We shall never defeat any of them, ladies, unless we stand together."

Those few moved by social mores quietly returned to their seats.

"Our quest begins by seeking franchise with the vote. It is our just voice in governance. It will not be won easily—radical reform seldom is. But we shall win our rights, for freedom and morality are with us. The vote begins the battle, followed closely by the property rights of married women. A woman and her children must never lose their home because of the loss of husband or father. We also have maternal rights to assert on behalf of our children and the schools in which they are educated." She paused, allowing the import of her words to fill the room.

"I have here with me tonight petitions advocating the basic rights of women. I ask all of you to affix your signatures thereto as a means to join the battle. By signing, you give your support to the Moneka Women's Rights Association, which shall use your authority to raise our collective voices where they can be heard to good effect. We shall gain a seat at the constitutional convention to be held this summer in Wyandotte. We may not win the whole of our cause, though we shall endeavor to that end. We can hope for some of it. But we must engage all of it with persistence. We must never waver from our holy cause until we take our rightful place in equal society with men. Now, please come forward and sign your support for this work."

She sat at a table, greeting each woman who signed. The line stretched to the back of the room. Clare was among the first to reach the table. She signed *Clare Mason.* Miriam stood at her side. Clarina Nichols caught her eye.

"Will you sign, dear?"

She hesitated, then nodded.

"Do you write?"

"I do."

She wrote *Miriam*

"Do you have a surname, Miriam?"

She shook her head.

"Then make a mark for your friend to witness."

She squared her shoulders. "Lord only knows what Caleb will say, but I do now."

"Do what?"

"Has a last name." She wrote *Madison. Miriam Madison.*

"Why 'Madison'?" Clare said.

"Mr. Madison wrote the Bill of Rights."

"So he did," Clarina said.

They left, passing a long line of approving nods.

Sycamore

"Madison. You signed 'Miriam Madison.' Where'd you get that from?"

"From a book."

"From a book. We ain't got no Madison kin."

"We do now. We got you, me, Rebecca, and any Madisons as come after us."

"I don't know. Somehow it just don't seem right."

"But it is right. That's the point. Mr. James Madison wrote the Bill of Rights to the Constitution just like I signed us on to our rights."

"Signin' don't make it so."

"It does when we win."

"Don't nothin' never keep you in your place?"

"Why should it? You wouldn't know me if it did."

"I guess I better then."

"Better then what?"

"Has you teach me how to sign 'Caleb Madison'."

Wyandotte, Kansas
July, 1859

The courtroom was spare of opulence. Sunlight reflected on wood floor. Simple furnishing sufficed. The delegates sat at tables arranged in a semicircle around a raised podium and desk to accommodate the needs of the chairman. Additional chairs were set in rows behind the delegates to accommodate the press and invited guests. A solitary gray lady sat knitting in the front row of the guest gallery, her presence haloed in window light.

James Lane approached the chair where Charles Robinson was seated, preparing to call the day's proceedings to order.

"Who is that woman? She comes here each day to sit and knit."

"She does more than knit, of that I can assure you. She listens until we adjourn for recess; then she plies her purpose. You simply haven't yet had the pleasure."

"But who is she?"

"Clarina Nichols. She represents the Moneka Women's Rights Association."

"What in hell is that?"

"That, my friend, is the voice of near a thousand women of this territory who seek to assert women's rights."

"Women's rights—what are you talking about?"

"I'm talking about the right to vote, the right to own property, and that's only the beginning."

Lane scowled over his shoulder at the woman sculpted in domesticity. "That's nonsense. Who ever heard of such a thing?"

"Don't be too quick to dismiss it, James. There is sympathetic sentiment in this assembly. We've seen the outcome of elections where we lacked a majority of right thinking people. One way to secure our interests is to enlarge the franchise to vote."

"With women?"

"Possibly."

"Risky business, I say. Give them the vote, and it won't stop there. You hear them nattering against demon rum; are you ready for that?"

"Of course not. I'm merely saying don't underestimate the power of pie."

"Now it's pie. What the devil are you talking about, Charles?"

"Pie. Every name on those petitions is signed by a woman who feeds husbands, fathers, brothers, and sons every day. Do not underestimate the power of that little lady back there with her ball of yarn. Her cause speaks with a powerful voice at near every supper table in Kansas."

Lane shook his head and set his jaw. "I've language to propose on the matter of the franchise. Permit me to introduce it at the appropriate time."

"As you wish, James."

The chamber turned warm toward late morning. Delegates fidgeted, some at growling stomachs anticipating lunch. Robinson rapped his gavel, restoring order to the proceedings.

"The chair recognizes the honorable James Lane."

Lane stepped to the podium to address the delegates, respected men of the territory all, though Democrats among them remained favorably disposed to slavery. He fully expected all could agree on this proposal, with possible exception of the gray lady quietly knitting in the first row of the gallery.

"Fellow delegates, I introduce for your consideration the following language for inclusion in the draft constitution." He read, "The franchise shall extend to all white males having attained their majority."

"Second!" someone said.

"We have a motion and a second. Discussion?" Robinson said.

"I would amend," another said. "The franchise shall extend to all white persons having attained their majority."

"We have a motion to amend. Is there support?"

"Aye!"

The debate joined, dragging through to the noon recess. "Gentlemen, the hour of our luncheon recess has arrived. I call this body into recess until two o'clock." Robinson rang down his gavel.

Lane stood at his desk to gather his papers. A light touch at his elbow begged attention.

"Mr. Lane, a word if I might, sir."

He'd half expected this. "Of course, madam."

"We've not been introduced." She offered her hand. "Clarina Nichols, of the Moneka Women's Rights Association."

"My pleasure. What can I do for you?"

"I beg your indulgence to consider the amendment to your franchise language and perhaps even to further amend it."

Lane smiled. Timid did not enter into this woman's concept of femininity. "You know, of course, that amendment would have the effect of extending the franchise to women."

"Of course I do. You must know that's why I'm here. And here with the petition support of nearly a thousand women who are citizens of this territory."

"Do you seriously believe there is sufficient support in this body to uphold such an action?"

"Perhaps not yet, but with the support of a leader such as yourself, anything might be possible."

Flattery. The woman had a flair for politics. You had to give her that. "Madam, you flatter me; but I seriously doubt this body has the appetite for so radical a departure from tradition."

"But don't you see that in time they must. It is our constitutional right."

"That interpretation escapes me. While we are indulging this discussion, you mentioned something further to the amendment. What might that be?"

"Only that the franchise might be extended to persons who have achieved their majority."

He laughed. "You would then by the stroke of a pen, enfranchise the Indian and the Black man along with their betters?"

"I would."

"Madam, your time and talents would be better spent putting up preserves for the winter rather than advocating for such foolish notions."

"The only thing foolish about such a proposal, Mr. Lane, is the blindness of those who fail to see right where there is wrong."

"Right from wrong is it, or idealistic folly from common sense? Now, if you please, I bid you good day, madam."

Chapter Thirty-Six

Lawrence
September, 1859

Clare and Miriam arrived early enough to claim seats without having to make the long march to the front of the room. The constitutional congress ended without gaining women the vote, though some accommodations were made. Tonight, they would hear what Clarina Nichols had to say on the draft constitution and the state of their cause.

The Eldridge House dining room filled slowly toward the appointed hour. The president of the Ladies Aid Society called the assembly to order and introduced Clarina. She took the podium and let her eyes wander the group, pausing to nod to Miriam.

"Good evening, ladies. When last here, I reminded you we might not win the full measure of our cause; and so we did not. We failed to win co-equal status with men under the law. Our efforts, however, were not totally in vain.

"Firstly, with your support and the weight of our numbers, we secured a seat at the proceedings. A seat we were able to use to vigorously advance your views on those matters central to our cause. While we fell short of equality, we were able to achieve some standing for women under the law as wives and as mothers. You should all take satisfaction in that.

"Now, by provisions of the constitution we have a right to own our husband's property should the need arise. The right, while regrettably limited to white women, is a start from which we should all take heart. We further achieved a voice in our children's education. We did not win the franchise to vote in all elections, but we did win the right to vote in matters of school governance. That voice, too, is a start from which to further advance our cause.

"So, we now come to the matter of ratification. The sober fact, ladies, is that our hard fought gains are not assured. The Congress itself divided over adoption of this constitution. It divided over the issue of slavery. The constitution as proposed is a partisan document divided by morality. Republicans and free-soil Democrats signed in approval. Slavery's proponents refused to approve a free-state document. It is up to our menfolk to decide the fate of the constitution in next month's election. Here, we must once again defer the franchise to husbands, fathers, brothers, and sons. While we may lack the vote, we do not want for influence where these matters are concerned. I urge you all: exert your influence in your homes and your churches. Secure approval of the Wyandotte constitution for our future and that of our children."

The room broke out in thunderous applause as the women of Kansas took to their feet. On October fourth, the Wyandotte constitution was approved by a wide margin.

Sycamore
November 1859

The wagon lumbered across a sienna sea of winter prairie grass like a giant beetle. A rumpled, woolen sky rippled east on a cutting, chill wind. Micah held the lines behind a team of twitching ears. Caleb rode the wagon box, carbine ready. With the harvest in, meat and fuel for the winter claimed their attention. Roaming buffalo herds catered to both needs. Firewood was precious scarce on the plains. Buffalo chips provided fuel for the fire and cook stove. Buffalo and deer provided meat that could be dried or frozen this time of year. Hunting trips ranged west along the river, where herds might make their way down to water. Micah drew the team to a stop on a ridge overlooking the river valley below.

"There." He pointed. "See where the grass is trampled down the ridge to the river?"

Caleb nodded.

"I'm guessin' we'll find chips along there and down along the riverbank."

"Let's get to gatherin', then. We be good at it. Last month we gather wheat. This month we turn to shit."

"To put a fine point on it."

"Ain't nothin' fine 'bout that point."

"Keep you warm in the winter."

"It do that."

"Then be grateful."

"Grateful? Grateful for shit. So be it."

Micah clucked to the team. He drove the wagon to the center of the trampled field and turned downslope before drawing a halt. He set the brake and hopped down. Shovels in hand they fanned out on either side of the wagon, gathering dried chips they loaded into the wagon box. They worked their way down the ridge to the valley below, gradually filling the wagon box. Micah noticed it first. A faint tremor in the ground.

"Caleb! You feel that?"

"Feel what?"

"The ground." The tremble grew stronger.

"They's comin'."

"I believe they are."

They took cover behind the wagon as the first shaggy brown heads bobbed over the crest of the valley wall, trotting downslope to the river. On they came, raising a dun dust cloud over their backs as the herd fanned out in greater number. The leaders reached the riverbank and waded in to drink. Others slowed behind them, browsing prairie grass as they made their way to the river.

The herd spread along the riverbank, spilling toward them. Caleb handed Micah the carbine.

"You takes the first shot. Makes sure we get one."

"They make a fine target."

"So do a barn. You takes the shot."

Micah shouldered the rifle, selected a big bull, and took aim. The carbine bucked a charge of blue powder smoke. The bull staggered, bellowed, and fell to its knees. The herd retreated away from their fallen brother without giving up the plenty of water and graze. Micah handed Caleb the rifle.

"Your shot."

He reloaded. "They ain't so close as they was."

"You're the one who said I should take the first shot."

"Don't make this shot no easier." He dropped aim on a yearling and fired. The animal squealed, wheeled, and ran from its wounded shoulder, spooking the herd nearby. "Damn!"

"Reload."

"I can't make a shot that long."

"Then we make it shorter. Reload and follow me."

Micah led the way across the valley floor to the fallen bull. They crept up behind the warm carcass. "Now you got a shot."

Caleb picked out a good-sized cow, took careful aim, and squeezed. Smoke bloomed. The cow fell. The herd retreated up the river valley. Caleb smiled.

Micah clapped him on the shoulder. "I told you, they make a fine target. Come on. We can't carry any more than that. We got some butcherin' to do. We'll head home in the morning."

Sycamore
December 15, 1859
The fire snapped and popped, sending sparks up the chimney, flavoring the parlor with savory cooking smells and pleasant, smoky scent. Clare and Miriam bustled about the stove and pantry preparing Sunday dinner. The girls played quietly in Elizabeth's room. Micah folded his copy of the *Lawrence Republican.*

"They hung him."

"Hung who?" Caleb said.

"Brother Brown."

"Over all that ruckus at Harper's Ferry?"

"Yeah." Micah shook his head. "According to the paper, the raid on the armory was a failure, but the notoriety he got for his cause may have secured moral victory."

"Hangin' be a moral victory?"

"According to the charges at his trial, he planned to free the slaves in Virginia by arming them and leading an insurrection against their masters. The plan failed when the slaves refused to rally to his side."

"He should a' knowed better."

"Why?"

"No black man gonna follow a white man agin' his massa. The minute the white man remember he's white, them Negroes be good as dead and dead in a bad way. So where do he get moral victory out a'that?"

"He said plenty at his trial and while he waited for his execution. He made his purpose God's sacred duty to right the wrong that is slavery. He stood by what he did with no regrets. He lit an abolitionist fire under God-fearin' folk in the north. He carried it off all the way to the gallows. Folks say they never seen a hanging like it. He never flinched. Marched up them steps calm as a man headed for Sunday services."

"Some ways he was."

"He's dead and gone, but the fuss he stirred up ain't nowhere near over. Folks in the south is nervous over what might come of it. They got the Democrats all riled up to blame all the abolitionist free-state talk on Republicans."

"You think them upstart Republicans might do somethin'?"

"I don't know. Democrats pretty well run things. The Republican party is new and not very strong yet. They're right about Republicans favoring free soil and abolition. Seems like Brother Brown put the fear of God in 'em."

"Den maybe the Good Lord be welcomin' him home."

Chapter Thirty-Seven

Sycamore
New Year's, 1860

It snowed New Year's Eve. Clare and Miriam trudged through blowing snow down to the dugout house. Once the house and cabin were built, they'd turned the dugout into a combination root cellar and frozen meat store. Inside Clare struck a lucifer and lit a lamp. Dressed deer and buffalo carcasses hung from the rafters. Dried, salted, canned, and pickled meat, vegetables, and fruit were stored on rows of shelves. They'd saved a fat goose, taken in late fall, to celebrate the New Year. Miriam took it down from a hook.

"You think a bird this size will thaw out by morning?" Her words went up in wisps of steam.

"He should. We'll cook him slow most of the day. He'll be just fine by supper time. How about some of these sweet potatoes?"

"Don't never have to ask Caleb twice 'bout them. I'll take some a these dried apples and boil 'em up to a pie for dessert."

"Then I'll bake the corn bread."

"My mouth's hungry already."

Clare huffed out the lamp. They climbed the bluff path into the teeth of the storm and hurried off to the warm comforts of home.

★ ★ ★ ★ ★

The storm raged outside the Mason home. Inside a cheery fire crackled, warming the hearth. The girls played, quiet mostly with their dolls in a back bedroom. Clare and Miriam cleared up the last of the supper dishes. Micah retrieved a bundle from beside the door.

"I got somehin' for you. Didn't get here in time for Christmas, but now is as good a time as any for you to have it."

"What's this?" Caleb said.

"Open it."

He took out his pocket knife and cut the twine binding the long, heavy package. The cloth sacking fell away, revealing a beautiful long gun. "I ain't never seen a gun like this afore."

"It's a Colt revolving smoothbore shotgun."

"Revolving?"

"Like a pistol with five shotgun loads."

"My, my."

"I figure this is the perfect gun for you."

"You figure I might hit somethin' with this?"

"I do. Here, let me show you." Micah took a second sack down from a peg beside the door. "You'll see once we load it."

Caleb watched as Micah measured powder and poured the charge into one of the chambers. He held up a ball.

"This here is .75 caliber." He dropped it into the chamber. Next, he counted out five smaller balls. "These are buckshot." He fed them into the chamber. "When you fire, all that shot spreads as it travels to your target. Now you got six chances to hit something, not just one."

"I like that." Caleb grinned.

"Thought you might. Next, we need to keep all that lead where it belongs." He took a square of corn husk and packed it in the chamber with a ramrod hinged to the barrel. "Now, you try."

Caleb loaded the next chamber with a little help. By the time he finished the fifth chamber, he had the procedure mastered.

"This next part is real important," Micah said. He opened a tin, axle grease by the smell of it, and filled each of the chambers to the top. "The grease keeps the powder in the one chamber from catching a charge from the chamber bein' fired. That's called a chain fire. You don't want no part of that. If it happens, the closest thing to get hit might be you."

Caleb nodded.

"This here's the last step." He held up a cap. "Fit this over the nipple at the back of the chamber like you do with the carbine, and this baby's ready to fire. Best not to add the cap until you mean to use it."

Micah handed over the shot, powder, corn patches, grease, and caps. "There's this little bit more." He handed Caleb a smaller wooden box. Inside was a tray of smaller balls and paper cartridges. "These cost more, but they're handy in a fight. The balls are .31 caliber pistol balls. Each chamber holds three. The cartridges get you powder and patch in one so you can reload faster in a fight."

"Let's hope we don't need 'em for that."

"We can hope, Caleb. We can hope, but we live in violent times. We're best off prepared. Now, you figure you can shoot that thing?"

He grinned and shouldered the gun, sighting along the barrel.

"Not that way. Hold it here." Micah moved Caleb's off-trigger hand from under the barrel to a position under the trigger guard.

"That don't feel natural."

"It's not. Ever notice the powder burn that comes off the cylinder when I fire my pistol?"

Caleb winced. "Ouch."

"Ouch is right."

North Ferry Crossing
March, 1860
Cold rain took over at midday. Thorne wished he'd chosen a different day for this errand. No good to be had for it now but to see it through like it is. The black Rogue slogged his way up stiff muddy ruts not yet given up of their frost. Thorne drew rein at the tavern rail and splashed down in a puddle. He tied off a rein and stomped mud from his boots on the boardwalk. Inside the dimly lit, smoky tavern, he shook rain off his hat and cloak, allowing his eyes to adjust to guttering lamplight. He spotted Herd at his usual table, the stub of a pipe clenched in his jaw, with Quantrill at his elbow. Good. Quantrill could be counted upon to favor his purpose. He crossed the room.

"Titus," Herd said. "Nasty day to be out and about. What brings you by here?"

"For a start, whiskey to rid my bones of this chill."

"Have a seat. You know William."

"I do." He nodded to Quantrill.

The bartender appeared with a glass. Herd poured. Thorne tossed it off for a refill. He let the whiskey burn warm his inwards.

"That's better."

"Now we got the chill put by, what brings you up here?" Herd said.

Thorne glanced around, making sure no one was in earshot. "The Mason place."

"Not that again. It didn't work out too well for me and my men last time."

"I'm not after the darky this time. Hear me out."

"Air's free."

"I want Mason burned out. I'll make it worth your while. As I recall, you got a five-hundred-dollar offer from Morgan Walker for return of those two runaway slaves. I'll give you five hundred to burn 'em out. Make it look like bushwhacker work. If you get the two of them in the bargain, you stand to make a thousand dollars."

"Hmm. What you got against Mason?"

"I want his land. By rights it should have been mine all along. He just beat me to the land office."

"When do you want this done?"

"Before his crop goes into the ground. If he can't plant, he'll have to give it up sooner or later."

Herd lifted a questioning brow to Quantrill.

"A thousand dollars would cover some lean times about now."

"Half now, half when the job's done," Herd said.

Thorne reached for his wallet.

Chapter Thirty-Eight

Sycamore
One Week Later

Caleb bolted awake to the sound of shattered glass.

"What's that?" Miriam stared, eyes wide-white.

"Trouble. Get Rebecca." He grabbed his shotgun at the bedroom door. A blazing brand rolled along the floor, spreading devastation across the wood until it crashed against the rough-cut dining table in a shower of sparks. Flames climbed the curtains on either side of the shattered window. Horses' hooves and shouts sounded beyond the cabin door. Miriam appeared at his side with a sleepy-eyed Rebecca. Choking smoke began to fill the parlor.

"Take the child to the root cellar and stay there until I tell you what to do next."

"What about the smoke?"

"You can open the cellar door a crack, but only a crack. That's our best way out of this. Now go." He crossed to the front door and opened it a crack. Muzzle flash and ball from mounted silhouettes bathed in firelight bit the door frame. Caleb dropped to one knee, brought up the shotgun, and kicked open the door. He sighted on the nearest raider and cut loose a charge behind a powder flare and plume of blue smoke. The man screamed and pitched from the saddle, dead before he hit the ground. Caleb rolled away from the door before the smoke cleared as a volley of ball answered his challenge. He scrambled to the back door as flames followed the ceiling beams toward the back of the cabin. He pulled up the trap door in the kitchen floor and descended short steps to the dark root cellar below.

"I's scared, Pa," a small voice said.

"Hush, chile. We be fine."

Clare and Micah awakened as one.

"What was that?" Clare said.

"Gunshots." Micah pulled on his britches, hitched up the suspenders, and grabbed his pistol belt off a peg beside the bedroom door. He strapped on the holster and started for the front door.

"You take Elizabeth, get down, and stay down." He paused at the door. Gunshots and shouting sounded to the south toward Caleb and Miriam's cabin. Flames danced through the trees beyond the barn. *Good God.* He dashed out the door. He no more than stepped off the porch when he saw them. Riders on the wagon road, heading toward the barn, torches bobbing in dark shadow. Micah froze. Two riders peeled away toward the barn. Others loped down the tree-lined lane toward him. *They mean to burn us out, too.*

He clambered back into the shadow of the porch and let the lead rider turn up the drive to the house. Crouching in darkness he let the dark figure close. He leveled the heavy Colt on the oncoming silhouette. The pistol bloom burst white orange in the dark. The rider's horse bolted. The wounded raider dropped his torch and toppled from the saddle, landing on the flaming brand. His coat afire, he rolled on the ground, shrieking at the flames like a rabid animal. Micah took aim at the flame and fired. The man jerked still, shrouded in burning wool.

The second rider pulled his horse up short. He fired wildly, wheeled his horse, and galloped back up the road toward the barn.

Smoke seeped through the trap door into the root cellar. Heat began to rise. They couldn't stay here much longer. Caleb lifted the outside cellar door. A muzzle flashed in the trees off to the north in the direction of the barn. The ball whined overhead. Caleb shouldered his shotgun and followed the shooter's powder smoke with a charge. A horse reared, silhouetted among the trees. The rider wheeled his mount and retreated toward the barn through tree trunks and branches painted in orange light, shadow, and smoke.

"Take the chile and hide in them trees yonder by the creek."

"What you gonna do?"

"Try an' save the stock."

"They's stock."

"They's most what we got left. Now you get on, girl, before this cabin fall down on our head." He dashed off through the trees to the barn.

Miriam grabbed Rebecca by the hand and ran from the root cellar across the yard to the shadowy shelter of the trees along the creek bank.

Hidden in the trees north of the barn, Micah watched the torch carrying rider. He leveled his Colt and fired, diving away from the muzzle flash to the base of a nearby oak. The raider returned fire, harmlessly chewing bark from the tree where he'd taken his shot. A throaty shotgun blast boomed south of the barn. *Caleb. I hope.* Micah crept forward, firing two quick shots. A second shotgun blast sent the raiders scrambling in disarray. They collected their horses and wheeled away toward the road.

"Caleb, is that you?"

"It is."

Micah dashed out of the trees into the glow of the burning barn. "Can we save the stock?"

"We can try."

Micah threw the barn door open. Heat and smoke drove him back. Flames ate at the far wall, climbing toward the loft and its hay.

Miriam gazed at the barn ablaze through the trees. She held a trembling Rebecca against her skirt. Shots popped bright flashes in dark places. Horses pranced, their riders caught specter-like in firelight. Torches arced through the air trailing showers of sparks.

"Where's Papa? Is he all right?"

"Shush, child. Your papa be fine."

"Sure he will."

The man was on her in an instant, pinning her arms in a viselike grip. Rebecca screamed. Miriam twisted in a desperate attempt to free herself. The man laughed sour whiskey breath.

"You'll fetch a fine reward for this night's work—contraband and maybe a bit of sport before we find your rightful master. Now shut that child up lest I do it for ye."

"That's Rebecca!" Caleb turned and raced south toward the sound. *One shot left, best make it enough.*

Micah plunged into the heat and smoke in the barn. He untied the cow and chased the terrified animal out the door into the corral.

Sampson brayed, wide-eyed, rearing and kicking in the stall nearest the flame. Micah opened the stall door and grasped Sampson's halter. The mule dug his front hooves into the dirt, too terrified to budge. Micah dropped his suspenders from his shoulders and pulled his nightshirt over his head. He wrapped it around Sampson's eyes.

"Easy, big fella. Come along now." He got a tentative step for his trouble, then another and another. He led the mule to the corral and released him to join the cow.

Miriam struggled in her captor's grasp. He cuffed her across the side of the head. Rebecca screamed again. The man reached for his pistol. With her child threatened, Miriam summoned an unknown reserve of strength. She twisted toward her captor and slammed her forehead against the bridge of his nose. Bone splintered gouts of blood. His grip slipped. She drove a knee into his groin. He gasped foul breath and doubled over, losing his grip. She tore herself away, grabbed Rebecca, and, blinded by tears, ran in the direction of the barn.

Caleb burst from the trees. "Are you all right?"

"He's there!" she pointed.

The man staggered to his feet, gun in hand. The shotgun blast lifted him off the ground and slammed him into a tree, his chest reduced to a bloody maw.

They stood together, bathed in firelight, watching the barn burn to the ground. Sampson, Delilah, and the cow cowered at the far end of the corral safe from the flames.

"Why?" Clare sobbed.

"It be us," Caleb said. "We be nothin' but trouble. Time we move on."

"You'll do no such thing," Clare said.

"Where we gonna live them bushwhackers ain't gonna burn down?" Miriam said.

"You'll live in the dugout 'til we get this barn and your house rebuilt," Micah said.

"We? You got a crop to put in the ground," Caleb said.

"You're wrong. *We* got a crop to put in the ground."

Caleb shook his head. "How we gonna do both?"

"With help."

"Who's gonna help a black man besides you?"

"You'll see."

Two Days Later

Thorne drew rein on the road. Smoke still rose from parts of the burned-out cabin and barn. The Mason house still stood. Herd complained he'd lost some men. The sodbusters gave them a fight. Somehow, they'd managed to save the stock, and there they were, plowing a field, the very thing he'd hoped to stop. Herd and his men did damage, but was it enough? He'd paid good money to force Mason into a sale. It was time to ride in and find out if he'd succeeded. He wheeled the black up the lane to the house and swung south to the field. Mason drew the mule to a halt.

"Good morning, Mr. Thorne."

"Mason." He stepped down. The black man stood by with a sack full of seed.

"I heard about your loss. Thought I might come by to see if there is anything I might do to help."

"That's kind of you."

"I see you managed to save your house and the stock."

"We did. The plow and reaper, too. Luckily so, and luckier still no one was hurt."

" 'Cept a few of them bushwhackers," Caleb said.

"You think it was Missouri men then."

"Had to be. No one but slavers would have call to attack us."

"I suppose that's true. These are dangerous times. If I was you, I'd be concerned they'll be back to take retribution for the men you killed."

"Did I say we killed anyone?"

"No. I . . . ah . . . just thought, from what your man there said."

"He's not my man. He's my partner."

"Well, let's get to the point. You've suffered a terrible loss here. You may still be at risk. I've expressed my interest in this land in the past; I'm still interested. With the house still standing for an improvement, I'm prepared to offer you seventy-five cents an acre. It's a fair price, generous really, and enough to buy you a fresh start somewhere safer."

"Our loss is your gain. Is that it?"

"Misfortune has a way of bringing about generosity."

"Mr. Thorne, you've expressed interest in this land before. I've told you I'm not interested in selling before. I'm still not interested. How about you, Caleb?"

"Me, neither."

"There you have it, Mr. Thorne. Thank you for your generous offer."

"Mason, you talk like this man has a say over your property."

"He does."

"How so? A black man cannot own property. This parcel is deeded to you."

"How would you know that?"

"The records are public."

"We share crop."

"You share crop."

"We do."

"I see. Then I wish you both better fortune for the future. Good day."

He mounted his horse and picked up a trot back to the road.

"Persistent feller, ain't he?" Caleb said.

"It seems so. Makes you wonder if them bushwhackers had some other reason to raid us."

"You think he'd stoop so low?"

"I don't know. He's a man accustomed to getting what he

wants. Sometimes that makes a man ruthless. We best be on our guard."

Her boughs weighed down with a heavy heart from the pain of scorched scars. So much good built, now destroyed. Still she felt the presence of the spirit. Grit, determination, purposeful resolve. Some good might yet rise from these ashes. The yoke of evil driven back for a time. Time to rebuild. Time to plant. Time to grow. Dark clouds pass from time to time. They do pass when the sun shines once more.

Chapter Thirty-Nine

Sycamore
June, 1860

They arrived by wagon, buckboard, and on horseback on a sunny summer morning. Twelve, then twenty-five, fifty by midday—able-bodied men come to rebuild what was lost. Jayhawkers led by James Lane and Doc Jennison. They came with lumber and tools and womenfolk to feed the crew. They raised the barn and framed a new cabin. Caleb and Miriam stood in awe and disbelief.

"I told you, you'd see," Micah said.

"If I didn't see this with my own eyes I never would a' believed it. All these white folks helpin' a black man."

"Good people. Some of us are, you know."

"I knowed that. I just ain't never seen so many in one place afore."

They turned to the sound of an approaching horse. James Lane rode up to the cabin building site and stepped down.

"I see the barn's raised."

"It is," Micah said. "All thanks to you and Doc and your men."

"We Kansans need to stick together. We can't let those bushwhackers get away with this sort of thing."

"Even for a black man," Caleb said.

"Even for a black man."

"I'm so much obliged, Mr. Lane."

"You'll have your chance to do your share, both of you."

"How can we help?" Micah said.

"Join the Jayhawkers. Ride with my men. This fight won't be over until one side or the other wins. Right's on our side. The men who did this to you stand on immoral ground. We mean to take that ground, blood soaked if it must be so."

"Count on me," Micah said.

Lane lifted a brow to Caleb.

"You want a black man, too?"

"Who better to rise to our cause than one who has been wronged by the enemy? You fought with Stewart at Wakarusa Creek I hear."

He nodded.

"In case you hadn't noticed, we make it our mission to free slaves when the opportunity presents itself. As their numbers grow, they will fight with us."

"Then count on me, too."

"Good."

July, 1860

Dear Ma and Pa,

It is with a sad heart that I write to tell you the misfortunes of the slavery conflict have come home to our Sycamore. Early this spring we were attacked in the night without provocation. I can gratefully report that no one of our families was hurt. The raiders, we must assume Missourians, burned Caleb and Miriam's cabin and our barn before Micah and Caleb were able to run them off.

Caleb and Miriam believe the attack was owed to their presence here. It took considerable effort to persuade them Micah and I would have no part in their leaving. Coming on the eve of spring planting as the attack did, I cannot help but wonder if the intent was to run us all off our land. If that be the case, I am proud to say they failed in their purpose. Micah and Caleb were able to plant our fields in spite of the loss.

Then last month, the most amazing thing happened. Friends and neighbors from Lawrence and beyond came to our aid. They rebuilt Caleb and Miriam's cabin along with our barn. The outpouring of community purpose was truly heartwarming. Miriam could not believe white folks would show such kindness to colored people.

So, we return to peaceful pursuits, conscious of the cloud which lingers over this community. One wonders where it must end.

Clare

Wakarusa Creek
October, 1860

Little of the Stewart compound had changed since Quantrill's last visit, save the place seemed devoid of Negroes. The infernal railway's work again. Reverend Stewart greeted him returning to the house from the barn.

"William, what a pleasant surprise. Welcome."

He stepped down and extended his hand. "Reverend, I hope I find you in good health and circumstance."

"My health is fine. There is always room to improve circumstance, if that's what you have on your mind."

"Straight to business, is it?"

"Nonsense, my boy. Time for that over a cup of hot cider beside a warm fire."

"The perfect antidote to a blustery day on the trail."

"Come in then."

They drew up chairs by a fragrant, crackling fire with cups of hot buttered cider.

"Now what brings you all the way down here at the onset of autumn?"

"Missouri hospitality."

"I'm afraid you have the advantage of me."

"The last time we spoke, you said Missouri had grown inhospitable to you. I wonder if it might be less so by now."

"It may. What have you in mind?"

"The Morgan Walker prize has yet to be taken."

"Jennison turned you down then."

"He expressed interest, but interest and action are two different things."

"So you turn to an old man of action to assist in your enterprise."

"Exactly."

"As I recall, we discussed stock, gold, and a rather large number of contraband slaves."

"Thirty by last count."

"I recall tempering temptation with judgment at the time. Times change."

"They do."

"Hmm. They do indeed."

Franklin, Missouri
November 11, 1860
David Atchison poured a steaming cup of morning coffee by the gray light of a frosted parlor window. He collected his copy of the *Missouri Democrat* and retreated to a chair by the fire. The headlines screamed.

Lincoln Edges Crowded Field
Democrat Disarray Spells Defeat

Republican Abraham Lincoln survived his electoral battle with a deeply divided Democrat field to win the presidency by a narrow margin. With the Democrats unable to achieve party unity around a position on slavery, the party splintered along regional lines over territorial rights of popular sovereignty favored in the north by candidate Stephen A. Douglas, and steadfast support for slavery in the south as advanced by Vice President John C. Breckenridge. Southern support further divided over positions taken by John Bell and the constitutional Union party. Bell's moderates sought to preserve the union and harden states' rights as favored by the majority. The divisions spelled disaster for the party and cast the future of the union into doubt.

While Republicans claim victory, they do so by the narrowest of margins. When the final vote tallies are recorded, the margin should be no more than forty percent of the popular vote. Mr. Lincoln will come to office a minority president on a platform rejected by nearly two-thirds of American voters. What remains in doubt is how the outcome will be received in the south. At very least, the future of slavery hinges on the controversial premises of the Supreme Court's decision in the matter of Dred Scott and the uncertain popular sovereignty provisions of the Kansas-Nebraska Act. That risk can only be exacerbated by Republican support for building a rail route to the Pacific, the likely central routing for which is certain to breed a progression of free states and an end to the effective balance of power in the Senate. The political strength of the abolitionist wing of the Republican party is yet to be seen, asserting its influence on the new administration. Minority or no, the Republican platform favors a legislative reversal of the Supreme Court decision. That decision was warmly received in the south for its strengthening of slaveholder rights. Should the abolitionists have their way with the law, slaveholder rights would be weakened. States that do not affirm the right to hold slaves for their own citizens may no longer be obliged to recognize the sovereign right conferred by another state. By any estimation, the outcome of this election hangs a dark cloud over the future of slaveholding in the nation as constituted. With such ominous signs in the heavens, a storm cloud of uncertainty must hang over the union itself.

Atchison set the paper aside, sipping his coffee to a smoky crackle and warm glow. The election foretold dangerous times. Douglas had proven no match for Lincoln when stripped of Democrat support in the south. The south was further divided over allegiance to the union. Secession had been little more than a whisper up to now. Things were changed by the outcome of this election, changes that in time must be felt in fundamental ways. The gangly lawyer from Illinois was embarking on a perilous journey if he sought to fashion a policy bridge over this raging torrent of division. He couldn't possibly preserve a union so hopelessly divided. The die was cast. It was now no more than a matter of time.

Chapter Forty

Jackson County, Missouri
December 10, 1860

Sun dazzling a light cover of snow did little to warm a chill winter day. Quantrill rode at the head of a horse-drawn wagon loaded with five Stewart men. Two rode the driver's box. Three wrapped in blankets huddled in the wagon bed. The county pike meandered east toward the Morgan Walker farm. Quantrill called a halt at midday in a wooded thicket a mile west of the Walker farm.

"You boys hole up here. I'll ride in for a social call to get the lay of the place for tonight."

The men climbed down from the wagon and scattered among the trees.

"No fires," Quantrill said. "I'll be back before evening." He picked up a lope down the road. A mile east he passed the Morgan Walker place and continued on to the neighboring spread. He jogged up the drive to Andrew Walker's place, Morgan's son. He drew rein and stepped down.

Andrew emerged from the barn in back of the house, wiping his hands on a smithy's apron. "William, what brings you out this way?" He extended a hand.

"I come as a friend," he said with a smile.

"Come on in. We'll take the chill off with a cup of coffee." Andrew led the way up the porch to the house. Coffee warmed on the stove. He poured two cups and carried them to a rough-cut parlor table.

Quantrill warmed his hands on the cup. "I come with a warning and at some personal risk. If I help you, I shall need your protection in return."

"Warning of what?"

"Stewart men plan to raid your father's farm."

"How do you know?"

"The reverend knows of our acquaintance. He asked my assistance."

"Hanging around those Jayhawkers was bound to lead you to trouble sooner or later."

"I suppose you might see it that way. The facts are, I've managed to enjoy some society on both sides of the border."

"By playing the ends to the middle to your advantage. What leads you to betray that side to ours?"

"Times change. With the election of that Negro sympathizer, it is time to choose a side. I believe I have more sympathies on the side of states' rights than on the side of the bloody abolitionists."

"Curious the prospect of a little blood should turn you squeamish."

"There's blood spilled on both sides. I simply feel more akin to the cause of free white men than the moralizing preachers of Negro equality."

"And so, you come to us with a warning. I should be grateful for that."

"Can I count on you to afford me sanctuary from Jayhawk retribution if I help you?"

"You may. Now when is this raid to take place?"

"Tonight."

"How many men?"

"Five, not counting me, though I shall be with them to lead them into a trap of your making."

"Tonight . . . then we shall have to move swiftly. We've neighbors we can summon to assist. Come let's ride over to Father's farm and lay our plan."

Morgan Walker Farm

When they arrived at the farm, they learned the elder Walker was away and not expected to return before evening. Armed neighbors answered Andrew's call, beginning to arrive by late afternoon. Men were stationed in an outbuilding and at the side of the house where they had clear fields of fire in the area of the front yard and porch. As the sun drifted toward the horizon, Quantrill took his leave to rejoin the raiders. Morgan Walker returned home in lengthening purple shadow. Andrew greeted him on the front porch.

"Andrew, what are you doing here?"

"Mounting a defense, Father."

"Defense for what?"

"The farm is to be raided tonight. Stewart's Jayhawks plan to free your slaves."

"How do you know?"

"A friend came in warning."

"How does this friend know?"

"He rides with them."

"He rides with them, and you call him friend?"

"He warned us, Father. He will lead them into our ambush."

"Where have you set this ambush?"

"Johnson, Taylor, and Travis are there in the shed. Mather, Jethro, and Tucker are there." He nodded to dark shadows beyond the end of the porch. "Now come inside, lest we give ourselves away."

"You've done well, Andrew. With luck, we shall kill them all."

"Not our friend. I've given my word."

"To a Jayhawker."

"He's not a Jayhawker, Father. He is a man who has traveled between the sides of this dispute. With the election of the Negro sympathizer he has taken to our side."

"Can you be sure?"

"I have his word on it. If he holds true to this plan, his life will be forfeit to the other side."

Cold rain drizzled out of a rumpled sky. The wagon creaked up the road to the Morgan Walker drive. Quantrill drew a halt. Lamp light could be seen in the windows across the front of the house.

"We'll ride on into the yard. Sedgwick, you and Dean stay with the wagon. Morrison, you'll stand guard on the porch while Ball and Lipsey accompany me into the house. We will secure the occupants and undertake a search for the gold. When the situation is under control, Lipsey and Ball will handle the stock in the barn. Make sure you saddle horses for yourselves and Morrison. When Lipsey and Ball attend to the stable, that will be the signal to release the slaves and load them in the wagon. Is that understood?"

The men nodded.

"Good. Follow me."

Quantrill led the way up the drive to the house. He drew rein a few yards from the house and stepped down. Ball, Lipsey, and Morrison scrambled down from the wagon box. Morrison took his place at the porch step while Quantrill led the others up the steps. He rapped at the door. Andrew opened in response.

"William, what brings you here at this hour?"

Quantrill raised his gun. "We've come for your Negroes. Now inside."

Andrew stepped away from the door. Morgan Walker stood in the parlor, calm in the face of three armed intruders.

"What is the meaning of this?"

"We've come for your Negroes, your stock, and your gold."

"Have you asked my Negroes if any of them wish to go with you?"

"We have. They do."

"See they are treated well. Now, if you take slaves to freedom, that would seem to satisfy your misguided moral purpose. Why must you take my stock and my money? That makes you little more than a common thief."

"Shut up, old man, and fetch the gold."

Walker pursed his lips in a frown. "This way."

Quantrill followed across a hall from the parlor to a library. Walker handed him a small chest.

"You'll find no gold in there."

"We need only the appearance. Now back to the parlor."

They rejoined Andrew and the other two raiders. "Gentlemen, have a seat." Quantrill waved Andrew and his father to a settee with his gun. He turned to Ball and Lipsey. "We have the gold. I can see to these two. Now, off you go to the stock and the slaves."

The door no more than closed behind the two raiders when the night beyond blossomed a bouquet of muzzle flash and a tympani of small-arms reports. Morrison fell dead in the volley. Ball and Lipsey bolted for the wagon, trailed by blast and ball. Lipsey went down with an agonized scream. Dean wheeled the wagon and lashed the team for home.

"Dean! Wait, man, for God's sake!" Ball cried in vain.

"Agh!" Lipsey rolled in the yard.

Ball returned to his fallen friend. "Here let me help you. Can you make it to those trees?"

Guttural groaning through clenched teeth accompanied his effort to rise.

Ball encircled the man with a supporting arm and led a labored way across the yard to the shelter of brush.

Dawn

Fog muted early morning light. Ball and Lipsey made slow progress, pausing often for Lipsey to rest or staunch a wave of pain. At length he crumpled to his knees in the ditch beside the wagon road.

"I can't go no further, Ball. You go on."

"We've come this far. We're only in need of a horse."

"Horse don't do no good." Lipsey coughed. "I couldn't ride a lick."

They hid in a thicket a short way off the road.

Morgan Walker led Andrew and his men out at first light. Quantrill rode along. Fresh blood left a trail leading west. Less than two miles from the farm it led to a thicket north of the road. Morgan Walker paused, full sun at their back.

"You figure they holed up there, Father?" Andrew said.

"Aye, that's how I make it. Spread out lest they run for it." He drew his revolver and rode on at a walk. Andrew and his men spread out in a line, advancing on the thicket. Quantrill followed the old man.

The two fugitives huddled in the undergrowth. One blood spattered and ashen. The other drew his gun and rose at the riders' approach.

Morgan Walker leveled his Colt and shot Ball in the breast.

Quantrill rode up to Lipsey and stepped down. The raider's eye lit in recognition, realization, and alarm. Quantrill cocked his gun and blew out the light. His part in the affair would remain unknown.

Chapter Forty-One

Sycamore
January 29, 1861

A warm, cheery fire crackled on the hearth, beating back bitter wind howling outside. Miriam folded the newspaper in her lap, studying her friend in thought.

"It happen just like Missa Nichols said."

"It did." Clare nodded.

"We maybe had a little hand in that, too, didn't we?"

"We did. Kansas is admitted to the Union as a free state under a constitution that gives women a voice in some things."

"It's a free state for black folks like me. 'Cept for them fugitive slave laws."

"It's a step in the right direction."

"I reckon it is. Be nice if all peoples got free. Be nice if women got even with menfolk."

"It would. These things take time. Not long ago women had no standing to own property. Now we do."

"White women do. Black folk can't own no property. Dred Scott seen to that."

"That, too, will change. All in good time, my dear. All in good time."

"Newspaper says folks in the south is upset about us havin' a free-state vote in the Senate. They say that comes on the heel of electing Massa Lincoln. Some's talkin' 'bout secs-cession."

"Secession."

"What's that?"

"They're threatening to leave the Union."

Miriam gazed at the fire. "Them slave states do that, what happen to them fugitive slave laws?"

"Good question."

"You think Massa Lincoln gonna put things to right?"

Clare shrugged. "I think he will move things in the right direction. It'll likely take time, but things do change for the right." She added a log to the fire in a shower of sparks.

"Paper says Massa Charles Robinson be our new governor and our Massa James Lane be senator now. I don't know about Massa Robinson, but them slave-state folks ain't gonna like Massa Lane much."

"Charles Robinson is a good man. James Lane . . . he'll fight for what's right."

"So it's like you say, all in good time."

"All in good time."

Lawrence
April, 1861

A grave mood lay thick and dark on Eldridge House, matching the gray skies and chill spring drizzle outside. James Lane and Charles Robinson sat hunched in conversation.

"News reports are scarce, telegrams terse," Robinson said.

"Aye, but the consequences plain enough. South Carolina has fallen. They are shelling Fort Sumter. The secession dam has broken. The south is in revolt."

"Not all as yet. The border states have yet to declare. That will be a dicey walk for Mr. Lincoln's first test. Which brings us to our neighbor."

"And now we come to your test, Governor. What of Missouri? There is no shortage of slavery sentiment there as we well know."

Robinson gazed into the fire. "Have Missourians the conviction to leave the Union?"

"That remains to be seen. Leave or not, we are bound to face another round of southern sympathies across our border."

"The president has begun calling for troops. I expect his call will come."

"My advice: make your response spare. Your counterpart in Missouri is raising a militia. His sympathies are well known. War will come to the West. When it does, westerners must be here to meet it."

"I agree, James. We must prepare. Your Jayhawks along with Montgomery and Jennison's men must organize into our militia. Then we shall be ready, should Jackson and his ruffians come to call."

"Or we pay them a call."

"I'm not the military man you are, James. Diplomacy suggests we not provoke our neighbors' southern sympathies. The bond of union may be sufficient to hold them in check."

"I defer to you in that, Governor, though I fear such thinking may prove wishful."

"It may. If it does, at least war should not be of our making."

Sycamore

For a warm spring day, a somber mood hung over Sunday supper at the Mason house. Micah carved buffalo roast and passed the platter to Miriam.

"Will it last long?" Clare asked.

"Talk is the South will be whipped pretty quick," Micah said. "I'm not so sure. With Virginia on Washington's front doorstep, the capital is threatened by the mere outbreak of hostilities. We know how stubborn slaveholders can be."

"Gonna be a bloody fight," Caleb said. "Pass the potatoes."

"We gonna have us a stake in it?" Miriam asked.

"James Lane has put out his call to the Jayhawks. He's raising a militia at Governor Robinson's request."

"Den we gotta go," Caleb said.

"Not we. Me."

"I told Mr. Lane he could count on me."

"I know you did, and you meant it. But we need you here more. We can't both go off to war. You need to stay by and take care of these womenfolk and the girls. War or no war, we still got a farm to run."

"Why me? I could just as well go an' let you stay by."

"Time may come for that but not now."

"Why, cause I'm black?"

"I didn't say that."

"I know you didn't. Not everybody thinks like you."

"So you see my point. Our women and children need a man around. It's every bit as important as runnin' off chasin' Johnny Rebs."

"Why does anybody have to go?" Clare said.

"We've known for a long time slavery was headed for bloodshed. Now it's come. The South picked this fight. Freedom lovin' folks can't just walk away. I have to go."

The table fell silent for a spell.

Clare rose. "There's apple pie for dessert."

Once more dark clouds gather on the horizon, threatening the season's tranquility. Plantings succumb to matters of worldly weight. Thunder rumbles in the east. Lightning flash sizzles. Powder burns. Plow shears set aside to favor saber and ball. Men rally to furled standards. They march. They ride. They engage in blood, death, and tears. She spread her shelter over hearth and land and hopes in prayer.

Chapter Forty-Two

Sycamore
July, 1861

James Lane galloped up the wagon road to the Mason place, trailing a dun dust cloud into a sun-washed pale-blue sky. He swung down in the yard, pushed back his hat, and mopped a sweat-soaked forehead on his sleeve. Micah stepped onto the porch, drawn by the sound of the lathered horse.

"What is it, James?"

"I'm afraid it's time, Micah. Missouri militia clashed with the federal garrison at the St. Louis Armory. The Missouri legislature has declared a state of emergency. Governor Jackson has called out the Missouri Guard and placed Major General Sterling Price in command. General Nathaniel Lyon, federal commander in Missouri, has called for volunteers. He's preparing to march south to put down the rebellion."

"That sounds like a Missouri fight."

"If only it were. We know, given the chance, those bushwhackers will turn on Kansas. We already hear reports that Confederate forces under General McCulloch are marching north to support Price. This is the beginning of the war in the West, and it starts with a Confederate land grab. Governor Robinson has commissioned me to organize a Kansas brigade. I'm calling out my men, as are Jennison and Montgomery. Are you with us, Micah?"

"I am."

"Good. We rally in Lawrence in two days' time for the march east to join General Lyon. Now, if you've water for my horse, I must be off to call the rest of my men."

Lawrence

Micah sat at Lane's side astride a long-legged bay gelding Lane loaned him after appointing him his aide. He surveyed the ragtag formation drawn up on a steamy summer morning. Fifteen hundred strong, the Kansas brigade stood ready to ride. Micah knew little of military training and tactics, but to call these recruits "irregulars" seemed more than too kind. Still, they assembled in high spirits embellished by noble purpose, confident they would be victorious under the command of General James Lane.

"Are we fit for battle, General?"

Lane lifted a thick brow. "Perceptive question, Micah. If you ask me as a dispassionate observer, I say no. If you ask me as their commanding officer, I say they better be. Let's ride."

Ride they did. One-hundred-seventy-five miles southeast to join Lyon's column five days later at Lebanon, northeast of Springfield.

Morristown, Missouri
July, 1861

Jennison paced the thicket like a caged animal. His men lounged among the trees, smoking, dozing, or talking softly. He sent an advance man into town to give him the lay of the place. All he had to show for it thus far was sweat, air thick with humidity, and biting flies. Pacing shed his frustration and gave pretense to keeping the flies at bay. He'd been warned not to ride into Morristown blind. Price was known to be farther north, but persistent reports said Confederate forces were moving north to support him.

Movement on the road to town brought him up short. A rider trotted up the road. Finally, some word to report. The man known only as Ames drew rein and stepped down.

"They's there, Cap'n. Regular reb cavalry looks company strength. Likely an advance of the larger force we keep hearin' about."

"No more than a company?"

"If they's any more, they got 'em hid good."

Jennison gave a sardonic smile. "Where are they?"

"The green on the town square makes a natural campground for horses and men. I expect the officers is billeted in the hotel on the square."

"All right, boys, saddle up."

Jennison divided his men into three columns, approaching the town from the north, east, and west. Rebel pickets sounded the alarm, firing and falling back. The town square exploded in a frenzy as troopers scrambled to horse. Jennison led his column into town from the north. They encountered rear-guard resistance from reinforced pickets retreating house to house toward the square. His rear element rounded up livestock, food, and munitions, torching the town as they followed the captain's advance to the town square.

The east and west columns halted at their respective edges of town, awaiting the rebel retreat. The Confederates mounted, abandoning stores, tents, and bedrolls. The commander led his men south out of town, signaling Jennison's east and west columns to close on his retreat.

The north column secured the town center and rounded up elements of the rear guard abandoned in retreat. They continued sacking, looting, and burning the town until the east and west columns returned from routing the Confederate main body.

"What'll we do with the prisoners, Captain?" The scout Ames spoke.

Jennison scratched his chin. "Seems like these folks meant to give shelter to rebels. I 'spect we should oblige 'em. Have the prisoners dig a trench there on the green. Make sure it's big enough they all rest in peace."

The prisoners dug their ditch. Jennison ordered them lined up beside it and shot.

Harrisonville, Missouri
One Week Later

They stood huddled in the town square, the heat of a warm summer night intensified by the inferno enveloping their homes and businesses. Orange light rendered the scene a hellish pageant in leaping flame, dancing, dark shadows, and towering billows of smoke. Mounted raiders galloped to and fro up and down the street. Men on foot carried armloads of plunder from homes and buildings not yet torched, piling it in wagons taken from those being looted.

"Damned Jayhawkers!" someone shouted.

"Worse than that," said another. "Some of them is black men."

"The slaves is risin'! Lord a' Mighty, save us."

"Ain't their own doin'. That hellion Doc Jennison done freed 'em."

"Armed 'em, too."

"It's the work of Satan his-self."

"Hades has been visited on Harrisonville. May God have mercy on us all."

Lebanon, Missouri
August 5th

Lane halted the column on a ridge overlooking the road south. He drew out his glass and fitted it to his eye, inspecting the column further north on the road. Blue coats. He snapped the glass closed.

"It's Lyon, or an advance element of Lyon. We've caught them in time. We best not ride in on him unannounced. With no unit colors or uniforms he's as likely to take us for bushwhackers as friends. Micah, ride on down there and meet the column. Offer the general my compliments and the services of the Kansas brigade."

"Yes, sir." Military order still felt strange on his tongue. He nudged the bay down the ridge to the road.

"Dismount!" echoed behind.

He loped up the road to the north. The column drew a halt at his approach. He raised a hand in greeting and drew rein.

"General James Lane of the Kansas brigade sends General Lyon his compliments. Might you direct me to him?"

"You found him."

The intense man with fire in his eye seemed young for a general officer. Micah gave his best effort at a salute. "The general's compliments, sir. The Kansas brigade awaits your pleasure on that ridge yonder."

"Very well. Invite the general and his troops down to the road. We can discuss our coordination from there."

"Yes, sir." Micah picked up his salute and wheeled away at a gallop.

Chapter Forty-Three

Wilson Creek
August 9, 1861

Cicadas serenaded a camp at rest. Fireflies winked in the black void beyond the perimeter. Night air hung heavy like a sweat-soaked sheet. Micah stood at Lane's shoulder. The two generals hunched over a crudely drawn map spread out on a camp table. Lamplight lined their features in shadow. Sweat trickled down his chest and stung his eyes. He wondered what the two would make of it. The situation as described by the reconnaissance patrol sounded grim. They were outnumbered nearly two to one. Price's volunteers were ragged and raw, much like the Kansas brigade. The Confederate regulars under General Ben McCulloch were another matter. Lane broke the silence.

"Any word from General Fremont?"

"None."

Lyon's terse response was laced with contempt. Lane described the general's frustration with his commander the day after they joined Lyon's column. Despite Lyon's repeated requests for munitions and reinforcements, the Union commander in the west, General John C. Fremont, ignored the plight of his Missouri command as he basked in the glow of his own self-assured celebrity.

"Does he not understand? If Price takes Springfield, Missouri may fall to the Confederacy. If that happens, Kansas and the western theater cannot be far behind," Lane said.

"The fop can't see beyond his own glittering behind. If the West is to be saved, it falls to us to do it," Lyon said. He bent over the map, studying the dispositions.

"Price is the weakness." He traced the line. "He is dug in and fortified on Oak Hill, but his men are ill equipped and unprepared. He's vulnerable to a flanking maneuver. If we strike his soft belly hard, we may put them to flight."

"A gambit such as that risks all. Might it not be prudent to fortify Springfield and hold it until Fremont or some clear-thinking head comes to his senses?"

"We haven't the troop strength or munitions to hold it long. I wager we couldn't even withdraw given the strength of McCulloch's cavalry. Our only hope for victory is a successful attack. I'll send Seigel's Dutch to the flank. When they strike, we shall assault the hill. If we break Price, I doubt McCulloch will commit his cavalry against the high ground."

Lane bunched his brows. *High stakes.*

August 10th

Sigel's Dutch struck Price's left like a lightning bolt released in the morning fog. Lyon and Lane fixed glasses on the advance.

"Skirmishers and small-arms fire. Sweet sound," Lyon said.

"Sweet sound?"

"The absence of cannon."

"They're emplaced on our path."

"Look there." Lyon pointed. "They've broken through. The rebs are pulling back up the ridge." He snapped his glass closed. "James, I'll take the point with two infantry brigades. You hold here until we breach the breastworks. That will be your signal to charge the breach and secure the route."

Lane nodded.

Lyon swung into his saddle.

★ ★ ★ ★ ★

The throaty rumble of six-pound, smooth-bore howitzers greeted Lyon's advance. The ground shook with the impact of shot; gaping holes opened in the Union line. Lane swung his glass over the Oak Hill breastworks. Powder smoke marked out six battery emplacements. The line filled in the gaps and surged up the hill.

On the right, Sigel's advance slowed. Lane's glass revealed a breakdown in unit discipline. Men stopped their advance to rifle the possessions and pockets of the fallen.

"What the hell is he doing?"

Micah heard alarm. "Who, sir?"

"Sigel. The fool's advance is breaking down with the enemy in retreat."

Another cannon volley summoned Lane's glass to Oak Hill. Men dropped to the ground. Gouts of earth and bloody clots of gore rained down. Lyon exhorted them. They rose and continued the ascent.

"It won't be long now," Lane said.

The air split on the clarion call of a bugle. The banshee howl of rebel yell rose on a thunderous cavalry charge. The Stars and Bars wheeled around the Oak Hill far slope; chestnut, bay, black, and gray, the horde bore down on Sigel's exposed flank. The beleaguered general attempted to form a skirmish line. Too late. The cavalry overrode his position, scattering the Dutch line in disjointed retreat.

Lane swung his glass back to Lyon. They'd soon breach the breastworks.

"To horse!" Lane ordered.

The Kansas brigade scrambled to their mounts.

"Column of two's." The command echoed down the line.

"Forward!" Lane spurred his horse. He led the column at a gallop up the slope.

Micah held his mount on Lane's flank. He drew his Colt. His gut and knees turned liquid. Ahead on the summit a blue haze of small-arms and artillery smoke hung like a pall over the crest of the hill. The breastwork erupted in another thunderous roar. Incoming ball screamed in his ears, falling short and long in thunderous eruptions of dirt and stone. The column climbed through fallen bodies and carnage of uncertain provenance.

The infantry charge reached the rebel lines. Lyon urged his men on, visible by the red plume on his hat and the flash of his saber. Frozen in a moment, he turned, red gore at his breast. Lyon fell as McCulloch's cavalry wheeled toward the Union right flank. A brigade commander called retreat.

Lane wheeled his column right, sealing McCulloch's left. The Kansas brigade harassed the rebel cavalry, covering the infantry withdrawal down Oak Hill.

Price's men rose to cheer their victory. They showed no sign of pursuit. In truth, they were all but out of ammunition. McCulloch reined in his men, allowing the Kansans to cover the Union infantry retreat toward Springfield.

With no pursuit, the Kansas brigade rear-guard action followed the remnants of Lyon's infantry and Sigel's Dutch into the capital.

Springfield

The remains of Lyon's command turned to the daunting task of fortifying the capital under direction of the surviving brigade commander. Lane watched the hasty construction of breastworks with Micah at his side.

"They've no chance to hold it without relief," he said as much to himself as his aide.

"Surely Fremont will reinforce us."

"He's shown little inclination before despite Lyon's continual pleading. If relief is coming, it should be on its way by now.

With no word of that, I can only conclude anything now would amount to too little too late. No, I'm afraid Springfield is doomed to fall to the Confederacy and with it the whole of southern Missouri."

"Then what?"

"Therein lies the crux of the matter for Kansans. Price will need time to regroup and resupply, but, once done, his rebel overlords will order him into the West. That means our homeland, Micah. We must play the board one move ahead."

"What do you mean to do, sir?"

"Withdraw to Fort Scott and prepare to meet the assault."

Fort Scott
Kansas Territory

With the outbreak of war in 1861 the old fort found its way back to military service. Built and garrisoned in the '40s and early '50s, Scott provided a strategic outpost to confront Indian hostilities for explorers and settlers on the way west. Abandoned to civilian purposes in 1854, Lane and the Kansas brigade established headquarters there following their withdrawal from Springfield. In August, a courier arrived with word of the inevitable.

"General Lane, General Fremont sends his compliments." The courier held his salute. Lane returned it. He handed over the courier pouch. "Shall I await the general's reply?"

"Thank you, Corporal, that will be all for now."

"Very good, sir."

Micah showed him out.

Lane opened the case, unfolded the dispatch, and settled in at his cluttered desk. He skimmed over the flowery, imperial salutation and cut straight to the meat of the message. He refolded the order, giving thought to his reply.

"Anything the matter, sir?"

"Springfield has fallen. Fremont expects Price is preparing to march west. We are ordered to engage and stop the advance."

"As part of a larger defensive force?"

Lane cast a wry, sidelong glance. "Apparently, no. It would seem from the general's lofty perch, we should be all the defense necessary."

"He can't be serious. We engaged Price at four times our current strength and still were outnumbered two to one."

"I wish it were a joke, Micah. I'm afraid the old popinjay remains blinded by his own fawning press and self-glorification. It seems it is our turn to toe Lyon's line."

"How will you respond, sir?"

"Not as I should like, for all the good that did poor Lyon. We shall do our duty as ordered. The question is how?" He stood and crossed the room to a large map on the wall. He fingered the stubble on his chin, tracing a line from Springfield to Fort Scott. He paused at Drywood Creek.

"There. Micah, I need couriers to summon Jennison and Montgomery. They both have a dog in this fight. Reprisal for Jayhawk raids no doubt enters the blood in Price's thinking. I need them here, prepared to march as soon as they are able."

"That will help, sir, but even with their men can we possibly defeat such a force?"

"I don't intend to defeat Price, Micah; I intend to turn him."

"I'm afraid I don't understand, sir."

"Since General Fremont seems content to sit his ass above the fray while he lets others do his fighting for him, perhaps we can engage him if the fighting comes closer to his regal tail feathers."

"Now I know I'm a simple farmer."

"We are going to give General Price a bloody nose and leave him a clear road north."

"But doesn't that risk an even greater prize?"

"Perhaps. But the risk is no greater than asking a force as overmatched as ours to secure defense of the entire western theater. If we can turn Price north, Fremont will be forced to consider his part in joining a defense of the west. Now get me those couriers and a reconnaissance patrol to scout the road east. The first order of business is to find Price."

Chapter Forty-Four

Drywood Creek
September 2, 1861

Lane spread his line in the wood and scrub along the creek bottom southeast of the ford, flanking Price's line of march. He posted Montgomery's cavalry west of the ford at the point with a heavy mountain howitzer. The Missourians would cross a broad grassy plain, approaching Drywood Creek. They'd allow the advance element to cross the creek before driving them back with the big gun and Montgomery's assault. Lane hoped to create the illusion of a superior force. Montgomery would strike from across the creek, pressing Price's column from the south. Lane and Jennison would form the main body, disguising their inferior numbers by the trees and undergrowth screen along the creek bottom. Cover, surprise, and rapid-fire Sharps carbines must carry the day. If they could make Price believe he faced a superior force, his relief lay to the north. They waited.

The column appeared in the distance at midafternoon, winding its way to the creek. Montgomery studied the line that seemed to progress without end. In fact, Price's Missouri guard had grown in strength since Wilson Creek, now numbering nearly twelve thousand. As the length of the column grew in his glass, the size of the task grew evermore daunting. When at last advance elements spilled over a low ridge into the shallow creek bottom, Montgomery cast the die.

"Is the gun primed?" Mongomery inquired of his second.

"On your order, sir."

"Very well." He let the advance party cross the creek to the wagon road west. Thirty he reckoned, enough for his purpose.

"Fire!"

The howitzer thundered and smoked. The ball screamed hellish warning before shattering the Missouri column at the base of the valley wall.

Montgomery's cavalry stormed out of the trees, charging east down the wagon road and flanking the crossing from the south. The Missouri advance broke in retreat across the river, pursued by volley of howitzer ball and grape to the thunder of cavalry charge.

Price rallied his column to halt retreat from the creek bottom at the foot of the valley wall. The howitzer pounded the withdrawal, scattering undisciplined formation.

With Price's left flank exposed, the wood and scrub along the creek bottom erupted in sheets of small-arms fire. The Missourians were caught in the open with little cover save tall prairie grass.

Montgomery trained his glass on the defenses forming on the slopes above. He smiled as they wheeled up a battery of six-pounders. He passed his glass to his gunnery officer. The officer returned the glass with range and elevation orders to his men. The first Rebel gun disappeared in gouts of dirt and smoke before it could reload a second targeting shot. The other two soon followed.

Small-arms volleys raked the hillside and wooded creek bottom. Despite their numbers the Missourians were armed with older muskets and shotguns that lacked the range and firepower of the Kansans' arms.

As the sun began to sink in the west, Montgomery considered the need for a timely withdrawal.

Price, of a similar mind, thought better of the cost he might incur dislodging such entrenched opposition. He couldn't fully assess the enemy's strength, but he knew his own lack of firepower. He turned north to the promise of softer prizes.

Sycamore

Dear Ma and Pa,

It has finally come to war. We prayed it would not, but, in our hearts, we feared the worst. The governor has called out the militia in response to provocations in Missouri. I write to tell you Micah has joined the Kansas brigade. He is serving as aide to General James Lane. I pray he will not be exposed to the fiercest fighting, though I know war is uncertain. Caleb agreed to stay behind, so Elizabeth and I are well protected.

Our crop is in the ground, so with good weather we should be fine for the season. We hope and pray Micah will be home by harvest time. More so, I pray for his safety.

Clare

Thorne drew rein. Golden afternoon light spread over the ripening fields. Such a handsome crop would fetch a fine price if they could get it out of the fields. It struck him as a daunting task for one Negro and two women. She'd refuse his offer, of course, unless he might play on her fears. Yes, that was it. He kneed his mount up the wagon road to the house. He passed the Negro's wife returning to her cabin without acknowledgement.

Miriam watched him step down. *Now what deviltry is that man up to?* She hurried on her way.

Clare stepped out on the porch, drawn to the sound of horse and rider.

"Good afternoon, Mrs. Mason."

"Mr. Thorne. To what do we owe your call?"

"Might you have a drink of water for a thirsty traveler?"

"Dipper's there by the bucket. Fresh drawn this noon." He found his way to his drink. *He didn't stop to slake his thirst.*

Thorne wiped his chin on a linen kerchief. "I heard your husband is riding with Lane. The reports from Wilson Creek set me to wondering if you'd had word of him."

"What reports?"

"Heavy fighting, casualties, I understand our Kansas boys were there in the thick of it."

She winced at his words. "I've had no word. I'm sure Micah is safe. He rides as General Lane's aide."

"Yes, I suppose he would be fine then, though General Lyon fell in the final assault."

"Mr. Thorne, what bearing does any of this have on your visit? Am I to believe it is purely out of concern for my husband's well-being?"

"It does after a fashion. You've a fine crop in the field, Mrs. Mason. It would be a shame to see it perish for lack of harvesting. I am prepared to add a fair price for the crop to my offer for the purchase of your land. It's a handsome proposal. You receive the value of a crop you can't possibly harvest along with the price of your land. You and the child would be well provided for should something untoward have befallen your husband."

"That is the most despicable suggestion I've ever heard. Have you no scruples? Playing on the possibility of misfortune where there is none. Worse yet, seeking to do so at the expense of a man fighting to protect your holdings in this state. Now, I'll thank you to get off my property."

"I wouldn't be too hasty, Mrs. Mason. You are one telegram away from losing everything here. I am merely trying to point out the uncertainty of your situation and offer you safe passage to the future."

"Get out!"

"Now let's not get emotional. Perhaps you need a little time to think, a little time to see reason. I'm a patient man."

"You heard the lady. She said get out."

Thorne turned.

Caleb stood by, shotgun cradled in the crook of his arm.

"And what business might this be of yours, boy?"

"Family business."

"Family business? Do you always allow such uppity behavior, Mrs. Mason?"

"Caleb, Miriam, and Rebecca are family, Mr. Thorne. Micah asked Caleb to look after things while he is away, and that is precisely what he is doing. Now, good day to you." She turned on her heel and went back in the house.

"My advice is you be careful where you point that thing, boy. This ain't over by a long shot. You best be careful you don't wind up low hanging fruit."

"You pick you poison however you like, Thorne. You pick mine, I be happy to oblige." He shifted the Colt to his right hip, muzzle to the sky.

Thorne swung into his saddle with an angry scowl and wheeled away down the road.

Caleb watched him go. He cocked an ear to the house as Miriam turned into the yard.

"What's he want?"

"The usual trouble makin'. I can look after him. You best see to Clare. I think he said somethin' to upset her."

Miriam climbed the porch and entered the house. Clare sobbed beside the dining table. She crossed the room and put a comforting hand on her friend's shoulder.

"Say now, what's all the fuss here?"

Clare turned to her arms. "Thorne talkin' like Micah might be killed."

"That man don't know nothin' but mean."

"I know. The thought he might be hurt or worse is never far

from my heart. I keep it where it belongs unless someone throws it up in my face."

"There, there, girl. You said it yourself. The man don't know nothin'. He's just tryin' to scare you into what he wants. You ain't gonna give in to him, is you? No. You's gonna fight."

Clare nodded into her friend's tear-stained dress. "You're right." She sniffed and wiped her nose. "I shouldn't let him upset me so."

"It's only natural with your man off to war. He'll be fine and be comin' home soon."

"I pray you're right. I do pray you're right."

"Oh, I'm right enough. Miriam knows things."

"You do, don't you."

Chapter Forty-Five

Osceola, Missouri
September 23, 1861

Price marched north. Lane's Kansas brigade trailed behind at a safe distance, obedient to Fremont's order without risk of engaging the enemy. Fremont would have to climb down from his throne long enough to mount his own defense. All unfolded according to Lane's plan until they approached the outskirts of Osceola.

A messenger from the column's advance guard galloped down the road toward the main body. Lane drew a halt. The rider slid to a stop.

"Rebs, sir. Flanking the road into town."

"Can you determine their strength?"

"No, sir. We didn't take heavy fire. No cannon."

Lane scratched his chin. "Likely a thin rear guard or maybe a token force intended to turn us away from Osceola. Osage River port makes a handy supply depot. Also makes us a fat prize. Tell the men up front to hold their position. We'll hit 'em in force to see what they've got."

The column advanced on the town. The skirmishers withdrew, offering no further resistance. The town lay before them, peaceful and sleepy on a late summer afternoon. A prize ripe for picking.

"Spread out. Every available wagon to the warehouses on the wharf," Lane said.

They marched through town, commandeering wagons drawn by horses, oxen, and mules. They liberated warehouses at the wharf of useful goods, food stuffs, powder, shot, and kerosene . . . these the legitimate spoils of war.

Men began to slip away into town. Looting began quietly enough. The first fire started as though it might be an accident. Others followed. Micah waited for the general to put a stop to it. He didn't. A vision of his own barn and Caleb's cabin burned in his mind's eye. It didn't seem right. This was the work of border ruffians. Jennison and Montgomery were known to employ such tactics. He hadn't approved of those reports, but they spoke of distant events and anonymous places. Osceola was here and now. He had a hand in it, if by no more than standing aside.

The town burned. Smoke blackened the sky. The nobility of battle for a just cause turned ugly drenched in soot and ash.

It started as a trickle down dusty roads. Day by day it grew to a steady stream. Tributaries swelled to a dark river of humanity. Slaves, escaped from their masters, poured into the Kansas brigade ranks.

"They only make more mouths to feed, General," the sergeant said, shadowed in campfire light.

"He's right, sir," Micah said. "What's to be done about it?"

Lane sipped a cup of coffee. "We can't send them back. We don't have weapons enough to arm them even if we had time to train them in their use. They only know field work."

"We've got crops in the fields back home. They'll need harvesting soon enough," Micah said.

"We do, don't we. Seems like trading one master for another."

"There's a difference, sir. This time we ask them. If they do so, it is of their free choice."

"It is, isn't it?"

"It is."

They assembled the following morning. A ragtag band formed loosely in ranks. Hopeful faces glistened in the heat awaiting instructions. Lane sat astride his horse before them, the better to be seen and heard.

"Men, we welcome your support to our just cause. You have taken your freedom. Now it is up to you to put it to good purpose. We know you are prepared to fight with us. We applaud your courage. Unfortunately, we lack the arms and the time needed to train you to that purpose. What's more, armies march on their bellies. We live off the land barely able to feed ourselves. Your number is more than we can reasonably provender. You cannot come with us. You are free to go where you will and engage in purposes of your own choosing. For those of you who wish to help, I can tell you the men of this brigade left their homes with crops in the field. Those crops will soon need harvesting. You know that work. Should you choose to undertake it, we will provide you with a guide to take you to Kansas territory. How many are with us?"

A chorus of cheers went up in reply.

Lane nodded.

They marched west that morning, a relief column to the fighters' fields. Gone by choice in rebellion against the task master's command.

Sycamore
October, 1861

Two black men stood in the front yard, scarecrow thin, clothes hanging in tatters. Clare stepped out on the porch with a quick glance up the wagon road toward Caleb and Miriam's place. She saw Caleb coming down the road. Her anxiety eased.

"Can I help you?"

"We be hopin' to help you," the taller one said. "General Lane sent us to help with the harvest."

"He did, did he?" She smiled.

Caleb turned into the yard. "What these boys want?"

"Help with the harvest. James Lane sent them."

"Well I'll be. That solve a problem, now, don't it?"

"It does. One I doubt Mr. Thorne will appreciate. Caleb, why don't you show these men to the barn while I stir up a hot meal for them. They look like they could use it."

"You boys got names?"

"This here's Jethro," the taller one said. "I go by Joseph."

"I'm Caleb. That fine lady is Mrs. Mason."

"You the overseer?"

"We don't have overseers here. Just owners."

"You the owner?"

"Own some. The barn ain't much. Best we got just now."

"We ain't used to much."

"That'll make you feel right to home then."

Clouds of war brushed aside on a brisk autumn breeze. Freedom tended to her fields at harvest. They cut and raked and bundled. They loaded the wagon for the drive through the shade of her boughs to the river. Day by day, field by field, the work of the season completed. She turned out her finest color in pride and gave up a few leaves in farewell to the barge.

Jackson County, Missouri
October, 1861

They met at Andrew Walker's home on a blustery fall evening. A crackling fire warmed the chill with help from a jug of corn liquor passed freely. Firelight cast the parlor in an eerie, shadowy glow. The scent of wood smoke mingled with clouds of tobacco.

"It ain't right," Andrew said. "Somethin's got to be done to stop them damn Jayhawkers from raidin' our farms and terrorizin' our womenfolk."

Heads nodded around the solemn assembly that included Quantrill, Cole Younger, Frank James, and Bill Anderson.

"What do you figure we should do, Andrew?" Younger said.

"Fight fire with fire. The good book says, 'An eye for an eye.' Them damn Yankee sympathetics got no less comin'."

"We can all agree on that. That's what the governor appointed a militia for," James said.

"Where the hell are they, then?" Andrew said.

Quantrill spoke up. "Price nips at Fremont's heels and runs clear to Arkansas to hide behind a Confederate skirt. He figures he's wagin' war."

"That don't do us no good," Anderson said.

"No, it don't. Andrew's got a point. If anything's to be done for us, it'll be up to us to do it," Quantrill said.

"Then you best tell us what to do, William," Younger said.

"That's right," James said. "You got military experience to go with all that book learnin'. You be captain of the outfit, and we'll follow your lead."

Walker and Anderson nodded agreement.

"All right, boys, if that's how you want it, I shall take your captaincy and consider it an honor. We'll need more men, of course . . . horses and munitions, too."

"Bill and me can recruit good men," James said.

"Pa and I got horses. Cole can help too, I reckon," Walker said.

Younger nodded.

"Let's get to it, then. I'll start sniffin' for targets while we see what you boys come up with."

January, 1862

They gathered again, huddled around Andrew Walker's hearth, fending off a bitter cold. Outside a light snow fell, swirled on a light northerly wind.

"Fifteen capable men," Frank James reported.

"More will come when we show some success," Bill Anderson said.

Quantrill turned to Andrew. "What about horses?"

"I'd say we can mount them as needed."

Cole Younger nodded agreement.

"You come up with a target yet, William?" Andrew said.

"I believe I have. One that will serve a number of our purposes. We have a nest of Yankee sympathy in our midst we'd do well to make an example of."

"Independence," Anderson said.

"Aye, Independence. It's a prize that's ours for the taking. It will attract others to our standard and fill our need for arms, powder, and ball. Are ye with me?"

"Aye," said all around.

Chapter Forty-Six

Independence, Missouri
February 22, 1862

Morning fog shrouded the river town known to harbor Yankee sympathies. Quantrill and his raiders struck in a dawn fury of muzzle flash and powder smoke. The town retreated within itself as fifteen marauders stormed the central square from the east. Looting had little more than begun when federal cavalry entered the square from the northwest. They appeared out of the fog as a dark apparition pricked in powder flash and small-arms reports.

The counter attack caught Quantrill and his men by surprise. The raiders met the enemy charge with a volley of pistol fire as they scrambled to their horses. Quantrill wheeled away out of town on Spring Branch Road, with his men strung out behind and the federals in full firefight pursuit. The raiders pounded down the road, creating some distance from the Yankee regulars. Quantrill drew rein by the side of the road, waving his men to scatter.

With the last of his command gone by, he put spur to flank as a federal ball took his horse from under him along with a piece of his flesh. His horse went down hard, pitching him into a roadside ditch. He crawled into the undergrowth and scrambled up an embankment to the cover of some boulders. The Yankees stormed past in the heat of the chase.

The raiders' superior mounts pulled away from the regulars,

and in practiced guerilla tactic they melted into the countryside to regroup once the danger had passed.

Quantrill bound his wounded leg with a strip of cloth torn from his blouse. Left afoot, he walked to the home of a nearby sympathizer, where he sought shelter. He was soon joined by Bill Anderson, Cole Younger, and a few of their men. They set out pickets and took supper.

"Cursed luck, be those Yankees close by," Anderson said.

Quantrill nodded. "Did we lose any men?"

"I saw two fall besides yourself," Younger said. "Won't know if they are wounded or lost until we rally back to the Walker farm."

"And the Yankees?"

"Hard to track smoke in a wind."

"Good."

Younger collected the plates.

"Let's get some rest. We can return to the Walkers' in the morning."

10:00 PM

A soft glow of moonlight seeped through a rumpled blanket of cloud. The house stood in dark shadow.

"Quiet as a church yard, Capt'n." The civilian scout's words floated on the chill night air in soft puffs of steam.

"I can see that. You think they lit here?"

He spit a dark tobacco stream. "No way to know for sure. Quantrill's known to take comfort from sesesh sympathizers. This place be one of 'em."

"All right, then, let's have a look. Sergeant, form a line. Encircle the house. Port arms. Forward at a walk. I shall approach the front door."

Dark-blue shadows fanned out, arms ready, horses breathing a light, steamy fog. They moved forward on the creak of saddle leather and the soft jangle of bridle brass.

The captain rode ahead, crossing the yard to the house. He stepped down. The porch step gave out a mournful groan in greeting. He drew his heavy Colt dragoon, using the butt to rap sharply on the door.

"United States Cavalry, open up!"

Muffled scuffle sounded inside.

"Who's there?"

"United States Cavalry, open up."

"That's what I thought you said."

A section of the door exploded in a powerful blast, the ball narrowly missing the captain. He ducked low outside the door frame.

"Throw down your arms, Quantrill, and come out with your hands up. I have the house surrounded."

"Barricade the doors and windows, boys," came the muffled reply.

"Suit yourself, Quantrill." The captain swung into his saddle and returned to his line. "Fire at will!"

The Union perimeter erupted in a volley of muzzle flash and smoke.

The guerillas returned fire with heavy-gauge shotguns and revolvers.

"This is your last chance, Quantrill. Throw down your arms and come out, or I'll burn the place down around your worthless neck."

The raiders responded with yet another volley.

"Sergeant, fire detail. Burn it down."

Three men fanned out across the front of the house with lit kerosene lamps.

"Covering volley!" the sergeant shouted. "Fire!"

The men dashed forward behind a wall of ball and smoke. The man closest to center went down in return fire. The man on the left threw his lamp from afar. It fell harmlessly short, spreading a pool of flame in the yard. The man on the right made a mighty throw, dove into the dirt, and rolled away from the ensuing shooters. His lamp arced toward the log cabin wall. It shattered, spreading flame across the right face of the house.

"Time's on our side now, Quantrill."

"They sure 'nuf got it lit," Younger said.

"We best find a way out." Quantrill headed for the back of the house.

Smoke seeped through the window frame, chinks in the logs, and under the door.

"Back here, boys!"

Younger, Anderson, and the rest scrambled away from their posts to the back of the house.

Quantrill held up a lamp beside a trapdoor. "This leads to a storm cellar. There's a second door outside. Shotguns first. You boys lay down fire. The rest of us follow. Cross the yard to the woods and scatter. We rally at the Little Blue headwaters campsite. Spread the word."

The men nodded. Those toting shotguns climbed down the hole.

The ground threw open with a heavy, wooden thud. Shotgun blasts flared into the darkness. Horses bolted, shattering the thin Union line behind the cabin into disarray. Quantrill's guerillas poured out of the ground and scattered into the woods. The Union cavalry fired wildly at shadows backed by the orange glow of firelight. Muzzle flashes peppered their ranks as fleeing guerillas paused to cover their escape.

The night turned still, save the crackle of flames eating at the cabin timbers. The scout sent an orange tinged black stream to the ground, chuckling to himself. *Blue coats ain't never gonna find them boys in their home wood.*

Chapter Forty-Seven

Franklin, Missouri
July, 1862
David Atchison stepped onto the porch fronting his spacious home. He filled his lungs with morning air, a fresh prelude to the heat of the day. Birdsong floated on a soft breeze, rustling the trees and plantings adorning the yard and house. He took to his favorite rocking chair and spread open his copy of the *Missouri Democrat.*

Congress Approves Pacific Railroad
Central Route Will Take Years to Complete

The headline sealed the fate of slavery for westward continental expansion. The South might preserve itself if it could somehow prevail in the current conflict. They'd had early military success, though they'd not been able to achieve decisive victory. The South needed swift victory to survive secession. Slowly the Union massed industrial muscle to the fight. Defensively, they'd managed to prolong the conflict. A war of attrition and naval blockades would slowly bleed the Confederacy's agrarian economy beyond its scarce resources.

Preserving the Confederacy and winning territorial expansion would prove two different things. Some reasoned Texas with its vast lands would bode well for the cause; but this railroad represented the strong arm of commerce. Commerce would determine the future of the nation, giving the industrial North the pearl of westward expansion and, with it, free-soil populace.

The war in the West was fast deteriorating into guerilla skirmishes with little or no strategic direction. The South could mount no effective military campaign in the West, while the Union found little need to defend it. The full weight of the Union fell on the eastern theater.

It hadn't taken long to move the railroad forward once southern opposition departed the Senate. Commercial and political pressures favoring the central route were substantial. As a practical matter, setting aside his southern sympathies, the proposed rail routing would grace Missouri and Kansas with wealth and prosperity. Wealth and prosperity made a comforting balm to soothe the abrasion of losing their cause.

Sycamore

Caleb's hand whittled crude dolls. Outfitted in calico scraps and a little imagination, they were all the girls needed to amuse themselves. Elizabeth, seven, and Rebecca, almost six, played on a blanket in the shade of the old sycamore down near the creek. Their giggles punctuated the buzz of summer insects and the trill of lark song. Miriam rocked on the porch, adding a quiet creak to the lazy summer symphony as she read a week-old newspaper. Caleb sat on the porch, chewing a straw, keeping watchful eye on the young ones.

"Congress give 'em the money," she said. "They gonna build a railroad clean to the Pacific Ocean. Can you imagine?"

"Micah be right. He been sayin' that since before he settled here. Someday that railroad gonna ship our wheat clear across the country."

"Not right off. Says here they figure it to take four, maybe five years to build."

"Likely longer. Such things usually do."

"Such things like what? Nobody never tried nothin' so grand

as this afore."

"Oh, I don't know—they got from Baltimore to Ohio and Chicago. That be pretty grand. I don't doubt they'll do it. It just might take a little longer, that's all. Look at them two peas in a pod." He pointed at the girls with his straw. "You suppose things gonna change when Lizabeth go to school this fall?"

Miriam set down her paper. She knit her brow. "Not if Becca goes with her."

Caleb cut his eyes to his wife. "School is for white folks, Miriam. You knows that."

"Why? I learnt to read. So can my daughter."

"Then you best teach her like Miss Clare taught you."

"I can't teach her 'ritin' and 'rithmatic. I don't know."

"Now, don't you let yourself go thinkin' like that. You take that chile up them schoolhouse steps it won't do no good but cause a whole passel of trouble."

"Caleb, you ever wants to own this land? You ever wants to vote? None of that gonna come of stayin' put down. You gotta make your opportunities. No one gonna do it for you."

"Who gonna let you make those kind of opportunities?"

"Good folk, that's who. As for Becca goin' to school, I think I'll see what Clare has to say."

"Me 'n my big mouth. I should never a' brought it up."

Bright morning sun filtered through the trees, laying a carpet dappled in light along the wagon lane to the Masons'. Miriam and Rebecca crossed the yard to the house hand in hand. Elizabeth burst out the door to the porch with her doll. The girls skipped off toward the sycamore, their morning play under way.

"You stay away from the river," Miriam called after them.

Clare stood in the door, wiping her hands on her apron. "Fresh coffee's brewed. Care for a cup?"

"That'd go real good. I need a little advice to go with it."

Clare raised a brow. "Advice is free. Worth what you pay for it, though."

Miriam laughed. "I'll take my chances."

Clare poured two steaming cups and carried them out to the porch, in earshot of the girls' squealing. They sat on the porch step.

"What's on your mind?"

"School. School for Becca. You think they'd let Becca go to school with Elizabeth?"

"Hmm." Clare sipped her coffee. "It'd be a first, far as I know."

"Caleb said it'd be nothin' but a passel of trouble."

"It might, though I don't know why it should. Children go to school to learn. I don't see the harm in that."

"Most white folks don't think like you. Ole Massa Morgan Walker used to say book learnin' make Negro folks uppity."

"Morgan Walker isn't here."

"No, he's not. Here's my thinkin'. Black folks don't improve our lot none by stayin' down. If we wants to vote and own property and such someday, we need to know things like readin', 'ritin', and 'rithmetic. You taught me to read, and now I know things. I could teach Becca that, I s'pose, but I don't know none of them other things. She gonna better her lot than mine, she gonna need to know cipherin' and such. If that makes me uppity, maybe Ole Massa Walker was right. But that don't make me wrong now do it?"

"No, it doesn't. The least we can do is talk to Miss Allen."

"Who's she?"

"Cora Allen is the young woman they hired to teach school. She'll be gettin' the schoolhouse ready to start in a week or so. Why don't we take a ride into town and see what she has to say."

"You mean you'd go with me?"

"Of course. They're our girls, aren't they? Besides, the territorial constitution says we women get a say in such things."

"White women."

"Then I guess I best speak for the both of us for now."

"It's settled, then."

"Well, maybe not settled, but we'll sure give it a try."

Lawrence
Schoolhouse

Chalk, dust, and books. Clare recognized the smell imported from a one-room school house she remembered back home in Ohio. Bright morning sun and a warm breeze blew through the open windows. The one-room schoolhouse would be warm in the early fall.

Miriam took in the neat rows of desks, facing a blackboard and the teacher's desk. She wondered what it would be like to have learned to read on one of those uncomfortable looking benches. She recognized the familiar alphabet above the blackboard with the unfamiliar ciphers ordered beneath them.

"May I help you?"

The voice was soft and pleasant. A pretty young woman in a gingham dress with golden curls errant in the heat. Blue eyes met them as she straightened up from behind her desk, arms full of books.

"Miss Allen?"

"I am."

"Clare Mason." She strode up the aisle and extended her hand. "My daughter, Elizabeth, will be attending your first-year class this fall."

"Pleased to meet you, Mrs. Mason. I recognize the name from my registration list."

"This is my friend and neighbor, Miriam Madison."

Cora smiled and extended her hand.

Miriam took it for a good sign. "Pleased to meet you, Miss Allen."

"Madison, now there is a name of historic import."

She turned back to Clare. "What can I do for you this morning?"

"Actually, it's Miriam you might be able to do something for."

"I'm sorry. Miriam, what can I do for you?"

"I was wonderin', ma'am, if my daughter, Rebecca, might attend your first-year class, too. She and Elizabeth is like two peas in a pod. They'd help each other with their lessons."

"I see. That would be something of a departure from the way things are done, though I am sympathetic to your desire for your daughter to receive an education."

"I know schoolin's for white folk, but Mr. Madison's rights don't say nothin' 'bout rights bein' for whites only. I know that's how things is done now, but that don't make it right, and it don't mean things is always gonna be done that way."

"I understand your point, Mrs. Madison. In fact, I'm inclined to agree with you. If it were up to me, I'd allow it. Unfortunately, a decision such as that is not up to me. It's a matter for the school board. Are you familiar with that?"

"I am. It's the only office white women gets to vote for."

"It is. I'm impressed."

"You didn't get that vote without askin' for it. I helped. I signed the petition to the constitutional convention."

"And we won. I respect your right to ask that your daughter be admitted to school. Let me talk to some members of the school board and see what we can do."

A tear welled up in Miriam's eye. "Thank you, Miss Allen."

"I can't promise anything more than I'll try."

"I know. God bless you for tryin'."

Sycamore

A stylish Cabriolet drawn by a sturdy Morgan chestnut wheeled off the town road and up the wagon road to the Mason house. Cora Allen drew the carriage to a stop and stepped down. Late summer heat hung heavy in the yard. Clare stepped onto the porch to greet her.

"Where might I find Mrs. Madison?"

"Miriam's home is up the wagon road there past the barn. I'll show you if you like."

"That is very kind of you." She gathered a bundle off the carriage seat and fell in beside Clare as they set off up the rutted track.

"How did it go with the school board?"

Cora shook her head.

"I feared as much."

"How will Mrs. Madison accept it?"

"She'll be disappointed, though I doubt she'll be surprised."

"As am I."

"It was good of you to try. It can't have been easy."

"No. While I might have found a sympathetic ear or two, most were shocked at the very suggestion."

They climbed the porch step. Clare rapped on the door. Miriam answered, wiping her hands on her apron. She looked from one to the other.

"They said no, didn't they?"

"I'm afraid so," Cora nodded.

"You tried, Miss Allen. For that I thank you."

"There is something more we can do."

"There is?"

"Yes." She patted the bundle with a smile.

"Please, come in." Miriam led the way inside. "Might be best to sit at the dining table. We ain't got much in the way of a parlor."

Cora laid her bundle on the table and took a seat.

"It's true the board said no to your daughter attending classes, but I got to thinking there is a little something we can do." She untied the bundle and removed the cloth wrapping to reveal three books, a slate, and chalk.

"What's this?"

Cora spread out the books. "Reading, writing, and arithmetic," she said.

Miriam picked up the reader and thumbed the pages, running a finger over the words.

"Do you read?"

Miriam nodded.

"Splendid. Then you can help Rebecca with her lessons. The slate and chalk are for exercises. I'll send assignments home for her with Elizabeth. Elizabeth can help her, and I'll come by from time to time to see how she is progressing. We'll do our best to help her keep up with what is going on in class."

"You'd do that for my Becca?"

Cora nodded.

A tear trickled down Miriam's cheek. "I don't knows what to say. Thank you don't seem near enough."

"I'm a teacher, Mrs. Madison. Students learning is thanks enough."

"That's very kind of you, Miss Allen," Clare said. "I'll talk to Elizabeth. She'll be happy to help. Might make her own studies better if she knows she needs to teach her lessons, too."

Cora smiled. "It might, indeed." She turned to Miriam. "Rebecca will be ready when the doors to school are rightfully opened to her."

"God bless you, Miss Allen. God bless you."

Chapter Forty-Eight

Sycamore
January, 1863
Miriam read the week-old news account for the second time to the howl of the wind in the eaves. Tears streamed down her cheeks. Caleb threw a log in the stove and bundled a blanket about his shoulders to ward off the chill.

"Does you s'pose it really mean what he say?"

She put the paper down and wiped her cheek with the back of her hand. "Pre-si-dent Lincoln say it do. The paper say he e-man-ci-pated slaves with the stroke of a pen he call a proclamation."

"Can he do that?"

"He be the pre-si-dent."

"I know that. But can he do that?"

"He did."

"My, my. What do you s'pose be comin' of it now?"

"All them folk in the South be free now just like we."

"We ain't been free. We been well hid runaways."

"We ain't no more. We free now."

"Them runaway slave laws?"

"Ain't no slaves to run away."

"Them Confederacy states see it that way?"

She pursed her lips in thought. "I s'pect not. Not until they lose the war least-wise."

"So them runaway slave laws ain't gone for everyone."

"They gone for us and all those livin' in free-soil states."

"What about ownin' property and votin' an' such?"

"Paper don't say nothun' about them."

"Free may be free, but it ain't equal yet."

She set her jaw with a nod. "All in good time. All in good time."

Blue Springs
Jackson County, Missouri
March 1863

Quantrill and his men made their base camp at the headwaters of the Little Blue River east of Kansas City. The densely wooded area provided an abundance of fresh water, concealment, and escape routes, should the need arise. The camp comprised a small village of scattered dugouts and tents nestled in the wooded hills above the river.

Evening settled through the trees swallowing the smoke rising from cook fires. Quantrill sat by a fire, cleaning a brace of revolvers. A splash broke the slate-gray surface of the river. The clatter of hooves on the stony bank brought him up from his work. A lone horseman rode into camp under the watchful eyes and muzzles of a half-dozen guns. Cole Younger swung down. Other men moved in to hear the news.

"They've arrested my sisters. Yours, too, Bill."

Bill Anderson scowled. "Who's arrested 'em?"

"Federal garrison in Kansas City. They got 'em locked up in that two-story brick building on Grand Avenue between Fourteenth and Fifteenth."

"We'll see about that." Anderson turned to go.

"Where do you think you're goin', Bill?" Quantrill said.

"You heard Cole. They got my sisters. I'm goin' to bust 'em out."

"Forget it, Bill," Younger said. "Don't you think I would have tried? They're bein' held under heavy guard. You'd never get near the place without getting yourself killed."

"What's the charge?"

"Don't need no charge. They're our sisters. The federals are lockin' up any womenfolk suspected of tending to our needs."

"They can't do that."

"They can, and they did."

Anderson turned to Quantrill. "What are we gonna do about that?"

"I'm not sure, Bill. We're not gonna ride in there and take on the whole federal garrison; that much I know. We need to get the lay of the land. Maybe we can do something quiet-like."

"Figure it out if you must, William. Just figure it out fast." Anderson stomped off into the gloom.

Sycamore
May, 1863

The chestnut Morgan stood in the Cabriolet livery traces, browsing in the shade of a tall oak. Caleb sat on the front porch step, whittling on a lazy spring afternoon, biding time before Sunday supper. Their guest tutored Rebecca on her arithmetic lesson while Miriam paid rapt attention, learning along with her child.

"Now try this one." Cora passed Rebecca a slate with two numbers written in chalk.

"Fifteen plus six," Rebecca read. "Five plus six is . . ." She thought. "Eleven." She wrote "one" in the sum.

"Now carry," Cora said.

"The one, one plus one is two . . . twenty one!" Rebecca beamed.

"Very good," Cora said. She glanced at Miriam. "Do you see what she did?"

Miriam nodded.

"Let's try this one." Cora wiped the slate clean and took the chalk from the child.

Caleb watched Clare and Elizabeth turn into the yard from the lane. His mouth watered at the sight of one of Clare's fresh baked pies. Elizabeth ran ahead, smiling brightly at the sight of Miss Allen.

Miriam met Clare at the porch step. "Mmm, that looks good. Here, sit yourself down. Let me take that inside before that man decides to start his dinner with dessert."

Clare smoothed her skirt and sat on the porch step.

"Any word from Micah?" Caleb asked.

She nodded. "I just received a letter."

"What's the news?"

"They've marched deep into southern Missouri. It seems General Price and the Missouri militia have abandoned the state and taken refuge in Arkansas under the protection of Rebel troops there. Union forces including the Kansas brigade have halted their pursuit. Micah says it's one thing to engage Price and another to mount an attack on Rebel regulars."

"They plannin' on comin' home any time soon?"

"They are. General Lane says they can't accomplish much watching the border. He says the men are needed at home come harvest time."

"I'm sure for havin' him home in time for harvest."

Miriam clapped her hands. "Dinner's ready."

Lawrence
July, 1863

The Kansas brigade returned home without fanfare on a hot, windy summer afternoon. Townsfolk set aside their daily business long enough to watch and cheer the men as they rode down Massachusetts Street to Eldridge House. There General Lane drew a halt and wheeled his horse to address his command. He rode the length of the column as he spoke.

"Welcome home, gentlemen. You have acquitted yourselves honorably in support of our noble cause. The people of Kansas are indebted to you for your service. I am proud and privileged to have led you. We prevailed where we were needed. Now it is time to tend our needs here at home."

"The war in the East advances. Righteous freedom shall undoubtedly prevail. For now, we shall stand down, but hear me: keep your powder dry, your blades sharp, and your weapons by, as the need of them may yet again arise."

"You are hereby dismissed. Go to your homes."

The men cheered and began to disperse. Lane stepped down at the hotel rail.

"Will you be needing anything further, sir?" Micah asked.

"Only that you accept my thanks, Micah. I've come to value your ear and your wit. Should the need arise, I hope you will again serve as my aide."

"Indeed, sir. What of my mount?"

"You've earned him. Now go home to that lovely wife and daughter of yours."

"Thank you, sir."

Blue Springs
Jackson County, Missouri
August 15, 1863

The camp stirred, alert to the sound of a fast horse approaching. Horse and rider resolved out of the forest, galloping through the trees to a sliding stop. Bill Anderson leaped down from his lathered mount.

"They're dead." Tears streaked his cheeks.

"Who's dead?" Cole Younger asked.

"Your sisters and mine."

Quantrill and his men gathered around the new arrival.

"What are you talkin' about?" Younger said.

"That rat trap on Grand Avenue where they was keepin' 'em collapsed. All them inside was crushed dead."

"What!? How?"

"Termites they say. I say bullshit! If it was termites, they was Yankee termites. They done it on purpose to get us 'cause they ain't been able to catch us. Murdered 'em they did, sure as I'm standin' here."

Anderson and Younger turned to Quantrill. "What are we gonna do about it, William?" Cole demanded.

"An eye for an eye!" Anderson said.

Quantrill raised a calming hand and smoothed his moustache. "You'll have your eye, Bill. The questions are how, where, and when. We can't take on the whole Yankee garrison at Kansas City. That'd flush us out and play right into their hands. We got plenty of blood accounts to settle with the Yankees and them free-state Jayhawkers. First Osceola, now your sisters."

He clasped his hands behind his back and dropped his head in thought, giving his audience up to bird calls and buzzing flies. At length, he nodded to himself.

"Lane and his Kansas brigade finished chasin' Price with the Yankees. He's disbanded the outfit."

"So?" Anderson wiped tear-streaked grime on his shirtsleeve.

"That serves up a target ripe for our vengeance."

Recognition lit Younger's eye.

"Lawrence."

Quantrill nodded. "Lawrence."

"You call that an eye? One piddlin' town ain't no more'n a start," Anderson said.

Chapter Forty-Nine

Lawrence
August 21, 1863

Dawn. Quantrill headed a column swollen to more than four hundred strong. They sat in the tree line on the road into town. Morning fog rose over the river, draping a gauzy veil over homes and businesses slowly waking from slumber. Despite their numbers, he suspected some among his command might be overtaken with misgivings at the magnitude of their target. Fatigue brought on by a long night's ride drew a man's thoughts to home, hearth, and safety.

"There she is, boys. Home and comfort to James Lane, Doc Jennison, and the rest of them red-leg butchers. You've seen their work up and down the border. Is there a man among you who hasn't suffered loss or atrocity of family or friend by their hand?"

His words struck chords. Will stiffened.

"They've a thin garrison now. Not more than raw recruits to the Union side. They shall scatter before our winnowing blades. They've shown us no quarter. We shall show none in return. Every able-bodied man is a Union loyalist. Cut them down where they stand. Mark me now, bring no harm to womenfolk or children. Leave them unharmed to mourn the loss of their menfolk and the comforts of home."

He squeezed up a lope down the road to the north. They passed a farm. A handful of men peeled away. They found the owner milking a cow. They shot him before he could rise from his stool.

Quantrill dispatched lookouts west to Mount Oread and a detachment to secure the east end of town. He led the main body in a charge up Massachusetts Street to Eldridge House.

Lane woke with a start at shots being fired. *Quantrill!* The name burst both accusation and conviction in his mind. He leaped out of bed and stumbled into his trousers.

"What is it, dear?" His wife blinked back her sleep.

"Bushwhackers. Get dressed and get out of the house as fast as you can. Stay with the neighbors. You'll be safe."

"But what about you?"

"I must raise the militia." He ran down the stairs, two at a time to the back of the house. He dashed across the yard to a field, where he took cover in a drainage ditch. He watched the raiders spread through town raising dust clouds punctuated by gunfire and plumes of powder smoke. *There's a bloody business afoot here, and I likely top the list of those to be killed.* He looked west. *If I can but make it to Micah's, I can borrow his horse.*

Quantrill stepped down at Eldridge House as his raiders fanned out across the length and breadth of town with his admonishment to kill ringing in their ears. Osceola and all the Jayhawk atrocities would be avenged by the blood of Lawrence.

A company of recruits to a Kansas volunteer brigade was encamped on the outskirts of town. Bill Anderson and his men overran the camp. Men were trampled beneath horses' hooves or were shot down unarmed. Blue coats ignited a bloody black rage in Anderson. He carried four pistols, twenty-four shots in all. He cried for his sisters as he counted his victims with each shot he fired. He carried two fully loaded pistols when he wheeled away from the volunteer camp and galloped into town.

A Negro regiment, similarly encamped nearby, were alerted to the raid by gunfire. Not yet armed, they scattered, running for their lives in fear of guerilla forces for whom their new blue coats would serve only as a death warrant.

Certain commanders had orders to see to specific targets. These men, known Jayhawks or Unionists, were dragged from their homes and beds, marched into the street, and shot, to the horror of their families. Their homes and properties were put to the torch.

Raiders broke into saloons and whisky shops, pouring strong drink on raging blood lust. Before long, horsemen holding bottle and reins in one hand and pistol in the other raced up and down the streets shooting in the air or at any man daring to show his face. Anderson wasted none of his bullets on meaningless noise. Each one exacted a measure of vengeance for Union atrocities done his family and sisters.

Quantrill seized the livery cabriolet and drove out to inspect the progress of his raid. He found every hotel and boardinghouse in town under similar assault. Inhabitants turned out to the streets under pretense of safe passage. There, all were robbed and the women made to watch as their husbands, brothers, and neighbors were shot down in cold blood. With the killing complete, houses and properties set ablaze, a pall of black mourning smoke spread over the town, searing the tears of those helpless who had only to stand in horror and watch.

He drove on to the Lane house. His men found it empty. In anger, he ordered it burned to the ground. He turned back to the center of town, choked in thick black smoke, a hellish inferno walled in flame. He wheeled the carriage west out of town and drove to the summit of Mount Oread, where he took in a lofty view of his destruction set against the backdrop of Charles Robinson's home leaping in flames. He indulged a satisfied smile as smoke drifted toward the summit, a burnt offering to justice done in the name of vengeance.

Sycamore

The afternoon was well advanced when a lone bedraggled figure jogged up the wagon road to the yard. Micah hung Delilah's harness on a peg in the barn as Caleb called.

"Looky here."

Micah stepped into the barnyard. "General!" He waved and ran to meet Lane with Caleb at his heel. The man's clothes were mud-spattered and torn. His hair, seldom groomed, stood in wild disarray.

"What happened?"

"Quantrill hit Lawrence this morning."

"He what?"

"Look there."

The black cloud five miles away may have been a rain squall. "Lawrence?"

"Burning to the ground. Every able-bodied man murdered without quarter. May I have the use of your horse?"

"Of course."

"I mean to raise the militia, though I fear we shall all be too late."

"This way. Caleb, see if Clare might have a bite of something for the general."

"Shore 'nuf." He ran off to the cabin.

Micah led Lane to the barn and set about saddling the gelding.

Lawrence
September 1863

Late summer spread golden across northeastern Kansas masking the whisper of autumn to come. Only the burnt scar that was Lawrence marred the glory of a breezy sunny day. They pitched a tent behind the Eldridge House ruins by way of promise to rebuild. Charles Robinson sat at a camp table with James Lane and Titus Thorne, quietly talking over soft flapping canvas.

"The Kansas brigade is ready to ride," Lane said.

Robinson rubbed his forehead in thought. "To what purpose, James?"

"To avenge this." He spread his arms over the charred remains.

"And how will you avenge it? With more carnage, burnings, and lootings? Will that put it right?"

"This atrocity cannot go unanswered."

"No, it can't; but I think we might find a more suitable answer."

"I don't follow you, Charles."

"I must say I'm a little lost myself," Thorne said.

"The war in the east has turned against the south both morally and militarily. The Confederacy will be defeated as it most assuredly must be. War's end will be followed by a period of rebuilding. Here in the West, we have the opportunity to begin rebuilding now. The most powerful statement we could make to our rebellious neighbors in Missouri is to rebuild. The railroad is coming. The prosperity it brings will put an economic end to the evils of slavery more powerful than the triumph of the sword. We here in Kansas should be first to avail ourselves of the opportunity. Let us put aside our arms and channel our talent and treasure to a new beginning. Let's rebuild Lawrence and let her stand as a beacon to freedom, equality, and the prosperity of a newly united nation."

"Wise words," Thorne said. "Your vision is much as my own, though you phrase yours more eloquently in those grandiose terms."

"And what is your vision, Titus?"

"Only a more practical start."

"How so?"

"I propose we charter a bank to finance the rebuilding."

"That's the spirit!" Robinson said. "Do the right thing and get on with it. An excellent plan I shall thoroughly support."

"Thank you, Charles. Your standing and support will mean much to the success of the enterprise."

"A bank, Titus?" Lane said. "Now I must say, I'm a bit surprised. It doesn't exactly strike me as your cup of tea."

"Oh, I don't plan to run it. We shall hire a professional for that. I merely seek to organize the capital needed to start it. That, of course, and hold some stock in the enterprise."

"A necessary first step, Titus," Robinson said. "You shall have more than my moral support. If you've a place for me as an investor, I should be more than happy to join your syndicate."

"I'd be honored, Charles."

"Very well, then. Do keep me informed of your progress. Now, I must be off to another matter. Good day, gentlemen."

Lane watched him depart through the tent flap. He lifted a brow at Thorne. "Since when have you become so community minded?"

"James, you wound me by your obvious suspicion of my good intention."

"No suspicion to it, Titus. I know you."

"Ah, yes, there is that."

"There's more here than good intention."

"Perhaps. If you must know, the railroad comes with right-of-way land grants. Those grants must be developed. A bank provides a useful vehicle to participate in the prosperity sure to grow out of that."

"My faith is restored."

"I don't see how."

"You're still a scoundrel."

"Pleased I could oblige."

Sycamore

Dear Ma & Pa,

I am sure reports of the tragic raid on Lawrence caused you concern for our safety. I write to assure you we were spared this time. All our family and properties are fine. The same cannot be said for our many friends and neighbors in Lawrence. They were subjected to vile brutalities and destruction. Any men and boys the raiders found were murdered in cold blood, most within sight of their loved ones. Much of the town was burned to the ground, leaving the widows and orphans of the dead homeless. Mere words cannot justly describe the devastation. We are left to ask, where will it end?

General Lane intended to call out the Kansas brigade to seek retribution. Such would have taken Micah back into service. Thankfully Governor Robinson stood against it. The community devotes its efforts to rebuilding. Micah says the war in the East has turned against the South. He believes at long last it may soon be over. I pray he is right. The violence must end. We wonder if the conflict ever will. Feelings run deep and strong on both sides. The wounds are raw and painful. They will be slow to mend. One wonders if they are ever to be reconciled peaceably. We are left to pray. For now all is well.

Clare

Chapter Fifty

Sycamore
April 1864
Slowly spring sun roused her from her winter slumbers. Ice cracked, dripping crystal. Her creek ran a trickle, drawn to the river below. She lay bare, releasing stiff frost from her bones. The old tree stretched out mighty limbs to the breeze, watching over all. Redbud burst among pale, green shoots. Bluebonnet spread carpet patches. Gentle spring rain moistened her fields, beckoning a lover planting seed.

Sampson leaned into his traces, drawing the plough to a clean straight furrow. Caleb followed, guiding the blade, Sampson's lines draped over his shoulders. The scent of freshly turned earth mingled with a light spring shower on a gentle breeze. Micah followed along, seeding the furrow. Gray clouds drifted east among patches of blue. If a man was to ask for a favorable planting, he couldn't improve on the day. Caleb made the turn at the end of the row and drew the mule to a halt. Micah straightened and stretched his back.

"You feel like takin' the plough for a spell? It be a might easier on the back."

He shook his head. "I'll trade a little stiff back for your rows. I can't cut 'em near as straight as you."

"Better cuttin' my rows than them as belong to a massa."

"A man takes pride in what's his."

Caleb nodded. "Well, this field won't plough itself. Hup there, mule!" He pushed off down the row.

May

Seed clutched to her belly, sprouting green and tender. Roots dug deep, drawing precious moisture from the soil. Stems stretched out to blue sky and the promise of summer sun. Birdsong filled the morning air, stirred by gentle breeze. The old tree stretched to the horizon filled with new life.

The sky overhead arced bright and blue. Micah hoed, willing the dust away. Caleb walked the rows, snatching a weed here, a bramble there. Miriam fed the men and minded the girls. Clare gathered spring wildflowers in the shade of the old sycamore. Day by day, spring wiled into summer.

June

Each day sunrise cracked the darkness without hint of red or pink. Bright summer sun at midday bleached the sky overhead. Harsh wind blew hot and dry. She parched. Her seedlings thirsted. Their cries produced no tears. The old sycamore cast a long shadow over the land.

Clare took strength from the old tree. It must have seen all this before. It clings to a life force in the land. The Lord must have seen the land through this before. The old sycamore testified to that. She prayed the good Lord would see them through to the blessing of rain.

Caleb milked the cow in the morning and fed the stock. He turned the stock out according to the dictates of the day's chores. He cleaned the barn, mended harness, sharpened plow and scythe. Simple chores busied hands, pushing back at worry. He watered the stock each evening.

Miriam looked after the girls at play and freshened their lessons lest they forget. Morning play led to midday, rest, some lessons, and more play. The children played in the shade of the old sycamore. They took little note of the cracks in her earth. Play lacked worry. Their laughter was a counterpoint to the mood of concern hanging over their elders.

Micah squinted against the sun, searching the horizon for a sign of relief. None came, save the red sky at night bred of the old mariner's rhyme.

July
Hot wind whipped the land; swirling dust devils danced across her brow. Sun parched sprouts turned golden straw before their time. Barren ache replaced the verdant promise of spring. The creek slowed to a sluggish trickle. The river receded from her banks. The sycamore bowed her limbs to the earth.

Parched soil crumbled between Caleb's fingers. Limp plantings turned brown, shriveled grain. Micah shook his fist at a relentless sky. Miriam steeled herself to hard times. Clare stood beside the old tree, her eyes turned to the heavens, praying for rain.

Sunday dinners turned somber with worry. The girls giggled and prattled, gravity beyond their years. Their elders' thoughts seldom strayed far from parched land and the crops withering in the field. They joined hands around the table to give thanks for their meal. Caleb said the blessing. Miriam finished for him.

"And, Lord, if you might could spare us one more little blessing. We could sure use some rain on our fields."

"Amen."

"Here's hopin' the good Lord be listenin' this day," Caleb said.

"He always listens," Clare said. "Just sometimes He wants things for us we don't know we need."

"He only gots to look at them fields to know what we need," Miriam said. "If we be needin' somethin' else, I sure don't know what it be."

"We'll find out in good time."

"And if it don't rain, what then?"

Glances exchanged around the table.

Micah shook his head. "We'll lose the crop."

"What be coming of Sycamore if we do?" Caleb said.

"Nothin' good, I'm afraid," Micah said.

"Pass the potatoes."

August

Rain did not come. Hot summer sun bleached the sky blue-white in a ball of shimmering heat. Tender shoots of spring died at their root. Once filled with tender promise, she ached, dry tears barren with loss. The old tree stretched out her limbs to the loss of her fold and moaned to the wind.

September

They stood shoulder to shoulder in silence, faces dark and sun-hardened to the burning wind. Dun dust clouds boiled across fruitless dry fields.

"What's to be done?" Caleb said.

"Plough it under," Micah said.

"Plough it under?"

"Plough it under."

"Then what?"

Micah looked to the sky.

"I don't know."

The dark rider drew rein. He looked out over the windswept fields. A mule and ploughman plodded along a row in one field, raising a dust trail dissipated against a cloudless, white sky. He shifted in the saddle and smiled. This wasn't the precise opportunity he'd envisioned, but he seldom missed opportunity when he saw it. Loss of a crop would do its work quickly. Fillmore would accommodate the loss—he'd see to that. He squeezed up a lope into town.

Lawrence
October

Lawrence Union Bank occupied a one-room clapboard building on Massachusetts. Temporary housing for the bank was one of the first structures completed in rebuilding Lawrence. The bank housed a lobby with teller counter and safe. It accommodated the bank's business without the pretense of strength usually associated with a banking institution. A more suitable structure would surely be built one day, but, for the present, the bank was open to finance rebuilding the town.

The bank's founding directors recruited Thaddeus Fillmore of Kansas City to manage the bank as president and cashier. An experienced banker, Fillmore presented the picture of trustworthy prudence to the community and his customers. He quickly insinuated himself into local society, befriending the influential who made up the political and commercial class of town folk. He was seated at his back-corner desk engrossed in the previous day's ledgers when one of his directors entered the bank. He rose in practiced deference as was his custom.

"Good afternoon, Mr. Thorne. How may I be of service?"

"A small matter, Thaddeus." He gestured to a side chair. "May I?"

"Please, have a seat." They settled into their chairs. "Now, what can I do for you?"

Thorne made a steeple of his fingertips. "It's about the Mason place. Do you know it?"

"The one they call Sycamore?"

He nodded.

"I've driven past it on my way out to your place. What about it?"

"I believe they've lost their crop."

"Ah, this drought. Simply dreadful. It's brought suffering to so many. I wish we could help them, but, as you know, the bank's resources are limited. Our lending priority must be rebuilding the town. They'll seek a mortgage. Risky business when compared to our construction loans to businesses with going concerns."

"I understand all that. Nevertheless, I want you to mortgage their farm if they ask."

"What about the board? Our lending policy is quite clear."

"Leave the board to me."

"But the risk—what if the drought persists."

"What value might a mortgage place on the property?"

"A lender might extend credit up to half the value of the property. One can never be sure what the property might fetch in the event of foreclosure."

"Exactly. You see, you have no risk at all."

The banker knit his brow. "I'm afraid I don't understand."

"I'll buy that land at the face value of your loan."

"Aha, now I see."

Sycamore

They sat at the dining table all eyes fixed on Micah. The light of a single candle pooled on the rough-cut tabletop.

"We've no choice. We lost the crop. We can survive the winter, but we'll need seed to plant in spring."

"But doesn't a mortgage put Sycamore at risk?" Clare said. "What if the drought continues?"

"What's a mortgage?" Miriam asked.

"A mortgage is a loan from a bank. You put up the deed to

your property as security for repayment of the loan."

"What's all that mean?"

"It means if we don't repay the loan, the bank can take Sycamore and sell it."

"How we gonna repay this loan?" Caleb asked. "We done lost the crop."

"That's why we need the loan. We repay it out of the sale of the crop next year."

"Then like Clare said, s'pose the drought keep on?" Miriam said.

"That's a risk we have to take. If we haven't got seed to plant in the spring, the land don't do us no good. We'd have to sell the farm and move on."

"Sounds like we could lose our Sycamore either way," Caleb said.

"Not if we bring in a crop next year."

They looked from one to the other.

Miriam folded her arms. "Micah's right. We got no choice. Sycamore be the best chance we got, Caleb."

He nodded.

"We be with you, Micah."

"Clare?"

She nodded.

"Pray for rain."

Lawrence Union Bank

The bank opened at nine on yet another hot, dry morning. Micah waited on the boardwalk. He'd fretted over the decision to take a loan all the way into town. He didn't like the risk. They had no choice. It was that simple. What if the bank refused to make the loan? They could see risk as surely as he. The head teller appeared at the door. He turned the *Closed* sign to *Open* and unlocked the door, admitting him with a thin smile. Micah nodded and crossed the lobby bathed in morning glow.

"Mr. Fillmore?"

The banker looked up from a stack of papers. "Yes?"

"Micah Mason, sir. I'd like to talk to you about a loan."

"Ah, Mr. Mason, I've been expecting you. Sit down, sit down."

"You have? Why?"

"I heard about the tragic loss of your crop. Terrible thing this drought, terrible."

"Yes. I'd like to take out a mortgage on Sycamore."

"Your farm."

"That's right."

"How much were you thinking?"

"We've got three-hundred-sixty acres."

"We?"

"Me and my . . . wife and I."

"The title will be in your name of course, so as far as borrowing is concerned, it's your farm."

"Yes, sir."

"The bank isn't doing much mortgage lending these days. Our loan policy commits the majority of our resources to construction lending for rebuilding Lawrence. We might do something short term. Let's see, three hundred and twenty acres . . . market price is $1.25 an acre. We might go $125 on that."

"We got two houses, a barn, and stock pens on that."

"Yes . . . well, improvements such as that may or may not add to the value of the property. We are in the business of hard security. I'm afraid the best we can do is one-hundred-twenty-five dollars due in full in one year. Will that be suitable?"

"I reckon it'll have to be."

Chapter Fifty-One

Eldridge House
April 10, 1865
Day by day Lawrence rose from its ashes, personified by the defiant Eldridge House edifice. Much finish work remained to be done on the upper floors. Furnishings for the opulent lobby floor were in various stages of order and shipment. Still, they'd opened her at the first opportunity. James Lane and Charles Robinson sat at a rough-hewn table with tankards of tart apple cider. A special edition of the *Lawrence Republican* lay on the table. The headlines screamed.

War Ends
Lee Surrenders at Appomattox Courthouse

Lane lifted his tankard. "You surely had the right of it, Charles. We sit here today surrounded by your rebuilt vision."

"Thank you, James. Kind of you to see it that way, though, as you well know, much remains to be done."

"Less than would be needed had we not had the benefit of your foresight."

"The coming of the railroad promises to brighten our future still further, if it would only rain to assure we have one."

"Spring rains have been short of the need, but our luck must surely change."

"One would hope and pray so. Those able to plant this spring may be spending their all to do it. Another lost season would spell disaster for many."

"We can only hope for the best."

"The best holds different meanings for some."

Lane looked puzzled. "I'm afraid I don't follow."

Robinson lifted his chin across the lobby. Lane followed the gesture. Titus Thorne shook his cloak off at the door.

"Ah, some things never change," Lane said.

"He's used the bank to set his cap for the Mason place."

"I wasn't aware of that. A mortgage?"

Robinson nodded.

"You were quick to join his syndicate for the purpose of hastening the rebuild in Lawrence. His real purpose in wanting a bank is to partake in developing the railroad right-of-way. It seems he's decided land speculation also suits him. Once a scoundrel, always a scoundrel."

Sycamore

May, 1865

The new season began with all the promise of the last. Snow melt and frost left her soil some moisture. The season's planting filled her with promise. Shoots burst forth green and tender. The old sycamore sensed desperate promise. Clear and bright, bright and clear, day by day, spring passed into early summer.

Miriam fed the chickens and watched the sky. Clare hung laundry and watched the sky. The girls played and laughed merrily in the yard. Caleb milked the cow and watched the sky. Micah pitched hay to the mules and watched the sky. The sky arched cloudless blue.

Sycamore

June

Thorne drew rein on the road to town. Hot, dry wind washed

over him. Rogue snorted at a dust devil swirling down a wagon rut, winding northeast. Off to the left the fields grew slowly, the land parched. Crops wilted. Thorne looked to a clear, cloudless sky and smiled. Time would run out on these squatters at last. What should have been his from the start would be his soon enough and at a foreclosure price less than half its value.

Micah watched the rider from the barn loft. It hadn't occurred to him before. He heard Thorne had given his support to chartering the bank, the bank that now held a mortgage on Sycamore. *There he sits, like a vulture circling carrion kill.* He looked to the sky. *Please, God.*

July

Life slowly sapped from the folded rows in the fields. Her offspring grew weaker with each passing day. The creek's merry spring gurgle dwindled to whispers slipping away. Dust devils passed for tears. Not again. Only the old sycamore looked on in hope.

"Look there!" Caleb ran into the barnyard pointing west.

Micah emerged from the barn.

Clare and Miriam came running from household chores.

Dark stain spread across the western horizon, slowly building toward them. Mesmerized in hope, they watched it grow. The breeze freshened. Thunder rumbled in the distance. They stood transfixed, believing and not believing. Could it be? The cloud bank rolled faster. Wind gusts tore at loose clothing. Lightning flashed in the distance, chased by peals of thunder that reverberated to the soul of a man's inwards.

Fat droplets spattered upturned faces. Puffs of dust splashed in the barnyard. A gray sheet emerged in the west, hung beneath dark clouds stacked in banks. Life burst forth from foreboding darkness. Rain came in sheets of hope. Joy rippled and pooled in puddles. Sycamore stretched forth her limbs to gather it in. Nourishment fell on the land, softening parched roots, teasing tendrils to drink freely, straighten, and strengthen.

They ran to the shelter of the barn, laughing like children at play. They stood dripping, shoulder to shoulder, and watched. Rivulets ran from the barn roof, cascading across the open barn doors.

"Our prayers be answered," Miriam said.

They sank to their knees in thanksgiving.

Lawrence Union Bank
November, 1865

Cold, white light bathed the austere bank lobby in the promise of winter. Micah watched the banker count the bills, dip pen in ink, and satisfy his debt.

"Paid in full." Fillmore handed Micah the cancelled note.

Relief washed over him like summer rain belatedly come. They'd found their way out of a great darkness. They'd come close to losing it all. So close. He stood.

"Thank you, Mr. Fillmore." He turned to leave just as Titus Thorne entered the bank.

"I see you've paid your debt."

Micah nodded.

"Pity. I'd rather thought I might acquire that land of yours after all."

"No, sir. Not now. Not ever."

Thorne laughed. "Cocksure are we, boy?"

"Not sure. Determined. Good day, sir." He brushed past a slack-jawed Thorne and stepped out to the boardwalk.

"You'd never have gotten that land, Thorne." James Lane turned away from the teller counter.

"Oh? How can you be so certain, James?"

"I'd have loaned him the money to pay you. Should the need arise, I stand ready to do so again."

"Why would you do such a thing, James? What could possibly be in it for you?"

"Loyalty, Thorne, but I shouldn't expect you'd understand that. He served as my adjutant in the Kansas brigade. Served me well, too. I shan't forget that; neither should you. Good day."

Drought, rain, harvest, redemption. The old tree extended her limbs in thanksgiving. A few remaining leaves, ochre and orange, fluttered to the blanket spreading below, their work done for the passing of this season. Golden light lay mellow on fields turning to the contentment of a winter's slumber. The mule-drawn buckboard passed up the lane to the barn, turning for home. The old tree watched over her land, once more at peace.

Chapter Fifty-Two

February
1866

Micah awoke to Clare retching in the chamber pot beside the bed. Outside the wind howled, swirling sheets of fresh snow. Finished, she rolled on her back. Her body radiated clammy heat. Chill in the room gave gray mist to their breath.

"Are you sick?"

"Must be something I ate."

He felt her forehead. Her hair was matted with fever. "Can I get you something?"

"I'll be fine. Just let me rest."

Micah got out of bed. He pulled his britches on over his nightshirt and slipped into his boots.

"I'll empty this." He took the chamber pot out into the storm. Cold wind cut through his nightshirt. Snow swirled around him as he trudged out to the yard and emptied the pot in a drift. He returned the pot to the bedroom. Clare's breathing came labored.

"Are you all right?"

"I'm fine."

He went to Elizabeth's room and crawled in bed with the girl. She snuggled into his warmth. He couldn't sleep.

The situation did not improve by the gray light of dawn. Clare's fever worsened. Retching emptied her stomach, though she continued frequent need of the chamber pot. Micah made Elizabeth a simple breakfast and dressed her in her warm coat. Together they waded through the snow down the lane to Miriam and Caleb's place. Miriam met him at the door. She read his worried expression.

"Could Elizabeth stay with you a day or so?"

"Clare?"

"She's sick."

"Come in. Rebecca's in her room, child."

Elizabeth shed her coat and skipped off to join her friend.

"What's wrong with Clare?"

Micah described her condition. Miriam pursed her lips.

"You go along home. Get some soup in her if you can. I'll come by later to see how she's doin'."

"Thanks."

Afternoon light had turned gray when Miriam's knock came to the door. A winter gust followed her through the door.

"How she doin'?"

"About the same."

"Did you give her some soup?"

"I did. She didn't keep it long. She's resting now."

"You go along over to our place. I fixed some supper for you menfolk and the girls. I'll stay the night with her. We'll see how she is in the mornin'."

"Thanks, Miriam."

She patted his chest. "Don't you worry none. She be fine."

Micah returned home the following morning as Miriam came out on the porch carrying the chamber pot.

"How is she?"

"No change. You go inside. Do her good to see you. I'll take care of this and be right along."

Micah crossed the dimly lit parlor to the bedroom. Clare lay in the blankets looking frail and thin. He sat on the edge of the bed. Her eyes fluttered open. She smiled.

"Sorry to be such a bother."

"You could never be a bother." He took her hand. Her usual strength and warmth felt cool and birdlike. He wiped a sweat sheen from her feverish brow.

"You feelin' any better?"

"Some." She lied.

Miriam returned with the chamber pot. "I'm gonna go on home and fix some vittles for them young'uns . . . Caleb too. I'll be back later."

Day turned to night and night to day with no improvement in Clare's condition. She grew ever weaker by the ravages of fever and dysentery. Micah's concern increased by the hour.

"Why doesn't the fever break?" he whispered to Miriam when they were alone in the parlor.

"Sometimes they don't."

"You've seen this before?"

She nodded.

"What is it then?"

"I ain't no doctor."

"I'm goin' to town for the doctor."

"That might be best."

He turned to new purpose. Miriam watched him go.

"You know what's wrong, don't you?"

The voice was small. Clare stood unsteadily holding on to the door frame.

"Come along now. You get back to that bed. You need your rest, girl."

"Rest won't help, will it?" She took a supportive arm to obey.

"We don't know that."

"Yes, you do." She lay down exhausted. Miriam covered her. "The doctor be along soon. Then it be in his hands."

Gray winter sun was well past midday when the jangle of harness sounded in the yard. Old Doc Boyle followed Micah into the parlor. Miriam emerged from the bedroom.

"Any change?"

She shook her head.

"Let me have a look at her," the white-haired doctor said.

Miriam followed him into Clare's room. Micah paced. At length, the doctor returned, closing his case.

"What is it, Doctor?"

He held Micah's eyes, his watery for a moment. "I'm afraid it's cholera."

"Cholera? What can we do?"

"Not much, I'm afraid. I've done what I can. Now it's up to her."

Micah buried his face in his hands.

"I can see myself out, son. I'm sorry to be the bearer of such news."

Miriam appeared at Micah's side. "You go along to her. I'll be here if you needs anything."

He went to the bedside and took her hand. She smiled a small smile, a shadow of the girlish glow he'd first fallen in love with. She seemed to rest more comfortably in his presence.

Gray afternoon descended into evening. She slept. Micah rose. He found Miriam waiting in the parlor by candlelight.

"She's asleep. Go on home to your family. You've done so much already."

She shook her head. "No, you go. There's a little girl over there who need her papa. I'll stay by her. You get some rest. I'll come for you if anything changes."

He gave her a hug and left.

Winter moon rose over the old tree, bitter cold in its barren limbs. Micah paused on the porch. She loved that tree from the first time she laid eyes on it. He cast his gaze about the snow-covered yard to the frozen creek. She loved this land and all it stood for. They'd seen its promise together. They'd worked at that promise. All of them. He lifted his eyes to the heavens through frozen, gnarled branches to the cold light of the moon.

Please, God.

He hunched into the warmth of his coat against the wind and trudged up the moonlit lane to a little girl who needed him.

"Miriam."

She woke with a start in her chair. The candle burned low. She carried it to the bedroom.

"What is it, child?"

"Tell me what it is." A tear stained her cheek in the candle glow.

Miriam sat on the bed and took her hand. She took a confirming breath.

"The doctor say you has cholera."

Her chin dropped to her chest. "You knew all along."

She made no answer.

"There are some things I must entrust to you."

Tears glistened in ebony shadows. "Anything."

"Promise me you'll look after Micah and my little Elizabeth."

"You know I will."

"Micah's a good man. Sometimes he just needs a little woman's wisdom."

She smiled white teeth. "They all do. He is a good man. You both good people. You made us a promise of these here acres, and you kep' it when you didn't need to do neither. If I didn't live these past years with the two of you and that promise, I never would have believed white folk and colored folk could be like us. No, you made us a promise, and now I make you mine: I'll look after them two like they was my own."

"I feel better for hearing that."

"Don't you worry none. Now you get some rest."

It be in the Lord's hands now.

She shook him awake near first light.

"Micah, you best come now. He's here."

He bolted up. "Who's here?"

"The one the Lord done sent for her."

"How do you know?"

"Hush. Hurry now."

He ran up the lane through the snow, unconscious of the cold. Miriam followed along, alone with her thoughts. Much would need to be done. She closed the front door and listened. The murmur of faint voices seeped from the bedroom. She smiled. He'd reached her in time. She stirred the fire to light, made a pot of coffee, and sat down to wait.

He stood in the bedroom door by the gray light of dawn.

"She's gone."

"I know." Miriam rose. She crossed the parlor to him, took him into her arms, and let him cry.

Boots crunched up the porch steps.

"Caleb," Miriam said and let him in.

"What's to be done with her?" Micah said.

"When you ready," Miriam said, "we wrap her up gentle-like and take her to the dugout. She can rest there 'til we give her a proper burial come spring."

"Down by the old sycamore. She loved that old tree's leaves in the fall."

"Then she should lie by there so they warm her like a quilt when they fall."

March

Dear Ma and Pa,

It is a heavy heart that takes this pen in hand. I'm not much good at this. Clare wrote our letters for us. She can't write them now. We lost her to cholera last month. I write we lost her, but it is I who am lost. I am lost without my beloved Clare to light my days. Elizabeth lost her mother, and I am at a loss as to how to mother her. Her needs are simple now. In time, I don't know what I shall do. Caleb and Miriam have been a great comfort. Miriam seems to know what we need even when I do not. When spring comes, we'll put Clare to rest beneath the old sycamore. Perhaps then I can move on to planting.

Micah

Chapter Fifty-Three

Sycamore
Spring
She rested in her shade, comforted by a soft gathering of good earth and a bluebonnet spray there to take root for springs yet to come. Sycamore sighed with the wind in her boughs. Leaves bud forth, new shoots spring up, renewing their promises. Sun warmed her fields and sprinkled their offspring with gentle rain. Promise mingled with tears that planting season.

May, 1866
Sunday dinners continued to alternate between the Mason and Madison homes with Miriam shouldering cooking chores at both houses. This Sunday, with the planting finished, came as a special day of rest. Miriam bustled about the Mason kitchen while the girls played in the yard. Caleb sat on the porch and whittled. Miriam came out to the porch. She looked toward the river. Micah sat silhouetted in late afternoon sun beside the small headstone under the spread of the old tree.

"Seems like that all he want to do," Caleb said.

"He's grieving. It got to run its course."

"How long you figure he be like that?"

"As long as it takes. Folks all be different when it come to such things."

"I s'pect you be mournin' me like that."

She arched a brow. "You do, do you. You feelin' poorly?"

"Me?" He shook his head.

"Good. I don't know how I'd be mournin' you, but I don't have no need to find out."

"That's good enough for me."

"So how about me?"

"How about you what?"

"How about you be mournin' me?"

"Oh, I'd be mournin' you sure. Dinner done yet?"

"You wouldn't be mournin' me long. You'd starve to death soon enough." She stomped back into the house, concealing a smile.

Lawrence
September, 1866

School opened on a bright, sunny morning with summer lingering on the doorstep to autumn. Micah drove Elizabeth to school. Miss Allen stood at the schoolhouse door greeting her students. Micah drew rein. Elizabeth hopped down from the buckboard and ran off, lunch pail in hand, with a wave and a grin. Miss Allen smiled and waved as she put her arm around the girl and showed her inside.

Micah drove into town with Miriam's shopping list. He drove home past the schoolhouse later that day. He stopped on the road to watch the children at play over their lunch-time recess. Their laughter tugged at the wrappings of his sorrow. Miss Allen sat on the school steps keeping a watchful eye. He clucked to Sampson and drove along home.

Sycamore
October

The cabriolet parked in the Madisons' front yard on a pleasant fall afternoon. Elizabeth scampered over to join in Rebecca's lessons. The girls sat on the porch with Miss Allen. Miriam sat in on the lessons when she could. This day she busied herself preparing Sunday supper. Caleb went down to the barn to feed and water the stock. He looked across the Mason place down toward the river. Micah sat at her side watching the sycamore spread its orange-golden blanket over her.

Pretty. The air was still, a rarity on the Kansas plain in autumn. Leaves fluttered softly, red-orange raining out of a flawless blue sky. They covered the earth and soothed the hurt beneath. He listened, as he often did in his time with her. He heard her voice in the thoughts that touched him. Today, she felt the beauty of an autumn day and the comfort of the old sycamore. Her spirit rested. She was at peace.

Peace. It seemed like a long time since they'd had much of that. The war, the drought, Clare's illness. He hadn't found much peace since she passed. Today he felt some comfort in knowing she was at peace. The old tree shedding its finery seemed fitting somehow.

Elizabeth tugged at his thoughts. Girlish, womanly things of which he knew little would soon be upon her. He remembered his mother and sisters. Mother taught the girls the way; Father taught the boys. Her lessons taught cooking and washing and prettifying ribbons and such. How would he do for Elizabeth? You've left me a clumsy mother, Clare. She laughed. He heard it. He smiled. Clumsy indeed.

He sat still until the slant of the sun announced supper would soon be served. He pulled away. Watched the leaves cover the place where he sat, and walked up the lane.

He paused at the carriage parked in the yard and watched them. Elizabeth and Becca paid the golden-haired young woman rapt attention. They smiled and laughed at some conspiratorial secret passing between them. She glanced up and saw him watching. He came forward awkwardly. She smiled.

"You have a way with teaching, Miss Allen."

"Thank you, Mr. Mason. I enjoy it."

"It shows."

"You made it just in time," Miriam said from the door. "Supper's on the table."

Supper ended with coffee and apple pie.

"Miriam, this has been lovely," Cora said. "Let me help you with the dishes."

She raised a hand. "These girls here can help me with that. I don't mean to shoo you out of here, but I feel best if you get back to town before dark."

"Thank you for that." Cora rose.

"Thank you for helpin' Becca with her lessons. Me, too, when I sit in."

"You're more than welcome."

"May I show you to your carriage?" Micah said.

She smiled. "That would be nice."

Caleb cut an eye to Miriam. She winked as Micah followed Cora out to the yard.

She paused at the carriage. "I've enjoyed our time today, Mr. Mason. Elizabeth is such a wonderful girl. It's easy to understand why."

"Her mother gets most of the credit for that. Elizabeth thinks the world of you, you know."

"She reminds me some of myself at that age."

He gave her a hand up to the carriage seat. His touch might have lingered a fraction longer than needed. He unhooked the horse from the tie-down weight and hoisted it into the carriage.

"Thank you for your help, Mr. Mason."

"Might you consider calling me Micah?"

Her eyes smiled. "Then you must call me Cora, Micah."

He liked the sound of his name on her lips.

As the carriage pulled away on the road to town, Cora Allen felt the tug of something left behind.

So, it began. Over the winter, Cora tutored Rebecca Sundays, weather permitting. She became a regular supper guest. She and Elizabeth grew close, and ever so slowly Micah again learned to laugh. Cora invited them all to dinner at the Eldridge House at Christmas time in thanks for all the Sunday suppers. Miriam and Caleb declined, not wanting to cause a fuss, but Miriam insisted Micah and Elizabeth go. One night in March, as Micah tucked Elizabeth in bed, she informed him that when she grew up, she wanted to be a teacher just like Miss Allen. He kissed her good night and took his chair in the parlor by the fire.

Cora Allen. She was a beautiful woman inside and out. He'd grown comfortable with her. She truly cared for Elizabeth, and the child doted on her every word. Still, was any of that reason to think she might see him for more than the father of one of her pupils? Was he ready to see her for something more? He might be. And not simply for fear of his limits as father and mother. He thought it possible she could fill the empty space his beloved Clare had left in him. It was certainly something to bear further thought.

He went to the window and scraped at the frost. The old sycamore stood stark sentinel in moonlight blanketed in snow.

What do you think?

He listened.

Lawrence
May, 1867

An ice cream social followed Sunday services at the Lawrence Congregational Church. Micah, Elizabeth, Miriam, Caleb, and Rebecca took their sweet treat off to the shade of a gnarled beech tree. The girls finished their ice cream and ran off to play with friends. Micah watched them go.

Elizabeth skidded to a stop near a knot of townsfolk and ran to a familiar figure. He'd thought about it, agonized over the possibility really. He'd thought long enough. He licked the spoon in his empty bowl.

"That was mighty good. I believe I'll see if they have any more left."

Caleb and Miriam exchanged glances as they watched him take a wide route to the long table where the ice cream was being served.

"Beautiful day," he said at her elbow.

She smiled. "It is."

"Have you had any ice cream yet?"

She shook her head. Her eyes were blue as cornflowers.

"I was about to have a little more. Care to join me?"

"I'd like that."

She took his arm on the way to the ice cream table. They filled their dishes. Micah noticed Caleb and Miriam had drifted off from the old beech.

"There's a spot of shade over there."

They settled beneath the tree side by side.

"This is good," Cora said with her first spoonful.

"Nothing better on a warm spring day."

"Have you finished your planting?"

"We have. School will be out soon; have you plans for the summer?"

"Last summer I worked at Spencer's mercantile. I suspect Mr. Spencer will take me on again."

He felt his small talk drying up. He wasn't very good at it.

"Cora, would you mind . . . would you mind if I called on you sometime?"

"Mind? Micah Mason, I was beginning to think you'd never

ask. Of course, I wouldn't mind. Nothing would please me more."

He smiled. "I'm glad. I wasn't sure. I guess it took me awhile to get up my gumption."

"Well, you got some of it up, I'm happy to say. See if you can summon up the rest of it. We aren't getting any younger you know."

He laughed.

She laughed.

"This ice cream is good," he said.

Sycamore
August, 1867

The buckboard parked in the Masons' front yard. Sunday supper finished earlier these days, allowing time for Micah to drive Cora back to town and return before dark, though most Sundays he didn't make it back until well past sundown.

It rained while Miriam served dessert; a brief shower moistened the fields before the sun returned. Micah, Cora, and Elizabeth walked out to inspect the crops. Fields of golden wheat ripened on a hot breeze.

"Look there." Elizabeth pointed.

A rainbow arched across the fields disappearing into the river.

Miriam and Caleb stood on the back porch, looking out across the creek.

Off to the east in the distance, the soulful sound of a train whistle announced its scheduled arrival.

"Listen," Caleb said. "Every time I hear that sound, I cain't help but think Micah been right all along."

"He gets that part right; my guess he gets the rest of it, too," Miriam said.

"You mean about rights?"

"I mean about rights. I think about them every time I go

down to the dugout past that old sycamore. She speaks to me there. She say it'll all be right."

"Miss Clare speaks to you?"

"She do."

"They make a right fine lookin' family, don't they?" Caleb said, lifting his chin to the fields.

"They do."

"What you s'pose Miss Clare would say 'bout that?"

Miriam's gaze lifted off through the branches of the old sycamore.

"I believe she'd say I kept my promise."

Lo, the mighty sycamore, her roots entwine the soul;
So, the sycamore promises, evermore to grow.

AUTHOR NOTES

One of the creative licenses the author has used to manage the number of characters presented to the reader, in some cases, is to use characters appropriate to an event (Jayhawkers or Bushwhackers) who may not have actually participated in a specific event. For example, Jacob Herd and his north ferry bushwhackers were credited to the account of the trading post massacre as a vehicle to introduce William Quantrill to the story. Well-versed historians will be quick to pick up on these discrepancies where they occur. We ask their indulgence of an artistic device intended to simplify a complex chapter in history for the reader.

Selected Sources:

Ball, Durwood. *Scapegoat? Colonel Edwin V. Sumner and the Topeka Dispersal.*

Kansas History: A Journal of the Central Plains (Autumn 2010), pp. 164–183.

Reynolds, David S. *John Brown, Abolitionist.* Random House Vintage Books, 2006.

Leslie, Edward E. *The Devil Knows How to Ride.* Da Capo Press, 1998.

Thomas, Emory M. *Bold Dragoon.* University of Oklahoma Press, 1986.

ABOUT THE AUTHOR

Paul Colt's critically acclaimed historical fiction crackles with authenticity. His analytical insight, investigative research, and genuine horse sense bring history to life. His characters walk off the pages of history into the reader's imagination in a style that blends Jeff Shaara's historical dramatizations with Robert B. Parker's gritty dialogue.

Paul's first book, *Grasshoppers in Summer,* received finalist recognition in the Western Writers of America 2009 Spur Awards. *Boots and Saddles: A Call to Glory* received the Marilyn Brown Novel Award, presented by Utah Valley University.

To learn more visit Facebook @paulcoltauthor

The employees of Five Star Publishing hope you have enjoyed this book.

Our Five Star novels explore little-known chapters from America's history, stories told from unique perspectives that will entertain a broad range of readers.

Other Five Star books are available at your local library, bookstore, all major book distributors, and directly from Five Star/Gale.

Connect with Five Star Publishing

Visit us on Facebook:
https://www.facebook.com/FiveStarCengage

Email:
FiveStar@cengage.com

For information about titles and placing orders:
(800) 223-1244
gale.orders@cengage.com

To share your comments, write to us:
Five Star Publishing
Attn: Publisher
10 Water St., Suite 310
Waterville, ME 04901